S0-AQD-320

Carol,

Thank you so much for your willingness to "Bless". My prayer is that "Potato Pie" will be a blessing

God's Best!

Millonease Taylor

9-6-02

Potato Pie

By
Mellonease Naylor

Copyright © 2002 byMellonease Naylor

All rights reserved. No part of this book shall be reproduced or transmitted in any form or by any means, electronic, mechanical, magnetic, photographic including photocopying, recording or by any information storage and retrieval system, without prior written permission of the publisher. No patent liability is assumed with respect to the use of the information contained herein. Although every precaution has been taken in the preparation of this book, the publisher and author assume no responsibility for errors or omissions. Neither is any liability assumed for damages resulting from the use of the information contained herein.

This is a work of fiction. Names, characters, places, and incidents either are the product of the author's imagination or are used fictitiously. Any resemblance to actual events or locales or persons, living or dead, is entirely coincidental.

ISBN 0-7414-1236-5

Published by:

PUBLISHING.COM

519 West Lancaster Avenue
Haverford, PA 19041-1413
Info@buybooksontheweb.com
www.buybooksontheweb.com
Toll-free (877) BUY BOOK
Local Phone (610) 520-2500
Fax (610) 519-0261

Printed in the United States of America

Printed on Recycled Paper

Published August, 2002

ACKNOWLEDGEMENTS

….Thank you Holy Spirit of God…for everything; for the situations that ultimately inspired me to accept the challenge to write this book. I am grateful for Your wisdom, Your sensitivity, and Your compassion that have been my constant companions. I am overwhelmed by Your promises as revealed in Your Word, and the fact that You are faithful to do what You've promised You would…You *are* God, and I acknowledge Your sovereignty…

Thank you, Al, for being my husband and my friend at the times when I so desperately needed one, and for believing in me when no one else was so inclined...

Thank you Ryan and Kasai, for enduring who I was until God made it better...Tanesha and A.J., I'll keep loving you until it does.

Thank you Mommy and Daddy…Jen, George, and to all of my family for pushing me, motivating me, and helping me to climb above my limitations...

Thank you Bishop and Lady T for encouraging me to realize and accept that I have none…

Professor Horgan, thank you for challenging me and helping me to realize that I really have a gift...

Elder Pierce, thank you for your gift of worship… you taught me how...

Ryana, thank you for being born and reaching into the place where a grandmother's love comes alive…you can have…

And to those who are still here with me and those that have passed on---thank you to all of my friends,… you know if you are.

I LOVE YOU ALL,

Mellonease

"Potato Pie" is a work of fiction. It is the story of Mara Singleton, her life, her loves, her passions, her perceptions, and the things that led to the shaping of her convictions. Set in contemporary time, *"Potato Pie"* reaches deep into the heart of one Black woman's experiences. It explores and defines the motivations and rhythms that sustain her despite the numerous attacks that might cause a less fortified heart to cease beating. It examines the reality of urban dwelling, the *thens* and the *nows* --- the change in its complexion over time, and the impact these changes have wrought in a peoples' existence. *"Potato Pie"* gives us more than a peek in from the outside; it opens the door and welcomes us into the living rooms of its characters, indeed invites us to live with them ... if we dare to accept the invitation.

Through Mara, *"Potato Pie"* surveys the depth of relationships. Reaching out from a heart of compassion to comfort the grieving mother of a drive-by-shooting victim, Mara realizes and faces the greater practical need--- money to pay for his funeral. Added to this is the emotional and financial burden of providing for the young son he's left behind in a household that is devoid of father figures for generations...past and future. Mara reflects upon the plunge in morality as evidenced in the attitudes and behaviors of the people that now make up her neighborhood. Without being a busybody, she identifies with who they *are* while understanding the urgent necessity of infusing them with a greater and more pressing sense of who and what they can *become*. Mara transcends the handicap of her own limitations in an attempt to honor the subconscious whisperings of her ancestors, to recover and uphold the values that so many of them died to attain.

As she seeks to free herself from the bondage and curse of incest, Mara is forced to travel dark unfamiliar, mental back roads --- roads that lead her into emotional wildernesses that she is unequipped to navigate. All along these roads are the haunting images and voices of her past, a potential danger to all that she struggles to become. Her husband Buddy, her knight in not-so-shining armor, is sent to rescue her from her ghosts--- *and* from herself. He is her safe place to fall; a place where she can rest and be strengthened, where she finds love and a measure of fulfillment … for a time.

But so that she is able to successfully ride out the twists and turns in her life, Mara has need of someone greater … a soldier of higher ranking, nobility, and power than her loyal and beloved Buddy. She discovers what she needs in the relationship she has with God. But it's okay. Buddy feels no pangs of jealousy, he doesn't mind being outranked. And anyway, like Jello, there's always room for more … in *Him*.

"Potato Pie" doesn't preach; instead it encourages us to examine the meditations of our own hearts. It causes us to question the validity of our hopes and inspirations. It dares us to confront those obstacles --- mental, emotional, financial, or physical, which produce pain in our lives and hinder the manifestation of a higher reality.

MOTHER PEARL'S POTATO PIE FILLING

8 small to medium yams (or 4 large ones)
1&1/2 sticks of softened Land O'Lakes butter
1/3 cup firmly packed Domino's "dark" brown sugar
1 cup Domino's granulated sugar
3 large eggs
¼ tsp. McCormick's ground nutmeg
¼ tsp. McCormick's allspice
1 12-ounce can Carnation evaporated milk
1 tsp. McCormick's pure vanilla extract
1 tsp. McCormick's lemon extract
2 tsp. Sue Bee honey
a pinch of Morton's iodized salt.

Boil yams for approximately 45 minutes, or until they are
very soft when pierced with a fork; cool for 15-20 minutes
when done, then peel.
Pre-heat oven to 350 degrees.
While yams are still warm, mash with potato masher; add
softened butter and mix well by hand or with electric mixer.
Add eggs, mixing well after each one.
Add sugars, nutmeg, and allspice; mix well.
Add extracts, honey, and salt; mix.
Add approximately 6 ounces of milk, mix well, then add
remaining milk. Mix on high speed for about 2-3 minutes, or
until mixture is creamy.

Pour mixture into 9-inch piecrust shells, place on bottom
oven rack and bake at 350 for approximately 1 hour. When
filling has risen to a firm bubble, insert a butter knife in
center of pie. Pie is done when knife comes out clean .

Cool for 30 minutes. Makes 6-8 servings.

Chapter 1

Just as the freezer door swung open, Mara thought she heard a noise. She stopped, spoon in one hand, holding the door in the other. Was that footsteps? She didn't want anyone to catch her, especially not Buddy, her husband. "I mean, it's not like he doesn't know I eat ice cream, but I don't want him to see me eating my third bowl," she reasoned to herself.

Mara tiptoed upstairs to check on Mother Pearl, and smiled at her bonneted head resting on the pillow; she'd had a long day.

Mara had gotten up early to have coffee with Buddy before he left for work. By the time she rinsed out the cups and wiped off the table, she heard Mother Pearl in the bathroom. The two of them left and walked the block to catch the number 119 bus that took them to the old neighborhood. It had changed a lot over the years; though it was still there, even the Knotty Pine had gotten a facelift. Formerly a little "greasy spoon" that occupied one of the corners on East 9th and Nooker Streets, it was now a busy little restaurant. The owners had purchased the adjacent building, knocked out the wall, painted, and added wallpaper borders, new tables and some aluminum siding. And even though some of the faces in the kitchen were different, the down-home cookin' that had sustained them over the years was still being served--- along with the smiling, southern-style hospitality that kept the customers coming back.

"Lawdy, slap Mawdy...Mother Pearl, if you ain't a sight f'sore eyes!" exclaimed Gracie, wiping her hands on her apron as she came toward them from behind the counter.

"If you didn't hafta look at that ugly husband a' yours ev'ry day, your eyes might not be so sore," Mother Pearl teased as she returned the bosomy hug that engulfed her.

"You just mad 'cause Ah wouldn't marry you, you mean ol' biddy!"

"Walter Addison, if you had a' been the first man God created, Eve wouldn'a never sinned!" Mother Pearl threw back.

A man with mixed gray hair, who had been sitting behind the cash register at the far end of the counter, laughed as he wheeled himself over to where his wife was smiling and holding Mother Pearl around her waist. Mara could see how loosely his tie hung around his neck. 'Mr. Addison's sugar must be real bad', she thought, moving so Mother Pearl could lean over to hug him.

"It's good t'see your face. We sure do miss you, Pearl."

"An' I miss bein' 'round here, too. But what can you do…that's what happens when you get old. My baby, Mara, she looks out for me, though."

A voice shouted from one of the tables across the room.

"Hey, Mother Pearl! Can you still make potato pie like you used to?"

Recognizing the voice, Mother Pearl walked a few steps in its direction.

"Better than your mama could. That's why you and your daddy was always knockin' on my door, Rufus Littlejohn!"

The welcome that they received was just as expansive when Mara and Mother Pearl walked in the door of "Miss Tootsie's".

"Mother Pearl!" she screamed, frightening the customer in the swivel chair, before laying the straightening comb on the folded-up, terry-cloth, hand towel. She made sure that the pressing wax on the back of her hand didn't get on Mother Pearl's clothes as she hugged her old friend. They spent the next two hours catching up on things while Miss Tootsie "did" Mother Pearl's hair.

"There ain't nothin' like a good, old, hard press an' curl," Mother Pearl said later, admiring her hair in the mirror Miss Tootsie handed to her. "An' Tootsie, you always was the best."

After they bought eggs and "a nice cantaloupe" at the Farmer's Market, she made sure that Mara took her by the "five and dime", so that Mother Pearl could get a bonnet to put on her hair "so it don't get mussed while I'm sleepin'." Then they had gone to pick up Mother Pearl's orthopedic shoes before stopping by the Boston Market to pick up a value meal on their way to visit Ethel and Dorothy, the Diggs sisters.

Dorothy's husband had been dead for many years, but Ethel had only recently lost her husband, Arthur. The two of them lived together, but, just in case she might forget, Ethel never failed to remind her sister that it was "the house that Arthur bought for me." As she sat watching the two sisters who supported each other now, like she was certain they had when they were younger, Mara wondered what would happen when one of them finally passed.

"You must think I'm terrible, keepin' your wife out all day like this," Mother Pearl said when Mara called Buddy to pick them up from the bus station. Buddy smiled at the love he saw in his wife's eyes as he helped her "other mother" into the car. He was glad she had brought Mother Pearl over to spend the weekend with them.

Mara stopped on the way down the steps, listened again, and satisfied herself that Buddy was snoring peacefully before returning to the kitchen. Then she went about piling her "absolutely-last-bowl-for-the-night" with her favorite ice cream, Breyer's vanilla, chocolate, and strawberry, then tip-toed back into the living room, stopping to listen again for footsteps. Once Mara was certain that everybody else really *was* asleep, she sat down to watch her favorite, new late-night show, "Change of Heart."

"Oh, he's fine" she thought out loud as a tall, handsome, Black guy came out to take his place on the love seat. He was the "alternative date" the show had set up for Tamala, tonight's female participant. The premise of this show was that a couple (so far all of them heterosexual) came on the show with the intention of dating respective members of the opposite sex, their purpose being to demonstrate to their current mate the value of the relationship they now shared. But as she looked at the reaction of Tamala's boyfriend as he watched the chemistry between the two of them, Mara got tickled as she reflected on how D.L. Hughley, a comedian she'd seen on BET's "Comic View", would have described him. Next to this vibrant and unintentionally cool *and* good-looking young man, the alternative date, Rodney, looked like an '*old, broke Lou Rawls*'.

Mara tried to guess whether or not they were going to have a change of heart, or whether they were going to recognize that they really did have a good thing going and stay together. It wasn't too hard to figure out about Rodney. Tamala was the best thing that had happened for him socially in a *long* time. Tall, shapely and pecan-tan, with a better-than-average weave going on, she obviously had no trouble attracting men. It was keeping them after she opened her mouth, exposing her "ghetto" background and mental dwelling place, that would be her downfall. Mara couldn't be sure, she had to wait this one out.

Tamala decided that even though she and Rodney had "a history" and she had enjoyed her date with Mr. Fine, she'd elected to stay single. Hey, no fair! That's a Love Connection decision! Mara thought as she spooned the last of the melted swirl of her ice cream into her mouth. But then she thought, You go, girl! Tamala was one of those strong, Black women who wasn't defined by her relationship with a man. Either that or Mr. Fine wasn't all he was trying to *look like* he was either. As she reached for the remote control to go channel surfing, Mara mentally argued with herself about the practicality of finishing off the last of the half-of-a-gallon of ice cream. It wasn't enough for another real bowl, but enough to increase her embarrassment if anyone realized that no one else had had any of it. "I could just say that one of my friends dropped by earlier," she told herself. But she seldom had visitors, even among those who designated themselves friends. "I'll buy a new one, and it will look like I didn't have any ice cream at all." But then she remembered asking Buddy to "just put a little bit" on that slice of pie she'd set aside for herself.

As she surfed to the cable guide to see if there was anything on TV that was worth staying up for, Mara heard what sounded like fighting outside. Hefting herself to her feet, she went to the window to peep through the vertical blinds.

"Oh, I don't believe she let him come back! Now they're fighting again!" Mara whispered as she shook her head, looking for something to put on her feet

"Caleb! Luce! Stop it!" she yelled as she stepped out on to her porch. "This won't solve one single thing!"

As she walked into the street and pushed herself between the couple, she talked to her Hispanic neighbor saying, "What kind of thing is this for your kids to see, you out here in your underwear fighting and bleeding?!"

"My keeds ain't home, and thees m------- ain't gonna get away with thees b------- thees time. I'm seeck of his s----- was Luce's heavily accented and determined reply.

It appeared to be a stalemate, both of them tired and holding each other at arm's length. Mara was finally able to pry one of her hands loose, but before she could pull her away, Luce hauled off and punched Caleb just shy of his right temple, spitting at him *and* on Mara at the same time.

"Now wait a minute girlfriend, you spittin' on me!" Mara warned as she pulled Luce out of the street.

A grateful Caleb tried to adjust his tank top while inventorying his injuries.

"That girl is crazy!" he said, looking for his other Nike and discovering it hanging above his head on the telephone wires.

"That's not as crazy as I'm gonna get. I'm gonna f---- you up! Luce screamed as she threw his boom box into the path of an oncoming Jeep Cherokee.

"Hey, what the....!?" exclaimed the Jeeps' pilot as he braked just short of windshield destruction.

"Eef you don't like eet, drive down another g--d--- street!" yelled Luce.

The Jeep driver, out cruising for drugs, decided it was safer for him to take her advice and popped a wheelie getting away from there. After Caleb had slunk off into the darkness to go lick his wounds and count his losses, Mara was able to convince Luce to go into her apartment to, "at least wash the blood off and put on some clothes."

Picking up batteries and broken radio slivers from in front of their car, Mara walked to the back of her house to get a trash can. As the beam from the motion sensor light mounted on her neighbors' house fell across her walkway, Mara made a mental note to tell Buddy that some more shingles had fallen from the roof.

"We've got to get that fixed," she spoke to no one in particular.

Finished clearing the street of domestic shrapnel and starting back into the house, Mara decided "I might as well go to the market and get another half gallon of ice cream." She'd figure out later what to say to explain how it got there.

Chapter 2

"A mother is not supposed to bury her children," Mara said. "You're not even listenin' to me, Buddy."'

Trying hard to beam himself from football-land back to his own living room, Buddy scanned the room trying to zero in on the origin of this voice. Realizing that it was Mara's, he mumbled.

"Hunh? Wha'diju say?"

Wrinkling her brow and pursing her lips as she disgustedly peered at him around the newspaper she was holding, she repeated herself.

"I said it's just *not* what God intended when a woman has to look down at her child in a casket."

"Must be what God intended. He's the one who give life so He's the only one who got any say so about when you come and when you go," was Buddy's sage reply.

Folding the paper down over her lap, Mara snapped back.

"I don't think you believe that nonsense any more than I do! This is an evil, lawless time we're livin' in. Young folks don't know about God and sure don't care about you or me! I know that God is the one who gives life, but don't forget, the devil got a job to do too. The Word says he came to do three things... steal, kill, and destroy. Problem is, there's too many folks givin' him a hand with his work. But that's all right. His time is windin' up!"

As she went back to the paper, Buddy mumbled,

"... the third quarter is windin' up too....wish you'd shut up so I can see it."

Before she could answer him, the phone rang, and Mara pushed herself up out of the chair to go answer it.

"Praise the Lord... Hey, Zena! I called you earlier, but I didn't get no answer. I was callin' to see if you read about Naomi's baby in the Journal... Page thirteen. You know they always put it in the back when one of *us* gets killed. Go 'head, I'll wait for you to turn to it... I was just tellin' Buddy

7

the *same* thing! Seventeen! Just got here and gone already!.. I guess I'll make a couple of potato pies and take them to the house this evening... O.K., I'll call you when I get ready to leave.”

Mara looked again at the picture of Jamar before folding up the newspaper and placing it in the magazine rack. Shaking her head, she walked the short distance into the kitchen. As she reached for the big pot she used for boiling everything from potatoes to crabs, she reflected on this most recent tragedy. How many had it been, just in the last six months? It seemed that everywhere she looked, death was all around her. Death and dying. Oh, not everybody was dying of violence like Naomi's son. Some were dying a crack hit or a needle stick at a time. Some were deceived into trying to become other than what God had created them to be, contracting death a 'sexcapade' at a time. Too many were occupying that netherworld of leprous marriages where there were no longer any nerve endings; no love, no sensation, resulting in paralysis, decay and eventual wasting away. Still others walked like zombies through their existences, no purpose, no hope, their dreams on life support with no expectation of recovery. Life had the sickeningly sweet smell of a mortuary where the dying waited in attendance for those who had already succumbed.

It was a feeling, a way of being, that was hauntingly familiar to Mara; she knew the existence of the "living dead"---had been suspended there herself. And unfortunately she had walked a mile in Naomi's shoes... in a way. The thought unnerved her, repulsed her, and she struggled now like she had finally struggled then, to detach herself from the offensive memory.

"It just can't be like this, God. Where are you?"
Mara questioned the atmosphere around her.
"Where are you?!"

****

"I believe I'll run on, see what the end will be...I believe I'll work on, see what life holds for me." The strains of

Oprah's theme met Mara and Zena as they knocked and then stepped into the dark, cramped space that was Naomi's living room. Focusing so she wouldn't trip and drop the two pies she was carrying, Mara greeted everybody present and no one in particular.

"Hey-y'all!"

"Hey, Miss Mara. How you doin'?" replied a voice out of the darkness.

"Valeta, that you? Come on over here, girl, and take these pies and put'em with the rest of the food people been bringin'," Mara spoke in the direction of the voice.

"Ain't nobody else brought nothin' becept for Mr. Les over the barbershop gave us some Popeye's chicken."

This came from the floor, and Mara, her eyes discerning better now, recognized Jomar, Naomi's three-year old grandson. Her heart caught for a second as she realized how much he looked like his father. Jamar, too young himself to become a father at thirteen, now lying on a slab...a baby having a baby, dead before either of them had a chance to know him as a man.

"Well, Miss Mara brought pies and Miss Zena got a pot of string beans,"....

"And here comes Miss Ginger with a big pan of macaroni and cheese!"

Mara turned to see one of the members of the deaconess board holding an aluminum pan with two potholder mitts stepping through the back door leading into Naomi's kitchen.

"And it's hot right out of the oven. ... Hey, Mara, Zena. Figured I'd see you two here," she said as she opened Naomi's oven door to stash her edible treasure.

She then used her potholders to relieve Zena of the pot she was making her way into the kitchen with.

"Give me that, baby. I'll put it on top of the stove so they can heat them up. Oooh, Mara them pies smell good!" In a lower voice she said, "I sure hope you made one to leave at home so I can have a piece."

"You know me, don't you girl. You know I got one home. Don't *nobody* love my potato pie better than me!"

9

All three of them laughed at Mara's declaration. Zena turned back in the direction of the living room.

"I still haven't seen Naomi. Valeta where's your momma?"

Valeta walked into the doorway. "She's down at the funeral home, talking to Mr. Bradley."

"Sweet Jesus! Is that who has his body? He is one of the worst undertakers I've ever seen. Always makes his bodies look so pasty...too much make up!" clicked off Zena, waving her hands.

"Don't nobody have his body yet Miss Zena. My momma went to see if she could make some kind of deal with him so he could go and get Jamar from the coroner."

At this revelation, one they had all experienced too often in this situation, Zena instantly regretted her flippancy.

"Well, it'll be all right. Somethin'll work out. God will make a way," Mara tried to comfort, unconvincingly. "Come on, let's get busy! Valeta, does everybody have what they need to go to the homegoin'? Jomar's probably going to need some dress clothes. All Jamar ever bought for him was those too expensive tennis shoes. I tell you, what does a three-year-old boy need with seventy-five dollar Air Jordans?"

Mara wasn't looking in her friend's direction, didn't see Zena's raised right brow. If she had, she may have been able to read what remained unspoken. The eyebrow underscored the question Zena would not ask---could not ask Mara.

"And how would you know anything about what little boys need?"

****

"Well somebody has to do it! That girl will worry herself sick tryin' to figure out what's goin' to happen," Mara said to Buddy from her side of the table. "If somebody don't take up a collection soon, Jamar's body is gonna blow up! It's been ten days, they can't keep him much longer." Mara anguished over the situation she knew was torturing her friend. "It's bad enough that he's dead and to make it worse, she can't even afford to put him in the ground. It just ain't right, Buddy."

"Don't she have any insurance?" Buddy asked.

"And *that's* somethin' else that's a dirty shame. Naomi had just finished her trainin' to be a nurse's aide and got that job at Care House. But her benefits don't start 'til her probation period is up. So they won't even pay her for funeral leave! How's she supposed to work with her baby layin' in the morgue!?" Mara steamed at the injustice of it all. Standing up, she picked up the empty five pound coffee can. "I know we're all doin' bad, but not so bad that we can't help each other in times like this. I'm gonna knock on every door in this neighborhood. They can't say nothin' but yes or no. And if they say no, God help'em when their turn comes. Chances *do* go around you know."

Walking through her neighborhood, Mara mentally recorded all of the changes she saw. Houses that once were the homes of people who cared lovingly for them, had now become apartments whose outer adornments were graffiti, whose hallways were littered with filthy pampers and cellophane crack bags. Homeowners who had sacrificed hard hours of often, menial labor to qualify for over-inflated mortgages, had long since died or moved away. In their places were young, usually single mothers, surprisingly, White, as well as Black and Hispanic, recipients of both food stamps and Section 8 subsidies. But even *that* wasn't so bad...everybody needed someplace to live. It was the despair that had moved in with them, finding a place in their black, imitation- leathered living rooms; the apathy that snuggled with them and their illegitimate boyfriends in their black and gold lacquered bedrooms, more securely positioned in their lives than their houses full of Rent-A-Center furniture. It was the purposelessness of the psychological games they played with themselves and on each other; games where everybody except them wins a prize. Lining up every check day for their turn to sit, first, in the chair at the beauty salon where they'd spend hours waiting to have tracks of twenty-five dollar-a-pack *genuine human hair* glued or sewn in, emerging looking like an updated version of a 1960's

Bandstand bouffanted prom queen. Next it was on to one of the seemingly hundreds of Asian-staffed nail salons where, for another hour or two, they sat sharing the latest "4-1-1" circulating through the hood... *who was pregnant by who, which 'ho thought she "had it goin' on", which drug dealer had the "baddest" car.* They tended babies in strollers, answered pagers, placed calls on pre-paid cellular phones, never interrupting the progress of Kim, or SoonLee or whoever's responsibility it was to create unique, *"fly"*, airbrushed designs on their thirty-dollars-a-set, two inch-long-petrified-gelatin fingernails.

After treating their children to Happy Meals to pacify them (and to appease their own consciences at the guilt they felt for using their AFDC allotments to beautify themselves), they stopped in what now sufficed as the local shopping area. Here they purchased, from yet another Asian-born family of entrepreneurs, NFL or NBA logoed sweat suits, shirts, and caps, all cash-and-carry...

"No lay-a-way, no cledit, you pay cash!"

Or they tried their hand at bargaining with the Muslim street vendors, arguing that they could afford to "give a sister a break" because their *overhead* was low. When all else failed they could always depend on the One Price store, where for any "one price" between seven dollars and thirty-four ninety nine, a sister could put together a *half-way*, decent outfit.

All this was done in preparation for "going out"-translation: cruising the bars and clubs within walking distance of the hood, because *nobody* had a car. Or if distorted providence was with them, they could actually expect to be picked up and chauffeured in leased Explorers, Jeep Cherokees or Isuzus by whichever good-looking, Timberland-sporting, young hip-hopper they managed to attract. The cycle was perpetual and vicious, catching them up and spinning them in a whirlwind of blissful ignorance, only to drop them four babies and three Domestic Relations hearings later, back on the crumbling porches that they called home.

Mara saw it all, lifetimes and generations... past, present and future in one, eternal second. She walked around a Big Wheel and a Blunt wrapper as she climbed the steps. This was the building where that young, White girl Kaitlyn lived, she realized. She wondered who the coffee can would be for the next time.

****

"One, glad, mor-ning when this life is o-ver...I-I-I'll fly away!"

The voices of the Mass Choir lifted and then faded into the cathedral ceilings of the Zephaniah United Holy Pentecostal Church of God In Christ, formerly, St. Augustine Catholic Church, the tall stained-glass windows and intricately etched marble statues of various saints, tangible reminders of its previous religious association. Reflecting from her seat "with the family" as she looked around at the nearly filled pews in the five-hundred-seating-capacity sanctuary, Mara recalled that before, when the Catholics owned it, the parking lot hardly ever had fifty cars in it.

"What did that little bit of White folks do in this *great, big,* church?" she thought. She chuckled to herself as she envisioned them, sitting straight-backed and appearing emotionless, devoutly enduring the Latin liturgies of the priest. "When He looked down, God probably couldn't tell them from these statues."

She leaned over and whispered in Zena's ear, "I knew it was gonna be crowded. Jamar knew a lot of people."

"Only problem is, the majority of them was his customers!" Zena whispered back, too loudly. A man sporting both a new S-Curl and a shape-up, looked over his shoulder in Zena's direction. She smiled, nodded an acknowledgment, and started fanning herself with her own fold-up, Chinese fan. Ignoring her last comment, Mara leaned over again.

"Naomi's doin' good, considerin'."

Careful to lean a little closer so only Mara could hear, Zena remarked, "Considering that he's been dead for almost three weeks, she's already done all her cryin', I would think."

Refusing again to entertain Zena's comments, Mara focused on the young people still filing past the open casket. Many of the guys modeled new suits; orange with lime green muscle shirts underneath, royal blue with white, heavily starched shirts and matching ties, suspenders and hankies falling out of the left breast pockets of the jacket. Most wore the uniform of this generation: jeans, sweatshirts, varied styles of designer sneakers or boots, skullies, or caps, brim facing backward on their heads. Those who had some small regard for etiquette carried their headgear, exposing Iverson cornrows or Snoop Dog ponytails. The young ladies, ever on stage, took advantage of the opportunity to reveal their long, shapely legs through thigh-high splits in clingy black dresses or from beneath barely butt-concealing skirts. There was an assortment of midriff and halter-tops, displaying rose-tattooed shoulders and butterfly background navel rings. Many carried their babies over one hip, the boys looking like under developed clones of their absent fathers, the girls all dolled out in too much chiffon and too many barrettes. Both sexes sported diamond-studded or gold-hooped ear wear. Since many of them depended on the SSI, Social Security, and Welfare checks that came out at the beginning of the month, still eight days away, too many of these babies had eaten nothing more than a bowl of off-brand cereal this morning. Chances were that their bottles were filled with anything from Tropical Punch Kool Aide to Pepsi, because WIC restrictions had increased.

The disparity in priority making of this younger generation of people frightened Mara, and she wondered now, as she often did, if she had ever been this ignorant of life's realities. She was sure she must have been, every generation had its time. But then, maybe her realities hadn't been entrenched in a time as immoral and violent as this one. Yes, life *had* had its problems, from the need for persons to fight for Civil Rights to the battle against its not too distant cousin, poverty; both the respective offspring of racism and apathy.

14

Racism, a concept so firmly embedded in the hearts and thinking of those who were in position to wield its influence, yet who were surprisingly unaware of its presence within them. It lay there crouching, seemingly comatose, only to rise, fiercely yet subtly overpowering its victims, from the Sav-A-Lot to the Supreme Court. And racism's equally effective ally, *apathy*, homegrown with its roots deeply planted in the fertile ground of a peoples' ignorance. This ignorance was visible in a whole community's outspoken outrage at the inequity of governmental appropriation of funding and tax breaks for "them Chinks and Iranians". Yet this same community had walked past the empty storefronts where Mom and Pop corner stores had closed, defeated by the very people they attempted to serve. People who'd robbed them blind, or just as bad, spent their money somewhere else. These same people who verbally rejected the intrusion of these new businesses in their neighborhoods, supported them a chicken wing special and a Tommy Hilfiger knock-off at a time. They threw a quarter across the counter demanding Blunts,... *"and hurry up!"*, then rushed back to their houses to practice their social, emotional, and economic moonwalk in crack-smoke-filled bedrooms, while "the enemy" gathered their quarters and sent their own sons and daughters through college. Rejecting the God who had led their grandfathers out of the atrocity that had been legalized slavery, now a century later they had imprisoned themselves on their own plantations, one slave daring another slave to step foot on ground that still neither of them owned.

From a vehicle double-parked outside the church while its' driver paid his respects blared the words of a song by Jay-Z.

"It's a hard-knock-life, for-me"...

Mara was inclined to agree.

Chapter 3

Sitting on the side of the bed as she finished rolling up her hair, Mara shared the events of the day with Buddy.

"His baby's momma and three other girls carried on terrible! The people from the funeral home had to stop'em from layin' all in the casket, and one of'em just passed out, knockin' flowers everywhere! But then some big ol' guy came up and leaned over and said somethin' to the one girl, and *trust* me, girlfriend got up off that floor and got herself together. Valeta said that he was the guy she just had her baby by. Big boy wasn't *havin' it!*"

Buddy had perfected the art of pretending to listen to Mara while he actually was reading the highlights of the day's sports events from a muted CNN Headline News broadcast.

"And then guess who had the nerve to show up?... Buddy! You listenin' to me or watchin' that durn TV?"

He turned and answered her with his own question, placating her to avoid what could potentially be a sticky situation.

"Who?"

Satisfied that she indeed had his attention, Mara finished reporting.

"I looked up and who should be standin' in front of the church but Jamar's daddy! He ain't been around since Hector was a pup, and he *sure* didn't send Naomi a cryin' quarter to help take care of those kids from wherever he been hidin'. But he sure did step his self in that church today just *as if* he had been a real father. If Jamar had sat up and looked at him, he wouldn'a even known that was his daddy. It's a shame before almighty God! Naomi just shook her head... wouldn't even say nothin', just shook her head. It took her three weeks to get the money together to put that boy in the ground, *and now here he come*. It sure couldn'a been me. No, sir. Not me. I guess that's why God made us all different."

She paused to put on her headscarf.

"They had a young preacher who spoke today. He said some things I have *never* heard said in church before, but it was good. Timely. And those young people needed to hear it. Truth is, us old people needed to hear it too. Took his text from Job when he had started to ask God to let him die and God said 'Where were you when I put the stars in the sky? Who tells night when to go and morning when to come,' and uh, let me see. ... I looked it up when I got home."

Flipping through the Bible she kept on her nightstand, she located the scripture passage she was looking for.

"It's right here, 'who tells a lion to hunt its prey, or gives a man wisdom?' I tell you, he made people sit up and pay attention! Even woke up ol' Deacon DeBerry. He sure made people understand that only God is God, whether they like it or not. When the service was over, young people and old folks was standin' up and givin' their lives to Jesus. It was somethin' to see! I'm just blessed I was there to witness it. God *is* good... *all* the time."

Changing direction she said, "I don't know who made that potato salad, but it sure was good! I tried to bring some home for you, but whoever made it only made enough to feed to the family."

Buddy knew not to ask how Mara had managed to get some because she *certainly* wasn't a relative. He clicked off the television as she climbed into bed.

Mara slept fitfully, dreaming the dreams of the undead. These were not beings who occupied the realm of spirituality where angels and demons and those who had formerly possessed bodies lingered. They hovered, waiting to be beckoned, during hell-inspired seances, to cross back over the threshold into the land where the embodied live. Neither were they those birthed from beneath dusty bunk beds or shadowy closets in the terrified dreams and imaginations of four and five year olds. No, these were the deliberately faceless symbols she fought to imprison in a pad-locked compartment of her subconscious. Locked... because if they ever escaped, Mara knew they would wreak havoc in her safely furnished existence; faceless, ... because to entertain familiar countenances even in her minds' eye, was a fate too painful for her to envision.

Sometimes, like now in this tortured restlessness, the faces demanded to be identified and so, reckoned with. But Mara wasn't ready and, barring some miraculous epiphany, probably never would be willing to give them eyes, and worse yet, mouths. She cringed at the very imaginings of what those mouths might say, what those eyes might reveal they'd seen. She slammed shut the eyelids of her awareness on images of salivating lips pursed to whisper debauched assurances that it was "ok". She erased the hands that reached for her, groping to touch her in places those hands had no right to explore. She ran away from tiny hands and chubby feet and the faces that belonged to them, accusing her, albeit silently, of their existence only in *this* place, this eternal no place. Mara ran toward the mouth whose sound she permitted entry into this purgatory, because *these* lips provided a portal for escape, and this voice guided her to where it was.

"Mara! Baby, wake up! It's ok, Mara."

Buddy called her to the only safe haven she knew for right now. She shivered in his arms, wrapped so tightly around her, protecting her. As her breathing slowed and her pulse ceased racing Mara clung to him, her shelter in these nocturnal storms. Then she felt that *other* fear rising and gently, lovingly, sacrificingly pushed him away. Someone peeking in on this sacred scene may have speculated at what appeared to be her insensitivity, but Buddy understood. Mara became his protector as she pushed him *away* from her and *into* his rightful position in her life. She extracted herself from the temporary safety of his embrace, replacing his arms with other, *eternal* arms. She exchanged this temporal refuge for the infinite one, because Mara recognized *this* fear as the awe and reverence that she *must* have. She welcomed it as the only presence she knew that had the power to not only shield her from the dread of these faces, but to "in the fullness of time" give her the courage to confront them.

"I am the Lord your God...Thou shalt have no other Gods before me... for I am a jealous God."

Mara had no desire to arouse His jealousy or for Him to be anyone other than He was...her God.

Chapter 4

Sitting in one of the thirty or so green burlap covered chairs lined up in the unemployment office, Mara waited for her number to be called. When she'd heard the rumors that the hospital would be laying people off, she hadn't been worried. Mara had worked there for seven years; she had seniority. What she hadn't anticipated was the ever-widening, ripple-effect of what the hospital administration called "downsizing". As a cost-cutting measure, positions were being "phased out" all over the hospital. Though Mara couldn't understand how they could do it, Whitman Hospital had closed their emergency room, leaving its staff without a place to work. It was the labor union's responsibility to negotiate to find jobs for as many union members as possible. The result of the negotiations was that those with greatest seniority "bumped" those members with less seniority, taking their positions. It turned out that Mara's seven years as a ward clerk didn't stand a chance against the sixteen years of a nurse who needed a job—even if it only paid half of what she'd been earning.

Mara checked her purse again to make sure she had her paperwork. She had been here since nine o'clock when they'd opened, hoping like everyone who had been standing at the door with her, that she could get in, be seen, and get out. It was now ten- fifteen, and there were still six people to be seen before it would be her turn. She tried to read the newspaper she'd bought at the Wawa (just so she could get change for the bus), but when she opened it to the front page, there was Monica Lewinsky, staring back at her.

"I wish they'd leave Bill Clinton alone! He sure didn't do nothin' that any *one* of those other men wouldn'a done if they had the chance!", she thought disgustedly as she folded the paper and laid it on the seat beside her. "They just mad because he was doin' too much for Black people, that's all.

First time in history that there's ever been over *sixty* Black people in them high level positions in the White House."

Mara had gleaned this bit of political savvy from Buddy, who knew a lot about those kinds of things.

"Just look at what they had done to that poor man Ron Epsy. Made him lose his job and everything and *never did* find a thing he did that was wrong. I still think this Lewinsky business was a set-up. What woman does what they say she did and then saves the dress? Not none I know of, that's for sure", she nodded, emphasizing the point to herself. "Not that it makes it right, what he did," she debated silently. "He still had a family, even if it *was* Hillary and Chelsea."

Lost in the humor of her last thought, Mara didn't realize that the person standing near her was waiting to sit in the chair next to her until he spoke.

"Excuse me, is this your newspaper?"

Hastily picking it up, she apologized for her oversight adding, "*If* you think that Monica Lewinsky and Bill Clinton is still news."

They both laughed as he sat next to her.

"What number are you?" he asked.

"Nineteen, but as long as I've been sittin' here, it feels like a *hundred* and nineteen. What's yours?"

"Thirty-three, and I guess that's how old *I'll* be when I get out of here."

Gently hunching him in his side as they both laughed at that possibility, Mara thought what a nice young man he seemed to be. She prided herself on her ability to judge a person's character, even if she'd only known them a little while. It was something about the eyes and the smile. She sensed a trustworthiness about him that some called intuition, but that she'd rather call spiritual discernment, and she decided it was ok to tell him so.

"You sure are a different breed from most of the young men I know around here. You from out of town?"

"Well, yes and no. I was born here, but my mother died when I was seven, so I went down south to live with my father and his people," he explained.

21

"If I'm estimatin' correctly, that was about eighteen or nineteen years ago. How'm I doin'?" she asked, already noticing something familiar in his face.

"You're doing real good. It's been nineteen years ago last week."

"Turn around here and let me take a look at you."

Buddy always said she could trace sperm better than anybody he knew. Looking into the young man's eyes as he smiled amusedly at her attempt to figure out who he was, she startled him when she blurted,

"That's *just* who you are! You-are-Hortensia-Milford's-boy. Left here and went to, let me remember, ... Winston-Salem, North Carolina !"

Surprised that this woman whom he had just met knew so much about him, the stranger questioned, "You knew my mother?"

"Practically *raised* her. Your grandmother and grandfather lived across the walk from me when I lived in the projects. They were older than I was, but I liked bein' around them. We used to play cards on the weekends that your granddaddy didn't have to work the midnight shift. They would put your mother in my bed, then we'd fry chicken wings, drink beer and play all night long." She laughed, shaking her head at the memory. "We'd start off playin' bid wist or pinochle, then when Melvin would get tired of gettin' his head rubbed he'd pull out his money and say, 'Take out the eight, nines and tens and deal me a game of tonk!' I'd win all his money, and then me and your grandmother would split it the next day!"

Looking at him again, she said,

"I've got pictures of Melvin, Versiel, and yo' mother when she was a little girl. She was somethin', even when she was small. Didn't take no tea for the fever. Hortensia wrestled and climbed trees with the best of 'em; she didn't care if she had on a dress and patent leather shoes."

Walking back through her memories, she smiled at the images they flashed.

"She grew up to be a pretty young lady, but she still didn't take nothin'--- from the boys *or* the girls."

Whispering conspiratorily, she went on.

"They used to be jealous because the boys liked to be around her, but they didn't have a thing to worry about."

She leaned in his direction.

"Your granddaddy wasn't havin' it! His baby wasn't seein' no boys until she was *seventeen*. No, sir!"

Turning to him again, she reflected, "But your daddy came up here to visit his auntie the summer your mother was fifteen and changed all that. As soon as she saw those big mule-plowin' muscles in his arms and heard that southern accent of his, your grandmomma and granddaddy had trouble on their hands! Before they knew anything, summer was over, he went back home, and you was on the way!"

Staring at nothing, she remembered, "I thought Melvin was gonna die, it hurt him so bad."

Quickly turning her head back to him, she reassured, "But he was crazy about you from the very beginnin'. He used to say, 'That's Pop Pop's man. Took you everywhere he went."

Knitting her brows together she continued.

"I can still see that night him and Versiel had hollered in the screen door to tell me they were walkin' you to the store and to ask me if I wanted them to bring me anything back. I told them to wait while I got my money so they could bring me some ice cream, but Melvin said 'That's ok, I got it'. ... And that was the last time I saw him."

Shaking her head at even the memory of the senselessness of it, Mara went on. "Seems he was pickin' you up so you could point to the kind of ice cream you wanted when this man walked up behind him and hit him in the head with a baseball bat. He never knew what happened. By the time Versiel ran from the side where the bread was, you were on the floor and your grandfather was layin' there covered in blood."

Mesmerized by the details of the story he had only known pieces of, the young man reached for more.

"But why did the man do it? That's what nobody ever explained."

Sadly she looked at him, wondering if in her reflections, she had said too much already. Buddy said she did that sometimes. But seeing the pain of too many unanswered questions in those eyes that had all at once become so familiar, she knew somehow that he needed to know.

"Melvin used to talk to this girl who worked on the assembly line with him. Her husband would beat on her all the time, and Melvin felt sorry for her. He told her that she should leave him, and he gave her some money to help her go. But her husband found out and was waitin' for her when she got to the bus depot. He beat her up and made her tell him who had helped her, and when she did, he got the bat, went lookin' for your granddaddy and left him *right* where he found him. ... Versiel was so pitiful after he died. And Hortensia went buck wild. She started goin' to bars, stayin' out all hours of the night, and leavin' you with your grandmother. I'd keep you sometimes, just to give Versiel a break."

She sighed heavily, remembering the weight of her friends' pain.

"But one week-end Hortensia went to New York with some people and didn't come back home. Versiel worried herself sick, but she did the best she could to take care of you. She got a job at the day-care center so she could take you to work with her. When it was time for you to go to regular school, she started working at the cleaners. ...You were the *cutest* thing goin' to Catholic school in your little navy blue and white uniform and tie. Then one day she told me she got a call from Hortensia from *somewhere* and that she said she wanted to come home. Only she never did get here."

"I know, my father told me that they found her dead in the restroom of some filling station. He said my grandmother couldn't take care of me anymore, and that's why I came to live with them. I only came back one time and that was to my Grandmom Versiel's funeral," he said, replaying the

24

mental video tape in his own mind.

"I remember, I was there," Mara replied softly.

Only she hadn't been there, not really. She had rented a room in her own misery and kept herself locked inside. She came out enough to function on her job, to interact with the rest of the world to oblige necessity. Even the pain of Versiel's death had to knock to get beyond the door.

"I think she died from a broken heart. Everybody she loved was gone."

She remembered that her friend, Zena, had said the same thing the day she asked Mara if Versiel had any surviving family. Though she, of course, knew Versiel, she didn't have the relationship that Mara had with the Milfords. In fact, Zena was ashamed of the conflicting emotions she felt when Mara called her to tell her that Versiel had died. She didn't dislike Versiel. She actually felt sorry for her; first losing Melvin so tragically, and then the whole Hortensia thing.

But Zena still felt 'some kinda way' about the friendship between Mara and Versiel. Or Mara and anybody, for that matter. Not that Mara ignored her or that she wasn't included in what they did. Mara would call Zena and ask her to come over to play cards with them, and at first, she did. But she couldn't get the hang of pinochle, and she didn't like bid whist. Playing tonk was totally out of the question. Zena just couldn't make any sense out of why somebody would work all week long, to sit down and gamble away any part of their paycheck, and she made no bones about it. That it was about the camaraderie was lost in Zena's bean count, and she eventually stopped going. She'd make up some excuse about working late when Mara asked her why she hadn't come, which was more than she did when she'd see Versiel. Zena tried really hard to avoid dropping her clothes off at the cleaners when she knew Versiel was working. If she couldn't avoid seeing her, she always acted like she was in a hurry and didn't have time to talk; that is, if she bothered to acknowledge Versiel's smiling attempts to engage her at all.

Zena always hated herself when she acted like that. She really wanted to be friends; God knows she certainly didn't have many. But something that was an ugly part of who she was, met Versiel's every gesture of friendship with a kind of arrogance that wouldn't allow her to reciprocate. It was as though there was some invisible force field around her that restricted entry into her life-space of any one except those who had been properly screened and were free of emotional contaminants. That the force field limited her ability to bond in even minimal socialization, was a negative by-product of living within its borders.

Zena hadn't always been this way. Having been born the fourth child in a family of six children, invisibility was easy and came early. A dull thread woven into the fabric of a family whose greatest inspiration and legacy was mediocrity, there was little to cultivate esteem in her. She grew up uneventfully, occupying the place reserved for her among her three sisters and two brothers. Happiness for her was maintaining order in that part of the world that was hers. She kept her dresser drawer and her side of the bed she shared with her sister neat. The safety pins that held her skirts on the hangers were as evenly spaced as were her tennis shoes, penny loafers and Sunday shoes on the closet floor beneath them. When it was her turn to do the dishes, her mother never had to reprimand her for leaving some part of the chore undone. Her good grades reflected the attention she gave to her schoolwork. Though she had never been especially outgoing, she enjoyed the relationships that developed in the normal course of life. That is, until tenth grade.

Her sophomore year in high school signified a turning point for Zena. That was the year she met Jamison Hicks. She watched him run out onto the gymnasium floor as the names of Concordia High's football team were announced during the fall pep rally. In his burgundy three-button cardigan sweater and his grey sharkskin slacks, he was simply the most gorgeous thing she had ever seen. From the time her girlfriend LaVern Jackson stopped by her house on the way to school every morning, until Zena's mother made her come in the house after they walked home in the afternoon, Jamison was all Zena talked about. Until he started talking to her.

"Hey, locker four eighteen."

Terrified that he was actually talking to her and flattered that he knew her locker number, she gripped her notebook and turned in his direction.

"How come you know my locker number?"

"Because I made it my business to find out. I know more than that. I know you're on your way to chem lab this period."

"So what else did you make it your business to find out about me?"

"I asked some of my connections that have PE with you to find out if everything I see under that pink mohair sweater is real."

Blushing and slightly embarrassed by his reference to her body, Zena was so flattered by his attention that she didn't quite know what to do with herself. She wore her mohair sweater at least once a week, and started pulling her skirts up just a little higher around her waist. Though officially she wasn't permitted to 'take company' yet, she looked forward to Jamison meeting her and LaVern every morning at the gas station two blocks from her house. By the time that they got to the building, Zena had managed to walk just a little ahead of LaVern, so everyone would know that it was definitely *her* that Jamison was walking to school. They ate lunch together and smiled at each other as they passed in the hallways on their way to class. When the school day was over, Jamison would wait for Zena at her locker before he had to leave to go to football practice. Though he wasn't in the starting lineup, just being associated with a guy on the football team elevated Zena in the eyes of her peers. Wearing a school football jersey with his number on it distinguished her as "Jamison's piece".

When she turned sixteen the week before Thanksgiving, Jamison gave her a black and white pearl ring. Sitting in the bleachers, cheering for him in the annual game between their football team and Brandywood High, she knew that the other girls were talking about her ring. They could see it because in spite of the fact that it was a cold November day, Zena refused to wear the gloves that would cover her badge of acceptance and most prized possession. Though she had never consciously aspired to it, Zena found herself one of the "in" girls. No longer was she invisible.

Being picked to be in the Christmas Choir gave them more opportunities to be together. Since LaVern couldn't carry a note in a paper bag and wasn't in the choir, Jamison usually walked Zena home after rehearsal.

"Zena, all Mama's gonna' say to you is this. You know right from wrong; I know you do b'cause me and y'daddy taught you and your brothers and sisters. Now Jamison seems like a nice enough boy, but the fact is, he *is* a boy. And he's a teenage boy. That's the reason why he's sniffin' around you so much. Teenage boys usually have only a couple'a things on their minds,,, sports and girls."

It seemed like her mother was able to read her as easily as a first grade primer. Zena hoped that the heat she was feeling on the inside wasn't showing on the outside as she tried to keep her face emotionless. Lately, Jamison had been more insistent when she'd let him kiss her and feel her breasts in the walkway between her house and the Myer's next door. Always fearful that someone would see them, she knew that it shouldn't have gotten that far, but she wasn't sure what else to do.

"Zena why did you give me a quarter?"

"Because remember when we was in the cafeteria and you asked me if I had any change?"

"Yeah, I needed a dime for the milk machine."

"Well, when I gave you the dime, you said that you wanted me to start givin' you more than that. That's why I gave you the quarter."

She'd felt really stupid when he explained to her what he really meant. Now it seemed like her mother already knew that she had agreed to cut choir rehearsal on Wednesday and made plans to meet Jamison under the bleachers at the football field.

... Zena, are you listenin' to me?"

"Yes, Ma'am, I'm listenin'."

"So, like I was sayin', don't nobody want a soda pop that somebody else already drank out of. I trust you, Zee, 'cause you have always been pretty level-headed. But I'm not so old that I can't remember my first boyfriend. Just keep in mind that Jamison is only the first boy in your life; he won't be the last."

That was easy for her to say. Zena's fear was that if she didn't do what Jamison wanted, he might be her last boyfriend for longer than she wanted. She knew that there were a lot of other girls who couldn't wait to step into her shoes; she'd overheard them saying that they didn't know what Jamison saw in her anyway. She was aware that she had a nice body, but she had an over-bite, and her hair didn't grow thick and full like LaVern's. Zena's more pressing reality was that Jamison felt like he had bought the bottle long ago; now he wanted to taste and see what flavor she was.

"So how come Mr. Football Player's not walkin' you home, Zee?"

"Because he had to drop off his application. He wants to get a part-time job at the Shop-N-Sav. He's going to meet me at the football field."

"The football field's not on your way home. Why are you meetin' him there?"

She was asking herself the same question as LaVern turned and walked toward her house, leaving Zena to walk the three blocks to the football field by herself. She started to turn back twice, but went on, magnetized by her knowledge that Jamison would be waiting for her. She saw her typing teacher Mr. Harper drive by, then slow up when he realized it was her, but she waved him on. It started to snow just as she crested the hill near the housing projects that sloped down toward the field. Zena hoped it snowed harder and faster; then they would *have* to go home. But as she looked ahead and recognized Jamison's snow-outlined figure

29

walking toward her, her heart began to pound with both dread and anticipation.

It was kind of pretty and romantic, the snow falling and everything. And being with Jamison almost always made her happy. But as she laid down on the sleeping bag he had spread out on the cement floor of the hot dog concession stand, Zena couldn't help but notice the cases of sodas stacked in the corner. Or the recently discarded condom that she almost touched when she moved her hand. She held her breath to keep from smelling the stench of urine and cats. As he turned her head to kiss her, she saw an overturned trash can through the opening of the door whose lock Jamison had jimmied to get in. Something inside of her wanted to scream "Stop!" when the light from the street pole fell across an almost empty soda bottle amid the other debris that snow was beginning to cover. But it was too late; she winced and closed her eyes against the piercing pain and the image of the dripping brown soda staining the freshly fallen white snow.

The chill of the cold dampness she felt on that day was mild in comparison to the cold shoulder she began to get from Jamison. Zena was confounded; she had done what he said he wanted her to do. She had no idea how to respond to who he became. At first, he started patting her on her behind in front of everybody. Or, he was always trying to get her off somewhere by herself so she had to fight him to keep him off her.

"So now you gittin' new? You s'posed to be my girl!"

"Just because I'm your girl doesn't mean you have to be touchin' me all the time, especially not in front of everybody, Jamison!"

"I can't help myself. You know how much I like your body. C'mon Zee, don't act like that."

"I'm not actin' like nothin'. I just don't want you to keep doin' that. You act like you want everybody to know what we did."

And it seemed like everybody did. Just like they all knew before she did that Jamison was seeing a girl in the twelfth grade.

Zena cried the whole Christmas holiday. She was visibly invisible, and she didn't like it one bit. She knew about the parties that she would have been expected to attend, *if* she was with Jamison. But she knew that instead, she was being discussed and laughed at in those same circles as an upshot of their break-up. If she had had the benefit of 'O' magazine's articles on relationships then, she would have had a point of reference. She would have understood the acts of this emotional drama, the three *'D's'*; the discovery of her abandonment, the distress of her helplessness, and her ultimate detachment as a survival strategy. She might have understood that it was her need to be cherished, to be "sweetly, indulgently, loved", that she had been denied. Having tasted the intoxicating liqueur of even this conditional acceptance, Zena's response was characteristic of addiction; she experienced withdrawal.

Like a hand that has lost a thumb, unable to depend on what she no longer possessed, she compensated. Her desire for meaningful attachment took a backseat to her greater need for the security of order in her life, causing Zena to create a world of carefully rearranged priorities that she could function within. Retreating into her self-constructed emotional rehab, Zena developed a care-plan to facilitate recovery. She avoided the people, places and things that could trigger relapse. She cultivated new interests that didn't require another person's involvement, limited her associations, evaded emotional attachments. Invisibility fostered a confining comfortability.

Guarded though she was within her bulwark, Zena could not maintain her fasting from intimacy forever. She needed a friend. It was a temporary letting down of her guard that had afforded Mara access those years ago. Some momentary lapse in the effectiveness of Zena's force field had allowed for an osmosis of sorts, a crossing over the relationship membrane. Surprised at herself for engaging her, yet wary of Mara's presence within her space, Zena carefully scrutinized her for any tell-tale signs of insincerity.

Conversely, Mara's reality was that she had unconsciously and involuntarily assumed this position, carried along by the ripples in her own life at the time. Like a popsicle stick floating in the current of a curb-side tributary, Zena was the rock that temporarily interrupted her journey. They shared the early, undeveloped fruit typical of work-a-day relationships, that level of intimacy that grows out of sharing floor space, lunch hours, and office gossip. Their mutual need for what each of them subconsciously labelled as strength in the other, drew them closer in their superficial bond. Their respective weaknesses and longing to be cherished would lead them apart in pilgrimages to discover something that neither knew they were looking for... and then together again.

By the time Mara cycled back into Zena's life, both of the future best friends had experienced situations that would mold them into who they would become to each other. Mara's relationship with Versiel was part of Zena's sculpting; it was a tool outlining the intricate details that defined who she was.

****

"Number nineteen," the receptionist called, flipping the numbers on the counter and bringing both Mara and the young man back to the present. She held up her number as she collected herself and walked to the counter. Turning back to him she said,

"You'll prob'ly still be here when I come out. Write down your address and phone number for me and I'll invite you over for supper some time. I went on *so*, that I don't know a thing about what *you're* doin' here. You're probably married now with kids of your own."

After getting her instructions from the receptionist, Mara looked back to where they'd been sitting.

"Hey! Do they still call you P.M.?"

Smiling, he nodded. Most people who had met him since the last time she'd seen him probably assumed it was because his name was Parris Milford, but Mara knew different.

"That's because you was Pop-Pop's man."

Chapter 5

"So they told me that they didn't give extensions on unemployment any more. I'm only gonna get a check for six more weeks, so I guess we'd better start figurin' out what we need to do, Buddy."

As Mara reached to get the rolls out of the stove, Buddy mouthed silently, widening his eyes and pointing to her turned back.

"What *we* need to do? *You* need to start looking for another job."

Unaware of his antics, Mara placed two of the homemade rolls on his plate, careful not to put them too close to his turnip greens. Buddy hated for his bread to get wet. Sprinkling cayenne pepper over everything except the bread, Buddy reassured her,

"Somethin'll work itself out. We'll worry about that time when it gets here."

She had learned to trust this man, Mara had. It hadn't been easy; he was big in the dream department but not too good on the "how to", and she had learned to be a practical woman. But somewhere between the time she spent on her knees praying, and the problems that had sent her there, God would bestow His favor upon Buddy and the problem would be resolved.

Watching him eat, Mara thought back on the time that she'd had her surgery. Two days before she was released from the hospital, the furnace in their rent-to-own house had groaned one last time and then died. Interested only that they paid their rent on time, the landlord had refused to have the furnace repaired, and Buddy had to bring her home to a house with no heat and seven inches of snow covering its steps. They had emptied their meager savings when they'd had to replace a part of the roof just two months earlier. Caught between the proverbial rock and a hard place, Buddy just did what had to be done.

After driving the fifty-two mile round trip from his job at the automobile assembly plant, he would stop at the twenty-four hour Super G to buy logs for their fireplace. (She'd loved that fireplace.) He would come home, stoke the fire he had built before he'd left for work some ten hours earlier, pick up the five gallon kerosene can and drive to a gas station to fill it. Returning home, he'd replenish the two kerosene heaters with fuel and, after taking her temperature and checking her surgical scar for any signs of infection, Buddy would give Mara her medication. Tearfully, she recalled how he'd climb into bed, careful not to do anything that might be painful to her. Then he'd position himself so that she could get the benefit of his body heat before, exhaustedly, he slept the three or four hours before he would have to get up and do it all over again. As sick as she was, both from the surgery and the fumes from the kerosene, Mara could not bring herself to complain. She knew that Buddy was doing *all* that he could do... until God stepped into their case.

In a whirlwind of events that caused Mara to shake her head in wonder even now, they found out about someone, a deacon at another church who had a house for lease-purchase. Within a two-week period, they had met the deacon, seen the house, made an agreement, and moved in. She looked around at this kitchen that had been God's way-out-of-no-way for them, repeated the "thank-you-Jesus" she had offered countless times since, both for the house and this gentle, soft spoken giant-of-a-man, before leaning over to ask,

"Buddy, you got enough? There's more of everything if you want it."

Motioning to his glass he answered, "Just a little bit more ice tea and I'm good, baby. Everything's delicious. Thanks."

Mara just smiled as she put down her fork and reached for his glass.

****

"After I heard your message at Jamar's funeral I told my husband Buddy that I was going to visit your church the first chance I got," Mara said, shaking the hand extending from the sleeve of the Kente-cloth robe. "I've been here a few times but this is the first time I decided to stay and tell you how much I enjoy your services. And I just love your choir … even though I'm not used to standin' up that long." Realizing that she may have just made a boo-boo, Mara quickly added, "But it's not so bad, for *real*."

"Well, I always say the first time you come you're a visitor. After that, you're family," the minister said smiling, providing her a graceful escape.

"And every time I been here, I felt like I was at *least* a second cousin," Mara joked.

For the most part it was true. She had enjoyed his preaching, the first time and each of the times she'd had occasion to slip into one of the chairs in the rear of this school gymnasium-turned-sanctuary. But most of the time she felt like a spy because she'd been watching him, looking for *any* of those tell-tale signs that would confirm her suspicions that he was a phony, like so many of the others. Mara loved God, but she'd had more than enough of clergy folk in her church experience. From the gospel-singing, holy-dancing, closeted homosexuals and smoking, cursing, Gheri-curled womanizers, to the fire-and-brimstone-spouting, wife-abusing adulterers. Mara had seen them all and wondered, even marveled, at the open irreverence they showed for the God that they claimed to represent. That's what had motivated her to come here, hoping to find that indeed this man, unlike those others, was what he said he was. A man who loved, lived, and was governed by the Word of God.

She had been truthful too, about the choir and the singing. But she had been hurt by these psalmists before. Yes, they wrote and sang beautiful songs to God, telling Him how worthy He was and how much they loved Him. But when the glory cloud moved and the anointing lifted, the smiles of spiritual ecstasy disappeared, replaced by pasted on

36

caricatures of lips and teeth, barely able to conceal the disdain they had for their *"sisters and brothers, in Christ."* Mara had prayed and worked hard to overcome the pain and then the bitterness it left. She had made up her mind that she could do *God's* work without going in *His* house, having to deal with *His* people because *they* weren't much different from the ones who called themselves sinners. At least worldly folk were honest about who they were, instead of hiding behind spiritual excuses like "God isn't finished with me yet." If He wasn't God, He would be, she had thought often.

So here she was, contemplating giving this "church thing" another try. Watching as the pastor greeted first, a very well endowed teenager and then a foul-smelling man with dirty clothes and matted hair she had seen on the street, Mara saw that they experienced the same smile and warm embrace that she had. And both felt right.

****

"Muh'dear wanted me to stay until after I had the baby, but his new job said Parris had to be here by the first of the month. Ah knew li'l Parris would be missin' his father and Ah didn't want to be away from him for five months either. 'Hit was bad enough when he had to come up here to see if he could fahnd someplace for us to stay. I cawled him almost ev'ry day he was up here. Ah was a 'reck Ah'll tell you."

Mara cupped Jovanda's heavy southern accent and drank in its innocent sweetness as she observed the obvious adoration she and Parris had for each other. *Li'l* Parris, holding the sleeping puppy on his lap, was sitting in the big reclining chair beside Buddy, whom he'd already started calling Poppy.

"That's what ev'rybody cawls mah deaddy on account of he's got big ahys lak mahn," Jovanda explained.

"Only his ahys aren't as pretty as yowas." Parris both mimicked and flattered his wife causing her to blush and Buddy to exclaim,

"Lord have mercy! You two make my face red. Cut it out!"

They all laughed, including Li'l Parris who had *no* idea what he was laughing about.

"Parris Ah guess it's about tahme for us to head on home. Miss Mara, thank you and Mr. Buddy for invahting us. And thank you for Li'l Parris' puppy."

Mara waved her hands at them and said, "Any time, any time… a boy needs a puppy, teaches him responsibility. We enjoyed havin' you all. Do you want to take somethin' home with you?"

"If Ah knew Ah didn't have to go to the doctor, Ah sure would take a slahce of thet potato pah. 'Hit tasted as good as Muh'dears' pah, but Ah better not" said Jovanda as she hugged her.

Mara watched as Parris zipped up his son's jacket and then picked him up in his right arm before placing his left arm around Jovanda's thickening waist. Looking on as they settled Little Parris and the puppy in the back seat, she mentally patted herself on her back; she had been right again. Parris had grown up to be a fine young man; Melvin would have been proud.

As she and Buddy stood on the porch waving to them as they drove away, Mara looked across the street at the apartment building on the corner. She saw Luce on her porch, turning what appeared to be hot dogs on a small hibachi. Caleb was standing in the door watching her as her children, a girl and twin boys, played on the sidewalk in front of the building. Standing on the second floor balcony, Rondell, the leader of the Usherettes drill team, was looking right at Mara, defiantly smoking a Blunt. He was a young man but acted and dressed like a girl, even down to his extension braids which right now were pulled up in a ponytail. Mara had seen him locked in an embrace with a young man who visited infrequently. Initially she wondered if the visitor actually knew what gender Rondell was, but got her answer when she'd seen them leaving a motel as she rode the bus to work one morning.

Despite Rondell's obvious attempt to bait her into addressing his public use of cocaine and marijuana, Mara chose not to be drawn in. Instead she turned to follow Buddy back into their house when she noticed Zena's car pulling into the space Parris and his family had just vacated. Closing the storm door behind Buddy, she walked to the edge of the porch.

"And what brings you by here this nice evenin', Miz Baldwin? I thought you'd be watchin' the Lifetime channel by now."

"That's just what I plan to do, but I didn't make anything sweet for dessert today, and I knew you did because you told me that you were having company for dinner. So I drove over to get a slice of potato pie to eat with this sherbert I just bought," Zena replied.

"Who told you that I had potato pie, and if I did, who told you I had any left?" Mara teased.

"Mara Singleton, I have known you for thirty-one years, and if I know *anything*, I know this. If you had company, you made potato pie and since you did, you made an extra one for yourself. Because don't **nobody** love your potato pie better than you!"

Laughing, Mara said, "Well, since you know all that, you might as well come on in. I was just gonna clean up the rest of the dishes and then fix me and Buddy a slice."

As Zena reached to catch the door Mara was holding open, a blast of loud music came from the apartment building across the street. Looking back over her shoulder to see who it was, Zena saw the drill team leader dancing suggestively on the balcony.

"That poor child is con-*fused*, Mara. Don't know whether he wants to be his mother's other daughter or his sister's little brother. He needs Jesus!"

"All I can do is just pray for him, Zena. He's got a momma somewhere and I am not her," Mara said as they walked down the hallway toward the kitchen.

"Speaking of that, did you hear that Naomi's going to be a grandmother again?" asked Zena.

"And where might I hear that from, Miss Zena? You know I don't run in and out of peoples' houses carryin' dirt," Mara responded, hands on her hips.

"You don't *have* to run in and out of peoples' houses. All you have to do is open up your eyes like I do, 'Miss' Mara! I saw Valeta coming out of the clinic the other day, belly looking like there's no more room for Jello," Zena reported proudly.

"If there was such a person as Lady Luck, I'd shoot her on sight if I was Naomi. That's the last thing she needs right now, another mouth to feed. What is she goin' to do now?" Mara thought out loud.

"That's *your* girlfriend, Mara. Why don't you call and ask her?"

"I sure will," she replied, slicing and wrapping Zena's pie to go. "I sure will."

As she stood again on the porch a few minutes later to watch as Zena got in her car and drove away, Mara had cause to look across the street when she heard shouting coming from that direction. Quickly scanning the balconies, she tried to zero in on where the voices were coming from. This time it wasn't Luce and Caleb, though she suspected that before the night was over it would be. She looked to the third floor balcony where she saw two men wrestling. One of them, Rondell, was bent backward over the balcony wall while the other man had him by the neck in a stranglehold. Behind them, the young woman whom Mara knew to be Kaitlin, was screaming for them to stop.

Apparently the only audience member of this up-close-and-personal Jerry Springer show, Mara hesitated, wondering what, if anything she should do next. Noting that there were no visible weapons and gauging the height from the third floor to be about thirty or so feet, Mara realized that the wisest intervention would probably be by the police, so she went in the house to call them.

As she filled the dispatch person in on the whereabouts of the incident, Buddy looked up from the television.

40

"Baby, you can't solve the problems of the whole world."

Placing the receiver in the cradle, she sighed.

"I know. But I can't turn my head and pretend I don't see them either, Buddy."

Satisfied to see a patrol car stop and two officers get out and go into the building a few minutes later, she turned to Buddy and repeated the information Zena had given her about Naomi's daughter Valeta.

"Naomi sure could use a miracle in her life right about now, and somehow I bet you're tryin' to figure out a way to make it happen," Buddy said.

Setting his slice of pie on the table next to his glass of milk, Mara never heard him expressing *exactly* what she was thinking, so far had her thoughts already begun their expedition to Naomi's solution.

Picking up his fork and cutting into his pie, Buddy studied his wife. What he saw was a scene that was all too familiar to him, an almost ritual deja vu. Mara could not see someone in need and fail to respond if it was within her power to assist in any way. Her compassion was a quality that had endeared her to him, its depth surpassed only by the situations he often found himself in because of it.

Buddy often joked that he could be rich if he had a dollar for all of the cars he helped to push out of the snow. He could have started a business with all of the flat tires he had changed, though he had put his foot down about picking up hitchhikers. He had stood guard in the crowd when his wife reprimanded an elementary school bully for taking unfair advantage of his victim. His own natural inclination to help people had made Buddy carry an old lady's bags, but Mara wouldn't be satisfied until they had given her a ride home and put the groceries on the shelves of her pantry.

Buddy knew that her desire to help people was birthed from Mara's need to make the world right. That need was not a selfish one, but was compassed within the broader directive of God's command to 'do unto others as you would have them do unto you'. Buddy had come to understand that

41

Mara's "doing" was an investment in her own life and the lives she touched, one that had the Biblical promise of greater return. He knew that she responded to a higher motivation, that she would not be placated until she had exhausted every effort to help her friend now. Buddy could only wait to find out what his assignment would be.

Chapter 6

"You crazy ol' bum! Homeless faggot!"

"What kinda box you gon' sleep in tonight?"

"Aw, man you standin' in his kitchen!"

Mara heard the jeers of the kids gathered on the front steps of the apartment building before she rounded the corner, shaking her head at her *knowing* who they were talking to even before she saw them.

"You stink! You need t'go someplace and wash wit' yo funky self!"

"He actin' like he got dred locks 'cause he ain't combed his hair since last year."

Their cruel comments were aimed at the homeless man Mara had seen in the gymnasium-church that Sunday she had visited last. She'd seen him the past few mornings too, as she stood in the doorway to watch Buddy as he left for work. She had watched the man coming from the backyard of the abandoned house two doors down from the apartments, arranging his bags to begin his daily trek through the city. Her eyes had followed him as he'd searched the ground for a substantial cigar or cigarette butt, then, after lighting it, trudged down the street as if he had a time clock to punch. Her thoughts had followed him long after he was out of sight, wondering about the perceived senselessness of his life. Where did he go, and what did he intend to do when he got there? What had been the circumstance that led him to this nomadic subsistence, one far below what she was sure had once been his dreams and aspirations? What was the standard used to measure how far away he was from where he had intended to be at this point in his life, and what was the compass that could indicate the right direction should he desire to find the way back?

Who were his people, his *folks*, and why was he not there or they not here? Her Bible told her that '*God places the lonely in families, but that the rebellious live in a parched land.*' How great then, was the rebellion that gave cause to his parched reality? If rebellion was not the culprit, then who had wounded him consistently and deeply enough to make him decide he no longer wanted to occupy the same world that they lived in, opting instead to create his own little cosmos?

Her instinctive passion to right the world of its wrongs evoked a spirit of battle in her that oftimes led her into the demilitarized zone of someone else's war. And so it was in this instance.

"He must be rich 'cause he live in a abandominium, hah, hah."

The young people's loud and obtrusive derision of this man who already bore too much of the weight of life's contradictions moved Mara to his defense.

"Why don't you leave people alone? He's not botherin' you."

"Wha'on't choo mind ya bidness? You ain't got nuttin'a do wif it."

Their intent to intimidate her by their insolence was lost on Mara, for she had no fear of them. She *was* them, a generation or so removed, with a life-time of varied experiences and an endless storehouse of decisions, good *and* bad, from which to draw wisdom.

This was where they diverged, she and them, this "place" called Wisdom. It was here, as they traversed the wilderness path as yet unconquered by Wisdom, where the youthful impudence that they operated and placed so much of their trust in, was in fact the down-payment on the lives they would own in whatever futures they had. Many of those lives would bear amazing similarities to this one that they took ill-conceived liberty in mocking. Unbeknownst to them, it was *only* in this place of Wisdom that they could strike a deal with its owner, developer, and contractor to exchange the dwelling places they would erect for themselves, for the safely constructed ones that He had already fashioned for them.

44

"I go to prepare a place for you... come and go with me to my Father's house".

Mara understood that, now. But she could look at them and remember, too vividly, the times when her perception of what lay ahead was as opaque as these young people's. Her heart wept for them all ... those who had yet to find that place, the homeless man who rejected its refuge, and she who knew the cost that must be paid to live in Wisdom.

In the spirit of this appreciation, she could speak to them in a voice that somehow translated her empathy.

"You don't want to treat nobody like this. I *know* there's more love in you than that."

Their young eyes searched hers for a less-than-brief instant, finding something in them they recognized but could not explain. In the language translated in the heart, where love is the natural response to love did they avert their stares, turning their backs *to* Mara and *on* the continuation of their previous actions. Overtly conceding nothing, they now spoke to each other.

"She not my mother, she ain't talkin' to me!"

"Come on y'all. Let's go 'round *my* way where people not so *newsy.*"

They filed off the steps, going around the corner from which she had just come, hopefully taking with them some part of Wisdom's purchase price, leaving Mara to examine her own level of commitment to what she'd spoken.

Turning to the subject who was responsible for whatever had just taken place she said,

"How about if I go in the house, cut you a slice of potato pie and pour you a glass of ice cold milk. I'll bring it out and we can sit on my porch and visit awhile. Neighbors ought to get to know each other, the way I see it."

Mara wasn't *about* to invite no strange man into Buddy's house when he wasn't home, not any more. She had a heart as big as anybody's, but she wasn't crazy. Not by a long shot.

Hesitating for just the tiniest fraction of a second he asked,

"What color was the potatoes? I don't care too much for white potato pie."

"Then I guess today is the day God chose to bless you with the kind of pie you like. Don't get me wrong; I can make a good white potato pie too, but I just like yellow yams better," she answered him as they crossed the street to her and Buddy's house.

****

"I don't think it's such a good idea for you to bring *any* strangers here when I'm not home, Mara. 'Specially some homeless man that sleeps under the back porch of a house *right* across the street from where you live. You don't know what he might do."

"I know Buddy, and usually I would *never* do that. You know I don't even open the door for Jehovah Witnesses and I know some of them." Attempting to lessen his justifiable concern at what she had done Mara said, "But it was out on the front porch in broad daylight and.."

Buddy cut her off mid-sentence.

"People get killed in broad daylight every day, Baby. You know that."

Reflecting on the two hour rap session she had with the homeless man, Mara smiled and said, "Once you get to know him you'll see that if Garfield's got anything in him, it's not kill."

"And why would I be 'getting to know' *Mister* Garfield, *Missez* Singleton?"

It always made her smile inside when Buddy acted like he might be jealous of somebody having an interest in her, even though they both knew that this homeless man posed no threat. The fact was, no *"body"* posed a threat to Mara's commitment to this man or this marriage, for both were built on something more foundationally secure than any piece of paper could insure. It was those beings "without form and void" that haunted the hallways of this sacred institution, trying to terrorize her into abandoning its solace. These ghosts of lifetimes past rushed at her sometimes even in her conscious thoughts, booing and shrieking in their attempt to chase her out into the midnights of her life. They tried to lure her into her darknesses where shadowy images loomed large in her fearful anticipation of encountering them there.

Mara had once heard someone address those dark places. A preacher named Mark Chironna told the story of one day watching a TV special about Jacques Cousteau, the world-reknowned oceanographer. He held the acclaim of being responsible for the discovery of hundreds of different, beautifully colored species of marine life previously unknown to man. When asked how and where he had made these discoveries, Mr. Cousteau revealed that it was in the deepest and darkest parts of the ocean, the parts where most people either lacked the equipment and technical know-how or were simply afraid to go. The preacher said he asked God "Why did you hide some of your most wondrous creations in a place where no one could appreciate their beauty?" God's response to him was that their beauty was there for anyone who was willing to go into the deep, dark places; it was only hidden from those who could not or would not make the journey.

Mara understood, like the preacher had about himself, that much of the beauty of who she was lay hidden in some of the deepest, darkest places in her soul; places guarded by gargoyles of fear. She knew God was equipping her to go there to discover and rescue herself.

"Now who's not listenin' to who, Miss Deep-in-my-own-thoughts? I want to know why I need to get to know Mr. Gypsy-come-lately!"

"Now Buddy, that was not a nice thing to say."

"Who said I was bein' nice? Why can't you just sit in the house and watch 'All These Children' like ev'rybody else? I keep tellin' you, it's not your job to save the world, that's God's job. What're you doin', tryin' to put Him out of work?"

Mara walked over to where Buddy was reaching into the cabinet for his cayenne pepper. She put her arms around his

47

neck, waited until he turned his head to look at her, and gave him one of those old-time Sugar-pie, Honey-bunch kisses. Then she said,

"I think I got some work for *you* to do. And you won't be needin' that cayenne. I can make it hotter than that."

Buddy just closed the cabinet.

Chapter 7

Mara clapped her hands as she joined in the excited activity that was taking place all around her. She knew now to call it praise and worship, but there was a time when she thought that it was just a lot of religious caterwauling. She watched as the slender, young girls on the church's dance team gracefully stepped in time to the uplifting tempo of the music. It was certainly different from the old hymns they'd sung at most of the churches she'd attended in years past; it was a good different. And she was glad that they didn't have one of *those* "choirs": the kind where even a less than omniscient eye could detect the disparity between what they sang and what they lived. Mara smiled as she remembered the title a visiting evangelist had given these church-goers. She'd called them "Listerine Christians", the kind that cruised the bars getting drunk and whoring around Saturday night, only to get up on Sunday morning and in preparation for teaching their Sunday school classes, gargle to camouflage the tell-tale evidence.

Mara wondered again at how many people believed that this was an acceptable standard, that God *understood* their unwillingness to aspire to and maintain His standard for Godly living. I just don't know how it is, she thought, that we pray to God, and ask Him to come to see about us in our ugly situations; then when He does show up, we redirect Him somewhere else, expecting Him to sit down and wait until we get ready to talk to Him.

The image of God sitting quietly, leafing through magazines while nursing a cup of decaf, waiting to be beckoned into an office was enough to make Mara laugh out loud, and she did. Thankfully it was lost in the joyousness of the worship, swallowed up in the "Praise the Lords" and "Hallelujahs" of the people.

Mara added her own "Hallelujah", grateful for this new thing that she realized was happening in her. She watched as women lifted their hands in surrender to the move of God in their lives, yet she couldn't help but question the different dilemmas that motivated these surrenders. She speculated about whose daughter was pregnant, whose son was in jail, who had gotten a negative report from the doctor. Of the hands in the air, how many represented homes where the husband had moved out, or worse, was there in body only? How many of these hands had received pink slips or utility shut-off notices?

Observing that there were young hands raised, Mara flinched at the flashing realization that some belonged to little girls who were being abused, sexually as well as emotionally --- perhaps at the hands of men so haunted by guilt that it deterred them from lifting their own hands above half mast. Others were the hands of young males that had already held and pointed guns, or those already saddled with the premature responsibility of trying to be fathers. For too many of them this lifting of the hands had already come too late. This surrender had been last in line to the other ones that had busted in ahead of them; surrenders which, had they waited their turn in proper order, might have given their owners a real chance at life.

But now, these yielded hands were connected to lives already filled with too much "stuff". Mara's mind pictured checkout lines with these hands pushing carts overrun with life's junk food. Selections made selfishly and indulgently, by persons ignorant of their need for nutritious, well-balanced existences. Those selections had been and would be paid for in currency they could ill afford or charged on credit that would take a lifetime to pay back.

Mara struggled to free herself of the mental pile-up their problems were creating in her mind, and again focused on what was happening here and now for her. Momentarily saddened by the realization that these "shopping carts" were what Jesus died to pay for, she was instantly grateful that she had a God whom she allowed to do *her* life's shopping. *A-men*!

****

"Mama? Hey, how you doin'?" Mara asked as she peeked around the hospital curtains. Her heart wrenched just like it did every other time she had come, overwhelmed by each new change she saw. She anguished over every pound no longer present, yet so badly needed to fill out these sunken and hollowed cheeks, to fatten the curves of these bony shoulders just visible above the starched white sheet. Mara fought back the tears and straightened her face as these too-recently grayed-lashes parted to reveal eyes whose sparkle was missing and already missed. Softly, lovingly, she smiled down at this face she loved yet no longer recognized.

"He-e-y, Mama. It's me. Look what I brought you, it's potato pie." Mara walked around the bed and taking off the aluminum foil, held it up for Mother Pearl to see.

"I did everything you told me to, so if it don't taste like yours it's because you held back on one of your secret ingredients."

Struggling to part her dry, cracked lips into a smile, Mother Pearl nodded her head and said, "I told you everything, shuggah. It looks like mine. Put it over there, I'll eat some later." Though they both knew she probably wouldn't eat any of it, Mara was comforted in knowing that Mother Pearl recognized the pie as a labor of love.

Repositioning the foil and setting the pie on the windowsill, Mara was pleased, yet uncomfortable at the fact that she was Mother Pearl's only visitor. She'd expected to come in and mix in the muted chatter that usually went on among the many family and well-wishers who regularly stopped in, and she wondered now, what she would say after the hospital formalities had been observed.

She smiled as she mentally questioned, "How can you know somebody all of your life and not have nothing to talk about?" She knew part of the answer was in the years that separated them.

Pearl Foster was about the same age as Mara's mother, raised within the value systems and social morality of their generation, a generation only seventy-five years removed from the actual day-to-day face of slavery. It was only reasonable to try to imagine how deeply the caverns were etched in the attitudes and actions of people whose parents and grandparents had belonged to other people--- human beings who denied others the right to be identified as human, establishing an Emily Post-esque etiquette for inhumane treatment. These were the attitudes and influences that colored the canvas Mother Pearl's life had been painted on, but she had managed to side-step much of the fallout of this time.

Mara smiled as she looked over at her, sleeping again because of the medication. "Uh-uhn, not Mother Pearl. She was her *own* woman, and if you dared to get in her way, she'd let you know it in no uncertain terms," Mara said, not realizing she had thought out loud until Mother Pearl stirred. As her eyes found and held her face, Mother Pearl managed to mutter a phrase that brought tears to Mara's eyes.

"How's Mama's little white baby?"

Reaching out with her light-skinned hand to hold Mother Pearl's gnarled and shrunken mahogany-colored one, Mara thought out loud again.

"Better for havin' you in my life."

But Mother Pearl never heard it as she slipped back into sleep.

Chapter 8

Mara sat in Buddy's chair, her way of touching him when he wasn't there. Though the TV was on, she wasn't watching it, didn't even hear the announcer's

"Roosevelt Jones, come on down!"

As she sat staring into her own thoughts, there was a subtle intrusion on her mental movie. Out of the corner of her eye, Mara saw an ever-so-slight movement. When she focused on it, she saw a praying mantis on the windowpane. It sat there, only occasionally repositioning itself; an almost imperceptible flickering of its legs, a delicate whispering of its antennae.

She remembered knowing that the antenna was an insect's means of communication and she wondered what it was he was saying. Was he talking to another praying mantis about the events of their day? Or was he sharing philosophies with some caterpillar because insects understood each other in some kind of universal language? Just then, the mantis slid down the glass, landing on the wooden ledge of the window frame. Maybe his mere presence on her windowsill was an attempt to speak to something in her. Perhaps he was symbolic of God's having answered her prayers; a visible reminder that the answer was there, quiet and unobtrusive, waiting to be noticed.

Suddenly the insect turned toward where she looked out at him and appeared to stare fixedly into her eyes. Then he slowly lifted a foreleg and very determinedly began to tap, tap on the window. Did he represent the solution to her present situation, more insistently now, wanting to be let in? She watched as he climbed back up, struggling to regain the ground he had lost. He balanced himself precariously on the edge of the window screen, so useful in its appropriate season when all of God's creation was in full regalia and bustling with life.

It was during the spring time that she lowered the screen to give access to the warmth of the early sunrise, to see the haze as the dew lifted from its nighttime resting place on new, young blades of grass, only to return to its daytime abode somewhere in God's atmosphere. The screen exposed her to soft fragrances and cool evening breezes that were so welcome after the humidity of a summer day. It served to remind Mara of the summers of her lifetime when Gods' blessings were in great abundance.

How wonderful it had been to meet Buddy after her self-imposed seclusion. It had been almost three years after "the Nate thing". She had felt him looking at her as the family lined up in front of the church to throw rice when Mr. and Mrs. Wyatt's daughter, Mona, had gotten married. Later on, at the backyard wedding reception/family reunion, he walked over to her with the last of a slice of pie in his bare hand.

"I just thought I should come and pay my compliments to the cook. They tell me that you're the person I need to thank for this knee-thumpin' potato pie."

Feeling the rustiness of the door hinges where she and her socialization skills had been locked away, Mara peeked warily from behind the door's protection.

"You don't have to thank me, but I'm glad you liked it."

"You ought to make you up a sign and put it in your kitchen window. This pie is good enough to sell. Who taught you to bake like that?"

Mara ventured a little further out from her safety zone. Bringing the image of Mother Pearl to her mind's eye, she made a mental note to go by and check on her.

"That recipe belongs to a lady who was a friend of my mother's. I used to go to her house all the time when I was a little girl because she could cook anything and everything. When I got to be a teenager, she took me under her wing. She told me "Girl, men spend much more time in the kitchen than they do in the bedroom. So you better know how to cook.""

Realizing too late how close to too much information she had just given him, Mara clapped her hand over her mouth. But she needn't have worried, Buddy wasn't the type of man who would take advantage of her sudden vulnerability. She had no way of knowing that now, but she would learn that it was so as their relationship progressed.

For the rest of that afternoon they'd laughed and talked. He'd helped her fold the tablecloths after they had shaken the crumbs into the corrugated tin trashcans. He'd taken the folding chair out of her hand.

"You leave that alone, Miss Potato Pie, that's a man's job. I'll get that."

She'd peeked out the window and watched his strong muscles flexing as he helped the other men take down the tables and load them in Mr. LeGrand's truck. Something stirred inside her when he took off his white dress shirt revealing broad, sweat-glistening, brown shoulders to join in a game of horse shoes out under the tree. This stirring unnerved her as she realized when she'd felt something like it before, and she immediately challenged herself to control it. She wasn't willing to even entertain any of what had followed this feeling the 'last' time. It was almost as painful now, years later, as it had been then. And the ache of missing what she didn't have was ever present... like the pain of a toothache dulled by oil of cloves, the sweet fragrance of an attempt to fill a painful void.

But again, Mara had no cause for concern. She realized it as she saw him rush over to where Romayne and his brother Tremayne were fighting over whose turn it was to push little Vicky in the rope swing. In the midst of the struggle, Vicky had fallen out of the swing and ended up face down in the dirt. Buddy swooped her up with one hand and, holding her against his shoulder, reached out to separate the two boys. Reaching into his pocket he gave each boy a quarter and, after putting her down and brushing the dirt off her face and her 'pretty little frock', took her by the hand. Together the four of them walked over to the curb where the water ice truck was parked, and he saved the day by ordering "three cherry, a vanilla and a peach, please."

As the children sat on the porch licking their frosty treats, Mara was surprised to see Buddy walking in her direction.

"They don't sell sweet potato water ice, so I bought you peach. Unless you rather have vanilla," he said, holding both funnel shaped cups in front of him. "Vanilla is my favorite, but you're welcome to it."

And that's how it had been ever since then... she was welcome to the very best he had to give. And he worked hard to make sure he could provide it.

God had been good to them, and Buddy had been good to her. She didn't have to work if she didn't want to; in fact, Buddy tried to make her a stay-at-home-wife. But Mara had insisted--- she needed something to do, especially since they had never had any children. In this matter too, she had been blessed. As Buddy had courted her over those next months, there came the time when she knew she had to tell him... about Nate and all the other stuff that was that part of her painful past. He held her when she couldn't hold back the tears that spilled down her face as she forced the story out. And she believed Buddy when he told her that he was sorry about the mistake the doctors had made. She needed to hear him say that it would be all right, though it hadn't ever been all right since that horrible day she'd found out that she would never again have the chance to be a mother. As she looked into his eyes on their wedding day, she knew it really was okay. God wasn't punishing her; He had forgiven her. And He sent Buddy to walk with her on the long journey to forgiving herself.

Now, over the years, like the neighborhood where they had settled in to begin the next leg of this journey, many things had changed. Buddy was beginning to show the strain of working on a job that was physically challenging to men half his age. But what else was he going to do? Who was going to hire him now? Like a marathon runner, he knew he had to keep going until he reached his destination. He had several more years before he could even see the end, and miles to go until he'd finally cross the finish line to retirement and rest.

Mara considered this as she stared back at the praying mantis. The fair weather screen had now been replaced by the storm window, pulled down to shut out the cold and threatening winter with its death-like appearance of barrenness. The praying mantis had somehow missed autumn when it should have sought shelter from the impending frosts. Like Mara, the mantis was left to deal with the cold.

Turning away from the window, Mara joked with her Father.

"OK, God. I see you and I hear you and I'm willin' to let you in. But as for that prayin' mantis, well, it's still a bug and I'm not lettin' it in here."

Yet she continued to reflect on God's symbolic colloquy. Gone were the brilliant pinks and purples of her springtime, the pastel yellows and soft corals of God's abundance that had once bloomed so fiercely in her life's garden. Even the small, green buddings from which they'd sprouted seemed no longer apparent. It appeared as though nothing in her life was producing anything. She had, like the praying mantis, missed the time of preparation. She hadn't meant to. She was only trying to live right, to somehow make amends to them, to Him. So she'd stopped... everything. She had just continued to exist. She wouldn't let herself be pretty or even want to. That's why she was so surprised that Buddy had thought she was; she thought she had done a fairly good job of hiding inside herself. But he had loved her and nurtured her back to a moderate level of acceptance. It had finally become at least okay to be herself. Buddy had demonstrated enough love and made enough sacrifices to make her believe that she was indeed worthy of him. But maybe he had gone too far, because now Mara wanted something more.

Most people would be and were satisfied with the kind of comfortable existence that was her and Buddy's life to this point. But for Mara something was missing. Her life was like block letters, mostly lower case. Only inside of herself she needed capital letters; bold, italicized, underlined ones that spelled out the words describing a life that she could not find a way to live. It wasn't that she didn't appreciate her life; it just seemed empty, filled with a whole lot of nothing. And nothing added, subtracted, multiplied and divided still equaled naught.

She wondered if anyone else ever felt like she too often did of late, as though life had sprinted past her, passing her baton to someone who wasn't even on her team. And she had to watch while they ran and won a race that she had somehow been disqualified from before she could even show her stuff.

"It's not fair, God."

There; she'd finally said it.

A tear found its way down Mara's cheek, and suddenly she found herself in an ice storm of tears. They fell relentlessly on her breasts, hard and cutting, as if to pierce her heart, the very one that housed the doubt, fear and anguish that these tears were all about. She couldn't let that happen because then her heart would be exposed and everyone would see what was in it... especially Buddy. She would never do anything to make him feel as if his best wasn't good enough.

Slowly her tears changed into softer, 'snow-flake' ones, blanketing her emotions against themselves, comforting her. And anyway, so what if it wasn't fair? Fair meant you got what you deserved, and she didn't want God to pay her what they both knew she'd earned at some other time in her life. She only wanted what she wanted.

Eventually her tears dried completely, and Mara was able to take a deep breath.

I sure am glad that pity-party is over, she thought, blowing her nose into a Kleenex. Now let me get up from here and get in this kitchen and get these pots rattlin' before Buddy comes home.' It was always a comfort to know that he was coming home, and even more reassuring when she heard his key turn in the lock.

Later, much later, after he'd had his dinner and a nap, after he'd flipped through the newspaper to read about all the bad things that were happening close to him, after he'd watched the seven o'clock news and knew all of the horrible things that were happening all around the world, then they'd talk. Later they could have a discussion about the face of things to come in their house; they'd talk about how they were going to pay the bills now that her last unemployment check had come.

Mara pulled out her big pot and put some yams on to boil. Out loud she said "I'll make him a pie," while the rest of the thought stayed in her head, 'so he'll have something sweet to take with the bitter.'

****

As she lay in bed next to Buddy reading, Mara nodded in and out of sleep. Her catnap was interrupted by a noise. Afraid at first that the barely appreciable rustling near her ear might have been some creature occupying the bed other than Buddy and herself, she was relieved to realize that she'd been awakened by the beating of her own heart. Comforted by this awareness and Buddy's soft snoring, she did what she always did when she woke to find herself among the living. Unwilling to disturb his sleep, Mara *thought* her thanksgiving. Thank you, Lord, for waking me up on this side of heaven. She lay quietly in this moment, listening to the rhythmic cadence of her life force as it pulsed through her body, sustaining her. All at once she found herself again thrust into that place of overwhelming comprehension of the awesomeness of God. It was He who orchestrated the symphonic harmony of all that she was---her breath, her heartbeat, the blink of her eye, the quickening of her thoughts. He took pen in hand and authored every chapter of who she'd been and would become. He was the choreographer of her every movement and the administrator of the business of her perpetual existence, whether it was here on earth or in that place where He is. The best part of it

59

all was that He gave her, in glimpses of time like this one, the ability to understand His greatness. It was the God she loved who, by the enabling power of His grace and the magnitude of His mercy, created, in her deepest self, gratitude at the thought that He had chosen to love her first. Because she was assured of that love, she knew that the answers to the questions that she'd not yet asked could be found in Him.

"If any of you lacks wisdom, he should ask God, who gives generously to all without finding fault, and it will be given to him."

The cry of her heart rushed up, and out through her lips.

"Help me, God! Show me what we should do!"

"Hunh? Wha'choo say? Do about what?"

Buddy questioned, reaching out his hand to protect and provide for her, though yet suspended somewhere between wakefulness and sleep.

Placing her hand in his and moving to rest her head on his shoulder, Mara answered, "It's nothin', honey. You go on back t'sleep."

Even she had no way of knowing how prophetic her next words would become.

"It was just a dream."

Chapter 9

"These four go to Patsy's Pastry Corner, and these five to the Drop In and Dine. This one is for Sister Scott, and I'm taking this one to the pastor and his wife. The first four are paid for, but you'll need to get the money for these other six. I'll see you later in church. Okay?"

Buddy just nodded his understanding of her instructions, knowing that it was up to him to figure out how to deliver ten pies to three different places and get to church without being late, *all* within the next hour. Though technically she wasn't open on Sundays, Mara took special orders for that day and would get up at four or five o'clock in the morning to start baking. Because she liked to make sure that her pies would indeed be "warm and fresh from the oven" at Grandma's Hands Homemade Pies, Buddy was drafted to be her Sunday morning delivery service.

The fact was, he really didn't mind. Mara was quite the businesswoman, and even if she wasn't, Buddy loved her and would do anything for her. That's why he'd taken out a second mortgage on the house to buy the building that used to be Take Out Tacos and T'ings. Mara had been right when she'd observed that "it's got its own parking lot and they already zoned it for that kind of business."

He'd been impressed at how she had done all the legwork in researching what had to be done in order to get started. So impressed was he that he had talked a couple of the guys at work into helping him renovate the place for a couple of hours, two or three nights a week. One of them was a licensed electrician, and Buddy knew that he alone had saved them hundreds of dollars. When he shared this bit of information with Mara, she took it all in stride.

"I thank him and I'm grateful, but when God laid it on his heart to do it, he really had no other choice, Buddy. It's called the favor of God."

Buddy had understood what she meant. For years Mara had at different times mentioned and thanked God for His "favor" in the situations that had risen to confront them. At first, he thought it was coincidence, acting in cooperation with hard work and common sense. But one Sunday, after he had taken Mara up on her invitation to go to the gymnasium-church, he'd heard something that stood at attention in his mind, and ultimately caused him to follow through with the plans for Grandma's Hands.

"A good idea will never replace a vision, for vision is God-inspired. And where God gives vision, He gives *pro*-vision."

For Buddy, the pastor's statement had been simple yet profound, though being a very uncomplicated meat-and-potatoes kind of man, he would never have defined it in those terms. He considered Mara the intellectual one in their house. To Buddy it just made sense. And it made sense to him that God favored His children, that He indulged them, preferred them, and treated them with special kindness. Some people probably thought that this favor was unfair, especially as attributed to God. But even if they liked them a whole lot, loved them even, didn't people prefer their own children over someone else's, treating them with a kindness that nosed ahead of the kindness they showed everyone else? Conversely, (though Buddy had no idea that that word existed except on the news) since God favored His children, shouldn't they favor Him? Not only in special consideration for who He is, but shouldn't His children look like Him? Have mannerisms like His? Buddy thought so, and it had prompted him to answer the altar call that day. When he'd gotten in the truck after church was over, he'd reflected on the words of the altar counselor.

"Now that you've accepted Christ as your personal Lord and Savior, the Holy Spirit has come to live on the inside of you. It's His job to lead you and guide you in all truth."

Looking down at his chest for the briefest second, Buddy thought that his heart felt just a little different than it had before. As the truck motor revved, he looked over at his wife sitting calmly with that smug, 'I knew he would finally come' look on her face.

Suddenly Buddy was glad that he had someone else to help him find his way if he was lost. Sometimes Mara just knew too much.

****

"I can't get over how big he is since I last saw you, Jovanda! What have you been feeding this baby?"

"The ownly thang Ah give him besides his bottle is cereal and fruit, Mom Mara."

"Well then, it must be something in what they're givin' the cows. Valeta, come here and look at this baby! This is what you've got to look forward to."

Valeta waddled in from the other room over to the counter where Mara and Jovanda were standing.

"Hey Jovanda, he-e-ey JayVon. Look at you and your big, pretty eyes."

"Hey Valeta. Gi-ir-rl when are you gon' have thet baby? You sure you ain't got twins in ther? Jesus keep the book!"

"And He can keep one of those twins you talkin' about. I don't know what I'm gonna do with one baby. I sure don't need two!"

As the three of them laughed at Valeta's comment, a man cupped his hand over his eyes to peer into the shop's window. Something about his face flashed familiar in Mara's mind, but he moved on before she could pinpoint it. Furrowing her brows, she stared at the place where he'd just stood.

"Where in the worl' did you go so fast? One secont you were laughing with us and now you look like you're tryin' out for Jeopardy!"

"I'm sorry, Jovanda, but that man looked familiar to me for some reason," Mara responded, still trying to figure out why.

"I didn't even see him, but don't make me have to tell Uncle Buddy that you're creepin' behind his back with some strange man." This came from Valeta.

"Your Uncle Buddy knows I don't want nobody but him, and if I did, I wouldn't creep. I'd tell him right to his face. We don't have no secrets, 'Leta."

And it was true. On those rare occasions when she'd summoned the courage to explore her "deep, dark places", she'd shared with Buddy whatever revelation she received. Much of it was painful, but there was an added measure of liberty that came afterward, because God had held her hand and walked through those places and times with her. With Him as her escort, Mara placed her name on the visitor's list of those she'd mentally imprisoned. One by one, as she was able to, she'd opened her mind's eye and looked at the face that stared back at her.

"Prisoner number 16374"...her girlfriend's father. *"You have been remanded to this institution for perpetrating moral injustices and sexual acts against a child, left in your care."*

Mara remembered when she'd slept over at her friend's house and awakened to the horror of finding her friends' father nursing at her thirteen-year-old breast. She recalled the panic of not knowing what to do or what to say except to threaten to scream and awaken his wife.

"Who do you think she'll believe, you or me? And anyway, I've seen you in the alley with those boys. You like it."

Not sure whether he was correct in his assessment of her morality, Mara elected not to tell anyone. After all, she did like it when the boys her age showed her that kind of attention. Didn't everyone?

So he had become her first in a long line of prisoners. Only now, with God as the guard, she switched roles from visitor to warden. She was able to release him, not on good behavior, but because Mara knew he had long since died and posed no threat to anyone. And now, he no longer held the power to terrify her.

"Prisoner 22869"... her neighbor. *"Your crime is that of misappropriated youthful curiosity as committed against one incapable of protecting herself from its subtle yet emotionally lethal tentacles."*

"Let me just touch it...ok?"

The memory of how bad she'd wanted to belong, to be accepted, sprang up in her as if it had been just that morning. She'd known she shouldn't let him, but she'd known he wouldn't let her play Truth or Dare as they sat on the steps, late on those summer nights. He'd say she was too little and all the big kids would agree with him, and she'd be left out. She'd oft played a game of tag trying to avoid rejection, even at this tender age. Somehow, no matter how hard she'd run, at the end of the encounter she was always 'it.' So she'd had to give in and let him touch her...there.

She sensed the comfort of God's presence as she decided to release this prisoner too. She wasn't sure why, except somehow she knew that He wanted her to.

As the ghost of her neighbor departed for the habitation of emancipated torment, Mara saw others behind him, their arms straining through the bars, begging to be loosed. But she couldn't handle facing these others. Not that day. God patted her on the back He understood. He again took her hand in His and walked her back to her right now.

"Mom Mara, Parris' Deaddy's coming up this week-end. Me and Parris wont you and Uncle Buddy to come ovah for dinner after church."

This was a face from the past she could handle.

"All right, Jovanda. I'll tell Buddy. He'll probably be glad to taste somebody else's cookin' for a change. Except I will bring a couple of pies so he won't feel homesick."

****

"It sure was nice seein' DeMont again after all these years, Buddy. It brought back memories of Melvin and Versiel and the good old days."

"I remember those days too, and I don't remember that they was none too good."

"Well, maybe you're right, but it was fun talkin' about the old times. I'm glad that DeMont did the right thing after Versiel died. Takin' Parris with him, I mean."

"It was his boy, that's what he was s'posed to do, Mara." (Why didn't she leave him alone so he could watch the end of this movie?)

"Now Buddy, people don't of a notion do what they s'posed to do, even *today*! That man wasn't for definite that that baby was even his. He had gone on back south when Hortensia found out she was pregnant!"

"So what you're tellin' me is he never did see the boy 'til after Versiel died?"

"Well, no. He did come up when Parris was about six months old. And I believe I remember him being at Melvin's funeral. Then I remember he came up here that year they had the carnival at Midtown."

"I had forgot all about the Midtown Carnival. A group of us used to jump in the back of an old pick-up truck and drive over there from Albertaville. I'm surprised you remember that."

Of course Mara remembered. How could she forget? That was when "the Nate thing" happened.

Mara could almost smell the sticky apples and the corn roasting on the homemade steel- drum-barbecue-grill. She and Verseil had decided earlier in the week to take Parris to the carnival on that Saturday night after they had finished washing and ironing their laundry.

But the day before, on Friday, Mara had met Nathaniel. He'd sat down across the aisle from her on the number twelve bus as she was riding home from work. She had tried to act like she hadn't really noticed him when he'd stepped on the bus. But she had seen this tall, brown, handsome young man as he'd run along side of the bus trying to make it stop for him. She'd managed to avert her eyes only seconds before he'd turned around and nearly caught her checking him out when he'd put his money in the box. She had stopped at the Pig In A Poke after work to pick up some bleach and a few groceries and had set the brown bag on the seat next to her when old Miss Newkirk had gotten off at her stop. He had gotten on the stop after Miss Newkirk, she remembered, because she was mad at herself for having the bag on the seat.

She needn't have worried. That didn't stop him. Nothing got in Nathaniel's way when he wanted something.

"So what's for dinner?" he'd asked, motioning toward her bag.

She'd decided to be witty.

"Bleach soup and bread with mustard. Oh yea-uh, and some canned milk."

"Either I'm strange or you need some new recipes."

She remembered how startlingly white his smile was as they both laughed at his observation. Add one deep dimple *and* "good" hair, and he looked like something good to eat.

By the time they got to her stop, they were talking and laughing like they rode home together every day. She remembered wishing that they would.

When she'd gathered her groceries and turned to say goodbye as she got off the bus, she was pleasantly surprised to see him follow her down the steps. He reached for her bag and walked beside her toward her house. She wasn't sure what she was going to do when they got there. He was nice, but he was still a stranger.

She was glad to see Versiel and Parris outside on the little grassy area in front of their house. He was tossing his ball against the wall while his grandmother sewed buttons on his uniform shirt. Versiel looked up as Mara came up, taking silent inventory of her escort.

"Hi, Mara. Me and Parris have been out here for a little while. I was wondering where you were."

"Oh I stopped at the Pig In A Poke on my way home to pick up a few things."

"It looks like groceries isn't all you picked up on the way home."

Before Mara could answer her, Parris walked over. "Are you Auntie Mara's boyfriend?"

Mara's mouth flew open in embarrassment. "Parris Milford!"

Nathaniel laughed and stooped down so he was eye level to Parris. "I'm not her boyfriend yet, but how about puttin' in a good word for me?"

Something warmed inside her when she'd heard what he'd said. Her first mistake. But it had been a long time since she'd had a 'suitor.' Maybe her dry spell was over. Hallelujah!

Nathaniel stood and talked with Versiel when Mara went in her house to put away her things. When she'd looked out of the window on her way upstairs, it appeared that Versiel was enjoying the conversation. Melvin had been dead almost three years by then. The only men in Versiel's life were the ones at work who didn't look at her "like that", the ones in the neighborhood that already belonged to someone else, and her grandson Parris, so she was as starved for male attention as Mara pretended she wasn't.

"If God sends me a man, fine, and if He don't send me a man, it's *still* fine," she'd often been heard to say. But maybe now Mara wouldn't have to say that any more.

The four of them had sat out until after ten o'clock when Versiel took Parris inside to put him to bed. Mara and "Nate"(by then) had continued talking in between listening to WDAS's Quiet Storm until almost midnight. When she finally told him she had to go in, they had made plans to meet the next night at the carnival.

Mara was embarrassed at her own excitement. After all, she was twenty-nine years old!' she told herself. But she couldn't hide her anticipation as she'd rushed through her chores the next day. It obviously was all over her face as she and Versiel and Parris walked to catch the bus to take them to Midtown.

"You look really nice, Auntie Mara."

She'd put on her blue pedal pushers and her white pull-over sweater.

"Thank you, PM."

"You gonna' see Mr Nathaniel at the carnival?"

"Why would you be askin' me somethin' like that?"

"Mom-mom said that you was singing all day, even when you was foldin' your clothes. You *hate* to fold your clothes. And you got on those nice pants and you are ackin' really nervous."

Mara had made a mental note to act more composed when she got to the carnival grounds. If it had been that easy for Parris to see, she needed to fix something on the inside that wouldn't be so apparent on the outside. But as they'd gotten off the bus, Nate was walking up to meet them, and her brain was a synaptic traffic jam as her eyes fell on him.

They'd had a ball, eating hot dogs and popcorn and drinking lemonade. They all had ridden the Ferris wheel, but she and Versiel sat on the grass on the sheet she'd stuck in her carry bag, and watched as Nate and Parris rode the merry-go-round. He'd looked so "in place" standing next to Parris as the painted steed went up and down. When it was time to catch the bus back, Parris had fallen asleep, exhausted, and Nate volunteered to carry him home. It was so appropriate; Nate fit in their lives so well.

Versiel took Parris from off Nathaniel's shoulder and carried him in the house herself. No other man had been in Melvin's house since he'd been killed...not even the insurance man who usually just knocked and walked into the house of his customers who lived in the projects.

"Let me use your bathroom before I leave. All that lemonade we drank needs to come out."

Her second mistake. Only she wasn't fooled by his tactic. She'd recognized it for just what it was. The mistake she made was that she had wanted him to stay as much as he did. Her third mistake was that she had thought she could say stop when she wanted to. He had been such a gentleman last night and tonight.

"B----! What do you mean, stop?! You didn't say stop when I was spendin' my money at the carnival. You knew I was coppin' a feel on the ferris wheel and you didn't say stop then."

She'd known. She hadn't said stop. Did any one?

"You know why? 'Cause you liked it, that's why."

Mara grimaced at the familiarity of those words

"And you gonna' like this too!"

She hadn't. She hated the haughty smirk that replaced the smile that had so enchanted her earlier, as he tucked in his shirt and combed his "good hair". She didn't like the dull resignation that formed a lump in her throat and her mind--- resignation that announced her gullibility, as his reflection in her mirror winked at her before walking out her door. She didn't like the lingering smell of his cologne...on her blouse, in her nose, in her memory.

Neither did she like it when she missed her period the next month. And the next month. And for the next seven months after that. She hadn't liked realizing that she hadn't even known Nathaniel's last name. Or where he lived. Or where he'd come from.

If she'd known any of these things, maybe she would have tried to find him to tell him he had a son. And maybe he would have cared. But she didn't know. And she didn't care to have to raise his son, this one he'd probably never know existed.

So over Zena's attempts to console her, and her protests that Mara would regret it, Mara made up her mind. Ignoring Versiel's assurances to Mara that she could manage (Versiel had, hadn't she?) Mara made up that part of her mind that hadn't betrayed her, the part that led her to believe that she had a right to be loved. Despite the whispers of the people on her job, the knowing looks of her neighbors and the sideways glances of Miss Newkirk as they rode the bus, Mara signed the papers.

She'd looked at him only once before she'd given him back to the nurse before leaving the hospital that day. Mara had to at least look at him to see if he looked like her. She'd searched his face for Nathaniel's dimple. It was there. When she saw it, she knew she'd made the right decision. As she gently ran her hand over his head full of thick, black, "good hair", she was achingly certain. He was a beautiful baby and he deserved to be loved. Mara knew that she couldn't love him. She knew she couldn't love because she couldn't trust. Wouldn't trust. Any man. Any more.

As she'd stepped on the pavement outside the hospital, her belly and her arms empty, her eyes filled with tears. She'd looked down at her shadow on the ground and watched as a salt-filled droplet fell on the surface that was as hard as her heart. As she'd walked into the wind, her tears had blown behind her. They, like her baby, became part of her past.

"Mara, is that the same guy who shot the woman in the beginnin' of the movie?"

"I don't know, Buddy. … I'm not sure what happened."

Chapter 10

They had Valeta's shower in the prep room in the back of Mara's shop. Rondell, the leader of the drill team was ooing and aahing over the cute little baby things with all the other women. Even Luce had stopped fighting Caleb long enough to bring a gift. Everybody was there from the neighborhood, except Valeta.

She had gone into labor about three hours before the shower was scheduled to begin; it was too late to contact everyone to cancel. So they had eaten chicken salad and crackers and took pictures Valeta would see later.

As Naomi was helping Mara to clean up after everyone had left, Mara looked over the crepe paper streamers she was taking down to see the same young man she'd seen peeking in the window before. This time he was standing outside the door, as if he was trying to figure out if the shop was open. As Mara climbed down off the utility stool to walk over to the door to make sure the closed sign was showing, he abruptly walked away.

"That's why I told you to keep that gun under the cash register shelf," Buddy said when she told him about it later. "These young boys out here are always lookin' for trouble."

"And that's what they'll get if they come in Grandma's Hands wrong. Bakin' pies isn't the only thing I know how to do with these hands."

But this young man wasn't from around here. She had never seen him before that she knew of. Yet somehow he looked hauntingly familiar.

"Well Garfield will be fillin' in, at least until Valeta can get back. But there's no tellin' how long that might be."

"That's good. I'll feel better knowin' a man is there with you."

Mara smiled at the realization of what Buddy said, but she wasn't surprised. He and Garfield had become pretty good friends over the past few months. Buddy said that

Garfield had "cleaned up real good" since he had started helping down at the church. They had even given him a room next to the heater room in exchange for his help. Some nights when Buddy came home from work, they played a few games of checkers.

"You make sure you tell Garfield what he looks like. Maybe he can sleep in the back room at the shop a couple of nights a week."

"Oh Buddy, all that is not necessary."

"Well, I agree with Buddy," Zena said as she drove Mara over to the hospital to see Valeta and the twins later that evening. "You say you don't know him but he looks familiar. Maybe it's because you saw him on America's Most Wanted."

"You need to stop watchin' so much television, Zena." Looking out of the car window to scan the lot Mara said, "It's gonna be hard to find a parkin' space close to the hospital this late. Visitin' hours are over at eight-thirty."

"Mara Singleton, this was your idea. I could've stayed home and watched the Golden Girls. You were the one who wanted to come see Valeta's twins."

"Lord have mercy, Zena! How many times are you gonna watch those same re-runs? And *yes* I wanted to come. I want to see the look on Valeta's face myself. I know she was fit to be tied when that second baby came out!" She cackled to herself just thinking about it.

"I saw the same thing on the Discovery Channel one time. One baby was behind the other one and the doctor didn't even know it until after he delivered the first one."

Mara had heard about it too. It had happened to her, in a way. She was fifteen and she was pregnant. She'd known it. What she hadn't known was who she could tell.

"Prisoner number 41380"... her uncle. *"You have been remanded to this institution for the crimes of incest, corrupting the morals of a minor and forcing her to become the guardian of 'the power'."*

"This is just between me and you."

He'd told her that when she was younger, eleven or twelve. By the time she was fifteen, it was an unspoken rule. And anyway, by then she had "the power." She could make grown men do what she wanted them to do just by looking at them. They knew the look. And what it meant. There were times she got a cheese steak and a soda, or a pair of earrings. Sometimes she got ten dollars; most of the time though, it was five.

Yeah, she had "the power". When she walked into the room where her uncle was with all of the other adults pretending to be smart and all grown up, she could make him feel stupid because she knew he wasn't either... grown-up or smart. She knew he couldn't wait to get her somewhere by herself so he could ask her to *hold it* in her hand. She knew how to make him close his eyes and shake. She knew how to do *everything*... except make him stop.

Mara searched frantically in her "deep, dark place" looking for God. She knew she should never be here alone. There were too many things here to hurt her. Some of them wanted to hold her here against her will to further torment her.

Where was God?!... Oh! There He was, walking towards her. As she reached out her hand for Him to take it, He pointed right at her uncle.

Him too? I've got to release him too, God? But God You don't understand. If I release him, the others will have to be let out too.

He said nothing, but God's eyes said He did understand. His eyes said it was time.

Mara took a deep breath, and holding God's hand *re-eal* tight, she opened her mind and let her uncle go free. She wanted to slam the door shut so the others couldn't come out, but God's firm grip on her hand reminded her that she had to.

Peeping through barely slitted eyes, Mara held her breath as she watched 'them' come out. They were so tiny. And innocent. Why had she been so afraid of them?

Suddenly they came lunging at her, chubby fingers pointing, cherubic lips screeching silent, murderous accusations at her. It was true. Mara had killed them... both. Only she hadn't known there were two.

When she'd realized she was pregnant, she'd told her uncle. She watched as her power, "the power" turned him into a terrified fool. But then, later, he had helped her. He'd given her something to drink that made her stomach hurt. It made her bleed. And then something came out. When it did, even in spite of the horrible pain, she was relieved. She thought maybe now it would all be over and her uncle would stop. She wouldn't have the power any more, but that was okay. She wouldn't need it anymore.

But she'd gotten sicker. She'd had to go to the hospital, and she had to tell her mother why. Mara had rather it been Mother Pearl, but she didn't tell. She had to keep the secret. It was Mamie Ruth who took her to the hospital, but when she'd realized it was her brother that was responsible for getting her daughter pregnant, her loyalty caused Mamie Ruth to make an ugly choice.

Mamie Ruth betrayed her daughter and forever altered their relationship. In that instant she stopped being Mara's "Mama"; then, like now, she was her 'uncle's sister' as she joined the little ones demanding to be given amnesty and a pardon. But Mara didn't want her loosed. She refused to set her mother free even though, *somewhere*, she loved her. She deserved the sentence of infinite incarceration as her penalty for betrayal and abandonment.

So Mara slammed shut the gate and started mind running, trying to escape the umbilical attachment and the mute cacophony of those tiny lips. She tried to flee to the safety of her right now, but God arrested her in mid-flight.

Taking her hand in His once more, He and she watched these last two attach themselves to her 'uncle's sister' in some perverse familial kinship. They kept looking until this ghastly trio vanished to join the others she'd released.

When they were gone, He looked down and smiled at her as if to let her know that she too was free to go... until the next time.

"Come on, Mara. Hurry up before they close the nursery and we won't even get to see Valeta or the babies."

"Okay, Zena. Keep your shirt on. I'm comin' right behind you!"

Mara checked her purse to make sure she had her camera. She wanted to make sure she had pictures of *these* twins.

Chapter 11

The irony of where the christening was taking place was not lost on Mara. It was no where near as filled now as it had been the first time she'd examined these walls. In fact, there was an echo as the minister, Pastor Lynch, instructed the godparents Valeta had chosen for the twins.

"The responsibility you have agreed to undertake as god parents is a very serious one. If by some move of the sovereign hand of God or if through their own neglect, these two young people become unable to fulfill their obligation to raise these two beautiful gifts, the duty becomes yours to raise them. By becoming God parents you resolve to instruct them in the things and ways of God as outlined in the Holy Bible."

As he went on, Mara glanced over to where Jomar was sitting on the front pew with Naomi. It had been a little over a year since he'd sat on this same pew. She had gotten around to accepting that God had allowed this little man/child to be left without his father. She wondered how much of the events of that time Jomar remembered. Though she would never want him to experience the pain of understanding how death had robbed him of his daddy, she knew how important it was to Naomi that he have some memory of Jamar.

Mara knew first hand that the memories of the people significant to us are crucial to who we do or do not become. Knowing this, she hoped Jomar outlived and outgrew the sad legacy surrounding his father's death. No one should ever be haunted by their past like she was. Instead, the past should be used as a canvas on which to sketch the outline of life. That life could then be filled in with it's own colors as it was lived to its fullest.

Beaming with open-faced pride, she focused again on Pastor Lynch. God was blessing *him* as he was blessing the people around him. He had a heart for the community and recognized what politicians and other clergy folk didn't: it was the perceptions of its' people that needed to change in order to effect change in the community. He had set about helping to create at least the atmosphere where change could take place... and he elected not to do it by just standing behind a podium and preaching.

Though all of the paperwork wasn't yet complete, he would soon be a permanent fixture in this pulpit. There was a substantial congregation that had begun to embrace the vision God had given him to help revitalize them economically and socially, as well as spiritually.

Pastor Lynch had rolled up his sleeves and scrubbed graffiti *with* them. He formed a group of men to go out and confront the "street pharmacists", though he'd had to teach them how to do it peacefully because they too, were products of these same streets. Many times this group would physically go and rescue a person from inside the crack house. He encouraged these same men to go home and be fathers to their children *financially*, if circumstances were such that they couldn't do so physically. Unfortunately, this was very often the case because there were children that they'd fathered in more than one household.

He had plans to turn the gymnasium-church into a recreation center for the youth. The people responded by "bringing all their tithes and offerings into the storehouse" to help finance the vision, no small feat considering the economic oppression which threatened to suffocate them.

In this city of crooked politics and a nearly non-existent tax base, its administration could be observed leaving their downtown business offices and climbing into four-wheel drive vehicles to make their five o'clock exodus to suburban residences. As they drove away, they left their constituents behind, standing on the corners waiting for buses of an antiquated and limited transportation system. The buses took them from minimum wage jobs at fast food restaurants advertising "Now Hiring, up to $6.00 per hour", to deteriorating housing projects or run down rental properties owned by the migraters. If the bus riders had compromised principles enough and presence of mind to be registered with the right political party, they might stand a chance of getting hired on as a "sanitation engineer" or perhaps as a nursing assistant at the county nursing home. Barring some miracle of fortitude, entrepreneurship had been left in the hands of drug dealers or people from other countries who had come to their community bringing with them their culture, their language, *and* their gods.

Pastor Lynch had focused his efforts toward re-establishing meaningful relationship with the God in the lives of these people. He introduced them to the God who had sustained them through the malevolence of legal bondage. He preached to develop faith that the same God was present to help them through the contemporary plague that was their poverty-laced existence. A smile crept over Mara's face as she reflected on the efforts of this young man of God's gospel. Though she didn't have the formal education that would give her the words to explain it just that way, her "mother- wit" made her know that he was doing the right thing for the right reasons.

Jomar looked up and, thinking Mara's smile was for him, rewarded her with his own toothless and as yet, uncorrupted grin.

As they filed out of the church to go back to Naomi's for the after-christening-repast, she walked over to where Zena was standing.

"I still need to get a card for Valeta. Are you still going to the Walmart when you leave here?"

"Um hmm. They got that sherbert I like on sale, and I need some toilet paper. Come on, my car is parked around the corner."

"Hold on a minute. I want to ask Naomi if I can take Jomar with me. I been meanin' to buy him a little somethin'. I'll meet you at the car if you don't want to wait."

Looking over her shoulder as Mara helped him in the back seat a few minutes later, Zena said, "Make sure you fasten his seatbelt. I don't want him climbin' all over my seats or hangin' out the window puttin' fingerprints everywhere."

"Well, maybe I ought to just ride in the back with him to make sure he don't tear your brand new car up, Miss Baldwin."

"It might not be new, but it's mine *and* it's paid for. And you better not sit in the back seat because you ain't Miss Daisy, and I am not your *sho-fer!*"

As they made the twenty-minute drive to Havenbrook where the Walmart Super Store was, Mara commented on the various changes she observed along the way.

"Well, look at that! I didn't know they had a new bank out here. Seems like they would at least fix up the one in town."

"They got a new bank out here because they got money to put in it. What makes you think that they would fix up our bank? The only reason it's open is to give out welfare checks, food stamps, and to cash Social Security and SSI checks. And the way I heard it, they soon won't be doin' even that."

"Now you not gon' tell me they gon' stop Social Security and SSI, Zena."

"They better not, I been workin' all my life, and mine better be there when I need it. But what I *am* gonna tell you is that the welfare people are gettin' a card like a Mac card. Then when they go to the market, they'll use that card to pay for their food."

"You learn somethin' new ev'ry day, don'tchoo? What will they think of next?"

"I don't know, but it sure don't need to be nothin' that makes bein' on welfare easier. I can think of a million other things they could'a done."

As they walked through the automatic doors into the air-conditioned cool of Walmart, Mara walked over to get a shopping cart. Before she could reach down to put him in the child seat, Jomar climbed up on the front of the cart. She turned to Zena and said,

"I'm gonna take him to the toy department and then to pick up some pajamas. I'll meet you at the cash register."

"All right, but you better put that boy in that cart."

"Mah mom-mom let me ride on here 'cause Ah'm bigger'n gittin' in 'nere."

Mara smiled at him, ignoring Zena's lips pursed in disapproval as she and Jomar rolled off in the direction of the toy department.

"She ain't got chick nor child, so she don't know no more than I do. Me and you gon' skin *this* cat, hunh Marmar?"

"You ain't got chick nor child either, Mara!"

If only she'd had nerve enough to say it to her face, instead of to her too-far-away-to-hear-back. The sad fact was that she didn't. Sadder still was the reality that it never occurred to Mara that Zena would ever entertain such a response.

It wasn't that Mara wasn't a good friend. She was; she'd do almost anything she could for you. That Zena had often been a recipient of that charity was her paradox. There were the times when they had shared so much. When she talked to herself about it, she referred to their friendship as "the Lucretia Borge Syndrome"; it was sort of like being the favorite slave in the "Big House".

The close proximity, the day-to-day interaction meant that you knew what pleased the master, his likes and dislikes, his secrets, and sometimes his passions. Having this knowledge curried a favorable position, with an assumed power accompanying it. Bestowed authority legitimized that power, however slight or great it's boundaries above that of the slaves that worked in the fields. Absent one's own tempering reality, it was power with the ability to destroy one's self and others. The sobering bottom line was one's consciousness that you were still only a slave, an even broader line of mental demarcation that separated *you* from the master. Your acceptance of that reality was crucial to your privileged survival. It wasn't significant that you were intelligent--- and the importance of your feelings and perceptions were only marginal. It was only as you continued to be of benefit to the master, or in Mara and Zena's case, the *mistress*, that you retained that favorable position. Aspiring to greater aspirations would find you in the field with the others.

At its best, it was a cherished relationship; at its worst, it fluctuated between what could be labeled idolatry and something akin to hate. The ambivalence of her feelings and the passion with which she experienced them would alarm anyone, if anyone had known. Zena's struggle to suppress those feelings paralleled her struggle to believe that Mara loved and respected her; such was Zena's tormenting perception of their friendship. Whether or not it was a true representation, it was a position that Zena feared losing. Mara was still the best friend she had; it was still better to live in the "Big House".

****

The security guard squeezed Mara's shoulder as he attempted to reassure her.

"Don't worry Miss, he's got to be in here somewhere."

But she knew Jomar didn't have to be here or anywhere else that was safe. She avoided looking in the direction of where Zena was standing, because she knew what she'd find on that face. She couldn't handle the "I told you so" she knew was lurking beneath the concern for Jomar's safety.

She hated herself for having to admit that *this* time she should have listened to Zena. But she hated even more the peril that her decision had placed Naomi's grand-baby in. They had been looking at the bicycles and she had walked around to the other aisle where the small two-wheelers with training wheels were. He'd been walking right behind her, but when she'd finished checking the price on the shiny blue one with the florescent handlebars, she'd looked down and Jomar wasn't there. At first she wasn't alarmed, thinking that he must have gone back to the aisle where some bigger boys had been playing video games. But when she got there and he wasn't, she felt a slight sense of panic rising in her chest, increasing every time she looked down another aisle and didn't see him. Abandoning her cart and almost forgetting her purse, Mara snatched it and doubled back over the same aisles she'd just scanned, mumbling to herself to stay calm, while she called out his name.

By the time she'd gotten to the pajama section of the boys department, she was praying, asking God to let him have found his way there. She knew that for him to do this, he'd have had to be paying attention to her and Zena's parting conversation and then be smart enough to figure out that he might find her there. Her mind knew that this was too big a task for a four-year-old, but her heart hoped so anyway.

When Zena came up behind her, pushing a shopping cart with Scott toilet tissue, three pairs of Brown Sugar panty hose, and an eight-bar-pack of White Water Fresh Zest, Mara was talking to the sales girl. She was making gestures that looked like she was indicating height, and the salesperson was shaking her head. Thinking that she was asking pajama questions, Zena reached for a top hanging on a Power Rangers display rack, reaching out to hand it to Mara.

"I'm gonna wait and get my sherbert when we get to the check-out so it won't be too soft when I get home.... What's the matter, you not sure what size he wears?... Just try one of these tops. Send him over here and I'll try this one on him."

As she turned and saw the look on Mara's face, Zena knew before Mara said it.

"I can't find Jomar."

Zena opened her mouth to utter the obvious, but closed it at Mara's worried glare. She walked away from her cart, calling out his name though she knew Mara had already been doing that.

"Jo-mar, *Jo-mar,* come over here to Miss Zena, baby."

Standing at the customer service desk forty-five minutes later, Mara looked from side to side, hoping that somebody would emerge from one of the aisles carrying a little boy clutching a truck. She turned to ask the counter representative if she would mind repeating the announcement one last time, but the white-haired grandmother with the understanding face had been replaced. Leaning on the counter while she talked on the telephone was a gum-chewing young woman with black lipstick and fingernails who made it all too obvious that she didn't feel it was her job to find lost little boys. Laying the receiver on her shoulder, she told Mara,

"Ah'ma doowit dis time, but ah'm only coverin' for Miss Albright while she on huh break,...o-ka-a-ay?"

Speaking into the mouthpiece she said, "Ah'ma call you right back, o-kay?...All right den, hold on."

Pushing the intercom button she announced quickly, "If ennie-body seen a lost little boy, bring him to the service desk, o-ka-a-ay?"

Then, quickly clicking back to her call, she dismissed Mara entirely, turning her back and whispering loudly.

"Some woman lost huh little boy. She shoulda been watchin' him is all Ah can say, o-kay girlfrien'? So what happen' when he said the baby wasn't his?"

Overwhelmed by the situation and the insensitivity of the girl, Mara was just about ready to give her a piece of her mind when she heard someone call her name.

"Mara Ruthine Bothert! When have I seen you?"

Immediately recognizing the voice, she thought 'It hasn't been long enough.' Being too polite to say it, she fixed a smile on her face and turning, corrected the owner of the voice.

"It's not Bothert any more, and not since you came home for Christmas, five or six years ago, Raylinda Howard!"

"Girl, look at you. I know Buddy must love having more of you to hold on to. But it looks good on you though. How've you been since I saw you last?"

"Just fine thank you, Raylinda. And how about you? You cert'nly look well."

"You can call me Ray, *Mara Ruthine*. I never did like being named after my grandmother *and* my grandfather. It's so,... so **country** if you know what I mean. But anyway, I couldn't even begin to tell you all of the wonderful things that have happened to me since the last time we saw each other."

Forced to wait at the customer service counter, Mara swiveled her head toward Miss Fingernails and back to Raylinda. So involved was she in her story, Raylinda never noticed Mara's increasing agitation, her pacing or the way she kept straining to peer down the aisle. Raylinda had always run her mouth too much and Mara knew that she would begin *and* probably wouldn't stop until she was finished telling her everything that had happened since the last time they had seen each other. Holding out her left hand and proving Mara's point she said,

"My name is Ray *Richardson*. I remarried, you know."

From behind her Zena asked," Again? How many husbands is this, four or five?"

Turning to face the voice, then rolling her eyes upward in feigned exasperation Raylinda snipped back,

"If it was five or one, it would be one husband more than *you've* ever had, *Miss* Zena Baldwin!

"That's because you married anybody who looked at you more than twice. I had some dignity about myself."

"And that's all you have today is dignity □and a new can of hair pomade. When *are* you going to stop wearing that French roll?"

Her composure deteriorating, and wishing Raylinda would leave, Mara interrupted the ages-old rivalry. "Well, I'm happy for you. I hope this one works out."

Momentarily forgetting the urgency of Mara's situation, Zena dug harder.

"If he lives through it. Two of your husbands died if my memory don't fail me, didn't they Ray-*linda*?"

"And both of them were better to me in death than they could ever have been in life, God bless their souls. But Alvon is a healthy, young man, and we've got a long, happy life ahead of us."

Oblivious to Mara's pointed and pregnant glare, Zena got in one last stab.

"Un-huhn, □'*Stella*'. I heard he was young enough to be your son. Don't mess around and let your groove get '*you*' back."

Attempting to short circuit the current of their exchange, and hoping to get Zena's attention, Mara said, "How is your mother, Rayli □ uh, Ray?"

"Well, she's about as good as she can be, considering her age and everything. I'm on my way to the nursing home, so I thought I'd better stop in here and pick her up some slippers and a few dusters. Oh, and do you know if they sell Ensure? The nurse's aide said she likes the strawberry flavor."

Seizing the opportunity to rid herself of her gossipy friend, Mara said, "I think I did see it over by the baby formula, Ray."

Determined to leave her mark, Zena said, "That's good because she can get a case of Similac for her new husband while she's there."

Before Raylinda could counter with venom of her own, Mara grabbed Zena's cart and pushed it toward the checkout line. "Zee, this line is short. Why don't you pay for your things?"

"What for? We can't leave until we find Jomar."

"And who is Jomar? Mara, I know you and Buddy didn't wait all this time to have a baby, did you?"

Glaring at Zena for running her mouth, Mara got ready to explain. But before she could, Miss Fingernails called over to her.

"Miss! Miss! Dey called an' said dey wantchoo t'come to duh s'curity office."

Opening her mouth to ask for directions, Mara couldn't believe that 'Miss Fingernails' was already back on the telephone. Forgetting about Raylinda, she started off toward the rear of the store. She'd ask someone where it was on her way.

"Zena, meet me in the security office."

Relief and gratitude struggled for position inside her when she opened the door and saw Jomar sitting on a carpeted area in the office. Tears welled up in her eyes as he turned when she walked into the room. Smiling, he held up an action figure.

"Look what the man gave to me, Auntie Mara."

"I see Mar-mar. That's nice." Picking him up and holding him to her, she smiled her appreciation at the security guard. "Did you tell the man thank you?"

"Him was gone, Auntie Mara."

Puzzled, she said, "There he is Mar-mar. He's not gone."

"It wasn't me who gave it to him, ma'am. It was the young man who brought him to the security office. He gave me ten dollars, the toy and him. Then he left. I didn't want to leave the little boy, so I just called customer service and waited for you to get here."

"Well, praise the Lord! You found him. Where was he?" Zena asked, puffing into the room. "He-e-ey, old man, come here and give Miss Zena a hug!"

****

"That *is* strange, Mara. I mean, why wouldn't he wait around so you could say thank you or at least see who he was?" Zena pondered as they walked to the car

"If I knew that, then I'd be God. I keep tryin' to figure out who he could possibly be. You want to put the bags in the trunk?"

"Yeah, and this time I want to put the seat belt on Jomar. One close call a night is more than I can stand."

Conceding to her friend, Mara said,"Okay" before pushing the cart over to the cart corral. As she walked back to the car, she looked up at the bus pulling away from the stop in front of the store. Thinking to herself, I didn't know the bus ran out here this late, she started when she caught a glimpse of the face looking out at her from the bus window. It was *him*. A little chill went up her back as he turned away. She told Zena as they waited for her car to warm up. "Well, if you don't tell Buddy, then I'm goin' to. Mara, that's dangerous! He's stalking you!"

Though she realized that the actions of this young man could fit the definition of a stalker, for some reason Mara didn't feel threatened. Looking over her shoulder, she smiled at Jomar in the back seat, contentedly playing with Mr. Biceps. He was so cute. She thanked God again that they had found him and that he hadn't been hurt.

And suddenly she knew. She knew now that she had known it all along, she just wouldn't let herself know that she knew. But now, truth jumped out from behind the curtain where it had been hiding.

Truth was like that. Like a single kernel of corn that had inside itself all of the genetic material necessary to become flowing acres of corn stalks with golden tasseled crowns, so did her truth have the potential to bring forth its own overwhelming harvest. She'd kept her truth in the "dark place", hidden away from the probing, enlightening eye of her knowing. Like some weird Lugosi-like mental catacomb, her truth lay dormant, living only in murky, midnight shadows. She knew that the daylight of her knowing would illuminate the disintegrating façade that had long stood in truth's stead.

She had tried to keep them separated☐ her knowing and the truth. When there was some chance that they might happen upon each other in the crosswalks of her mind, she'd have one or the other of them quickly turn a corner, prolonging what could only be the inevitable.

But now they had come face to face from seemingly opposing corners in a heavyweight mental contention bout, each vying for the championship belt. They were closely matched, truth and knowing. But now that the bell had rung, she somehow knew that truth had the greater endurance and so, would emerge the victor. And her knowing surrendered, in submission to her truth.

Chapter 12

Mara didn't say anything to Zena that night, or to anyone else in the days that followed. She said nothing, not even to Buddy. She had to find a place inside herself to put this while she worked on what she would or even could do about it.

So Mara kept busy in the bakery and then at the church. She volunteered to work in the nursery for the Saturday Night Youth Jimmy-jam, so that the young girls who kept popping up pregnant could come to church. That way they could get a break from the responsibility of mothering the children who were not much younger than they were. She was continually amazed at how much younger these mothers got all the time. But wisdom told her that it did no good to condemn them. She elected to become part of the solution rather than part of the problem. The reality was that these young mothers needed her, the babies needed her, and as much as she was reluctant to admit it, something in her needed them.

It had been hard for her at first. Every time that she was handed a little blue blanketed bundle or saw a tiny baseball cap peeking out of an infant carrier, she would immediately, albeit unconsciously search each face for 'that' dimple. Of course, it was never there....it couldn't be.

As she finished zipping Kavon's bottle into the pocket of his diaper bag, Mara turned to see Buddy standing in the hallway just outside of the nursery room door. After LeTeseya adjusted the diaper bag on her shoulder so that she could maneuver Kavon's car seat, Mara hugged her and walked her to the door.

Questioning his presence with her eyes, her smile affirmed her pleasure at seeing him as she took his hand and walked back into the room. Sensing that his being here meant more than she wanted to volunteer for, Mara allowed herself to be momentarily comforted by the scent of his cologne. That was another one of the reasons why she loved him, *if* she needed a reason. Buddy always smelled so good. That thought was almost enough to displace the obvious.

"Kavon was the last one that had to be picked up. Let me fold these blankets and put these toys back and I'll be ready to go."

Picking up the blanket, Mara got busy folding it, trying to avoid what her churning stomach and rapid heart pace told her she didn't want to know.

His arm encircling her ample waist as he gently turned her to face him, Buddy locked his eyes in hers as he answered Mara's intentionally unasked question.

"It's Mother Pearl, Baby... she's gone."

Involuntarily clutching her chest, Mara sucked in a breath and held it, the impact of Buddy's words backing her against the crib rails. With her other hand, she reached for something else to support her... like Mother Pearl's presence in her life had for so many years. Shaking her head an indiscernible 'no', Mara leaned on the strength of Buddy's reaching arms as she buried her face in his chest. Unable to locate tears amidst the whirlwind that was her pain, she stayed that way for what seemed a lifetime. As the eye of this emotional tornado moved on, Mara opened her eyes to the realization that something inside her had suddenly aged.

Turning out of Buddy's embrace, she reached for the Pamper Potty, busying herself again in someone else's life in an attempt to cope with this horror in her own.

"I don't know what she's been feeding Rynika, but that little girl had this room lit up. Can you put this in the dumpster out back for me?"

"Sure, Baby. Then I'm goin' to take you home."

The service was held in the small church where Mother Pearl had been a 'member in good standing' since Mara could remember. It was the church where Mara had gone to Sunday School and Vacation Bible School when she was a little girl. Mother Pearl had seen to that. She would go by to pick Mara up every Sunday morning. That is until that time when she had gone to pick her up and Mara answered the door, still in her pajamas.

"My mama didn't get me ready this morning, Mother Pearl. She still in her room wif' Uncle Sonny-boy."

Mara's mother hadn't answered the door when Mother Pearl knocked, but that didn't stop her. She opened it and stood in the doorway, blocking Mara from seeing inside the room.

"*You* need to get a job, Sonny-boy, and *you* need to keep him out of your bed 'til he do, Mamie-Ruth! It don't make no sense you layin' up here wit' dis' no count in front of this baby! Ain't even got enough gumption to get her ready for Sunday School and you *knew* I was comin' to get her! And what is that you trying to cover up, Sonny-boy? You sure don't have to 'cause it ain't nothin' I have not seen before. You seen one you seen 'em all! Don't stop what'choo doin' on my account! It's too late for that now. I'll get her clothes ready and take her with me. Mamie-Ruth, I'll talk with you when you are standin' up!"

After that, Mara spent Saturday nights at Mother Pearl's house. She would get her hair washed and hot pressed, and Mother Pearl would roll up the front of her hair with Dixie Peach and brown paper bag rollers before she put the stocking cap on. In the morning, after she washed up and brushed her teeth, she would comb Mara's hair and tie ribbons on it to match one of the pretty dresses she'd bought and hung on the big nail in the back room.

Then they would go into Mother Pearl's kitchen where she would fix Mara's favorite, pancakes and Habbersett's scrapple. Mara always had to put her bathrobe on backwards, 'so you won't mess your clothes up'. The two of them would bow their heads, thank God, and ask Him to bless the food in front of them. It was Mara's job to clear the table, putting the dishes into the white tin washbasin so Mother Pearl could wash them. While she was getting dressed, Mara would dry the dishes and, climbing up on the wooden footstool, put them away on the second shelf. After making sure that they both had their white gloves and a hankie in black patent leather pocketbooks, they would walk the seven or so blocks to the church.

Sitting on the hard wooden pew, Mara heard the minister talking, but it never occurred to her to pay attention. If she lucked up and sat next to another child, she would take out her tablet and they would play tic-tac-toe or hang-man. If not, she was able to amuse herself by counting the flowers on somebody's hat, or by folding and unfolding the pamphlet she'd been given in Sunday school until it was time for the offering. Then Mother Pearl would give her three quarters, "one for the table, one for the plate, and the other one for later". Later meant the ice cream cone or the two-for-a-penny washboard cookies and red hot dollars she would buy from Sis's Variety Store on the walk back to Mother Pearl's house.

When they got there, they'd change out of their Sunday clothes and retire to the kitchen where Mara would watch with fascination as Mother Pearl would magically have a meal of fried chicken, mashed potatoes and gravy, garden peas and cornbread on the table in no time at all. The menu would change from Sunday to Sunday, but the delicious taste of Mother Pearl's cooking never did.

Neither did the steady stream of Mother Pearl's customers. When they would knock at the back door, Mother Pearl would let them in and they would wait while she went into the pantry. They would stand, salivating over the pineapple upside-down cake or sweet potato pies cooling on the kitchen table. She'd return with brown paper bags of various sizes and shapes, joking with Big Pete or Daisy as she made change out of the small leather purse she kept tucked in her bosom. Often as they staggered down the alley-way behind the house, Mother Pearl's "customers" maneuvered with their bag in one hand and a slice of Mother Pearl's cake or pie in the other.

She was almost twelve years old before Mara realized that Mother Pearl ran a bootleg operation out of her home. Her own mother, Mamie Ruth, cleaned rooms in the motel out on Route 18, or sometimes she would make money by "putting a few curls" in her neighbors' hair before they'd go clubbing on the weekends. Mara had been too young to know or care how Mother Pearl got money. By the time she began to understand who the people were who stood in the kitchen, life was just the way it was. And anyway, there were several other things that Mara had become aware of by then.

Mixed in with those years of Mother Pearl Sundays had been the summer nights of Truth or Dare. Somewhere in those years she had left home a teenager anticipating the fun of staying up and talking about boys when she spent the night at her girlfriend's house, but she had come home someone else. It was during this period that her uncle, her *real* uncle, Russell, came home from his time in the army. He looked just like the pictures he had sent home from "overseas", so handsome in his uniform. That changed after he moved in with Mara and her mother and planted the seed that would grow into "the power". Maybe, just maybe, if she could have found the courage to tell Mother Pearl. But she was Mara's only safe haven, and in the immaturity of her twisted reasoning, she feared losing this refuge. This also was the time when Mara learned to question, and then deny her self-worth. This was the time of preparation for the later times of her destruction.

Mara was seventeen when her most recent "uncle", Rayfield, killed her mother. Actually he had been killing her from the first time she'd met him. He was cool about it in the beginning, when he'd dazzled Mamie-Ruth with his footwork on the dance floor at the Rainbow's End. His good looks, chemically processed hair, and two-toned shoes were more than enough to get him in the front door. His promises to marry her and give her the world earned him a key to the front door. Mamie's realization that his promises were empty and never paid the rent might have sent him packing if it hadn't been for a couple of other incidentals. If it hadn't been for the fact that she'd ended up pregnant and Rayfield "had never had a son", and it was right around Christmas and "wasn't this a wonderful present?" he might have become just another New Year's resolution. Add to this Mamie-Ruth's discovery, acceptance, and introduction to Rayfield's secret world of heroin addiction. At a time when Mara needed her most, her mother was lost, both to Mara and herself. Mamie-Ruth became the carpenter of her own cross,... or at least an apprentice.

Mara didn't know which was worse, watching her mother junkie-scratching herself into a nod, or seeing her pulling things from beneath her maternity tops--things she had shoplifted and brought home to Rayfield so he could go and fence them to get money for their next hit.

It became a contest for Mara to figure out whom she hated most, her mother, Rayfield, her *real* uncle Russell, or herself. Rayfield bounded out of the starting gate when he would slap her mother and make her cry. It was her *real* uncle, Russell, ahead by a nose when he used Mara to affirm his manhood instead of asserting it by confronting Rayfield for beating up on his sister. Mara's hatred ran neck and neck with pity when she'd listen to Mamie-Ruth make excuses for why it was her own fault that Rayfield hit her. Coming into the homestretch, Mara focused her hatred inward at her inability to change what was going on around her, pulling out in front and crossing the finish line first....a winner and a loser.

And then there was that day when she came home from school and heard Rayfield crying.

"Mamie, Mamie-Ruth! Wake up! C'mon, wake up Baby! Mamie!"

Mara ran up the steps and into her mother's room, stopping short at what she saw when she got there. Mamie-Ruth was lying sideways on her bed, and there was blood all around her. Rayfield was positioned on the side of the bed with no shirt or shoes on, the seat of his pants absorbing the blood he was sitting in. Mara couldn't figure out where the blood was coming from, but the possibility that all of it was her mother's struck panic somewhere deep inside of her. The chance that Rayfield had done anything to cause it made something bitter-tasting form in her throat. Before either emotion could rise and overtake her, Mara knew she had to do *something*, she just didn't know what.

She walked three more steps into the room in the direction of the telephone on Mamie's nightstand before she remembered that the telephone was turned off. When she stopped, Rayfield turned his glazed stare to where Mara was standing, his "'do-rag" hanging untied over one eye.

"I told her not to take that last hit... she said she needed to go to the hospital... but she couldn't go unless she got straight... she begged me for one more hit... I told her... I told her.... aw, Mamie...aw, Baby…"

Mara looked over his shoulder and saw Mamie-Ruth's face. That still picture told her it was too late. She didn't know that she was running, she didn't know that those were her screams, she didn't know where she was going until Mother Pearl opened the door.

"Mara Ruthine Bothert, what in the world is wrong with you?!… Who did it?… Talk to Mother Pearl….Stop, shuggah, you stop now so you can tell me what happened!"

Mara never did tell her. There was so much she didn't tell her. She couldn't. When she managed to lift the heavy, iron doors that had replaced her eyelids, she was in the emergency room and she could hear Mother Pearl talking.

"Well, if you think it's better for her to stay in here, then I'll listen to you, Doc."

As her eyes walked slowly around the room, they stopped where her *real* uncle, Russell, was standing in the corner. She tried to quickly shut out the image, but not soon enough to close out the ugly memory of him standing in a corner of her hospital room on that *other* occasion. She turned her face toward the opposite wall. Just then she saw a stretcher go by the curtained doorway of her room and heard the nurse whispering to the orderly who was pushing it.

"That's her daughter in there. It's a blessing that the baby lived."

"I don't know if it's a blessing or not, coming into the world with no mother and you *and* your daddy are hooked on heroin," the orderly disagreed.

It was probably right then that Mara appointed herself judge, jury, and warden; there was no need for a lawyer. In her mind they had no right to a defense. *Let the sentencing begin....*

"Defendant Rayfield Butler... and infant boy Butler... you are charged with the intentional, premeditated, murder of Mamie-Ruth Bothert. You both are hereby sentenced to death in the mind of Mara Ruthine Bothert, never to be thought of, never to be missed, and certainly never to be loved."

The gavel cracked just as Mara drifted off into somnolent escape.

Chapter 13

"I'll fly away... oh glo-o-ry-y....I'll fly away-ay-ay.....When I die hal-le-lujah bye-n'-bye.... I'll fly away....."
The choir sang the familiar funeral anthem as the preacher, followed by the family and friends that were still alive and could get a day off from work, walked down the aisle behind Mother Pearl's casket. Outside on the sidewalk in front of the church and across the street on the steps of the houses that faced it, people were sitting, standing and milling about. Women in full-length mink coats and men in navy blue pin-striped suits, as well as those in wrinkled blue jeans with railroad kerchiefs tied around their heads, had come to pay homage to Mother Pearl. Neighbors, friends, relatives, people she used to work with, some she used to work for...all those who could manage to, took a position in the crowd. Some were her customers, some were their children. There were several white people interspersed in this mix of old and new, the occasional dandelion in this field of assorted hues of wheat-colored faces, looking out of place, but unintimidated.

Mara tried to put names to the faces. She knew that Mother Pearl had cleaned the toilets and polished the silverware in the homes of some of them. Many nights she had stood long hours at their ironing boards, pressing and hanging, sprinkling and folding, until she was rewarded with the sight of the bottom of the clothes basket. Others were the children that she had taught manners to when their parents couldn't or wouldn't recognize the need to or were too busy entertaining at the country clubs Mother Pearl hadn't been allowed in.

She had been forced to stand on the corner to catch a ride in the jitney that took her and the other day maids out of the city in the morning. Their destinations were the homes of the college professors, business executives, doctors and lawyers who walked in the front door in the evenings. They sat down to place settings in dining rooms whose polished mahogany tables gleamed, to eat meals that had been shopped for, prepared and served by the people who came in and left by their back doors.

Mother Pearl told her about the propositions the husbands (and some of the wives) had made to her on the occasions that they would benevolently offer to give her a ride home.

"That's why I ride the jitney … 'cause at the end of the day I don't owe them nothin' and they don't owe me nothin' but a day's pay for a day and a half's work."

She shared with Mara the dysfunction that went on inside those stately brick monuments to their owner's material success.

"They cheated and beat up on their wives worse than we did, only they couldn't blame it on bootleg licka' or bein' poor'. They was just mean… just mean. And do you think that those women would leave after they got up off the floor? Un-uhn, they would just look at their diamond rings and new cars and act like nothin' ever happent!"

Mara heard these stories when she and Mother Pearl would sit in the laundromat waiting for their clothes to dry. Or they'd be sitting on the bed when she heard about Marybeth, the judge's daughter who had gotten pregnant and had to get married.

That had all happened after Mara had gotten out of the hospital…. after they'd buried Mamie-Ruth… after the trial, the real one. Mara had told them what she'd seen when she came home that day….and the days before that. She hadn't looked at Rayfield when she was talking… she couldn't … he didn't exist anymore.

She had moved in with Mother Pearl even before Rayfield had gone to prison. So it was Mother Pearl who made sure her term papers and her monthly cycle were on time. It was Mother Pearl who went out and got a job so Mara could go to the prom and on the class trip to Washington, D.C. It was on top of Mother Pearl's coffee table that Mara's high school diploma and graduation picture sat. And it was o.k., …for a while.

It wasn't until after Mara finished the eighteen months at business school and got a job at Maragon Mutual that it started to get ugly. She met Irvin in the cafeteria at work. She didn't notice him at first, not until Zena, the girl who was in training with her, pointed him out.

"Now he's not the most handsome man I've ever seen, but he is not hard to look at. And he got big hands too."

Mara looked up just as he was paying for his platter. She didn't understand why the size of his hands was such a big deal to Zena, but she had to agree that he was nice looking in his own way. He smiled at her and nodded his head as he sat down with some of the other men eating lunch. Mara was eating the slice of coconut cake Mother Pearl had wrapped in waxed paper when she'd packed their lunches the night before.

"That looks like homemade cake to me and I know homemade when I see it."

He was leaning toward the table where she and Zena were sitting. Zena saw her chance and jumped right on it.

"Well you must know your stuff 'cuz you can't get homemade coconut cake any better than Mother Pearl's, or potato pie or fried chicken either."

Mara raised her eyebrows and smiled as she wondered how it was that Zena had such a running commentary on Mother Pearl's cooking. They had just met a week ago, and all she knew about Mother Pearl was the little Mara had shared with her. But Zena was a woman with things on her mind and she was on a roll.

"From what I hear, you know a little bit about a whole lot, and not just coconut cake either… *Irv-in*."

"What I *don't* know is coconut-cake-in-a-brown-paper-sack's-name," he said, dodging Zena's lunge like a matador avoiding the horns of a charging bull. And that's how it started.

Mara couldn't wait to get to work every day. She started spending her paycheck on new clothes and weekly appointments at the beauty salon.

"If you want to impress him, show him that you got sense enough to save your money for a rainy day, 'cause mark my words, a rainy day is comin', Mara Ruthine Bothert!"

"Well, it's not rainin' to-day, Mother Pearl. And if it does, I'll just buy myself an umber-*rella!*"

When she'd decided that she didn't want to hear it anymore, she packed her things.

"Because I'm tired of you rollin' your eyes every time he comes here. You just don't like him! And anyway, it's time for me to be on my own. Me and Zena can share the rent."

Mara called her new friend and moved in with Zena, who was more than glad to have her. Except the rent wasn't the only thing she'd had to share. It turned out there were young ladies other than Zena who appreciated the size of Irvin's hands. Mara had no idea who the woman with the page-boy hair-do was when she heard her suck her teeth and mutter something under her breath as they passed each other in the hallway at work. She found out soon enough when they both ended up in the bathroom next to the claims office one day. Mara was washing her hands when she saw a hand, holding an envelope, appear next to her.

"Please let us know if you can come. We have to give the caterer a head count."

"I heard she was pregnant, and that's the reason why they were supposed to get married, but I wasn't going to tell you until I was sure, girl. I told you he was sneaky from that first day in the cafeteria" was Zena's reply when Mara showed her the wedding invitation on their way home from work.

She shook her head in disbelief at Zena's comment because she couldn't believe that Irvin had gone out of his way to deceive her. Besides that, Mara didn't remember any comment from Zena about Irvin's sneakiness. She wondered if Zena's warning would have done any good if she had.

But at work a few weeks later, it didn't really matter. With a stack of files in her arms, Mara backed her way into the stair landing, thinking, I wish they would put some elevators in this place. As she did, she encountered someone coming down from upstairs. She couldn't help but feel sorry for her when an embarrassed Arlene stopped, then rushed past Mara, knocking one of the files she was carrying to the floor. Stooping to pick it up, Mara again shook her head in disbelief at the lengths Irvin had gone to avoid responsibility for his actions. Mara thought that he was on vacation or out sick, but the ever-faithful gossip, Zena heard that Irvin had somehow been transferred to the district office in another state, two weeks *before* the wedding.

****

As Buddy walked her to the limousine, she noticed a Mercedes pull up to take its place within the motorcade preparing to travel to the cemetery. As the car passed by, Mara caught the driver's profile. Why did that face look familiar to her? She turned to say something to Buddy, but he was helping Jotta, one of Mother Pearl's great-nieces, into the limo. She looked for Zena but she had already gone to her car. Mara saw the same gentleman again later, pushing an older man in a wheelchair as they were all making their way to the gravesite. She pointed him out to Buddy this time.

"Who is that man, Buddy? He looks familiar to me for some reason."

"Is he the man that you saw on the bus at Walmart when you couldn't find Jomar, Mara?" Buddy asked accusingly.

"No, no,... un-uhn, Buddy. That was a much younger man than he is.

"Then I don't know, Baby. Maybe he's one of Mother Pearl's nephews. Is that man in the wheelchair one of her brothers?"

"I don't think so, Buddy. I didn't get a good look at him. If my memory serves me correct, she only had two and one of them died years ago, but maybe you're right."

Mara put it out of her mind as she watched Mother Pearl's casket being lowered into the ground. She was grateful for the time they'd shared, now and before, the good and the not so good; grateful that she'd been given the opportunity to mature and grow. Mara appreciated that she had lived to see and make it through some of the rainy days. She was grateful that she had the chance and the presence of mind to mend broken fences. Death was so final, no chance for a reprieve. Mother Pearl wouldn't get to sit out on her steps and watch the street lamps come on or smell the flowers that were lying on top of her casket. She had moved on. She lived somewhere else now... *I go to prepare a place for you, that where I am you may be also....For to be absent from the body is to be present with the Lord.*

"Hello, Mara Ruthine. How are you?"

The voice and the memories that accompanied it pierced her reverie. It was older now, but she recognized it. Her first instinct was to run, without looking back, like she did in her dreams, like she sometimes did in her mind. But this wasn't either of them. This was real, and it was right now, and she knew she'd look like a fool if she suddenly sprinted out of the cemetery. So she reached for Buddy's hand and turned to face the voice.

"Hello, Rayfield."

He was the one in the wheelchair. He hadn't danced in a long time, had no need for a doo-rag now. When her eyes found his beneath his nearly-bald head, she noticed that one of them was opaque.

"Cataracts," she thought out loud.

"Yeah, I been debatin' whether or not to have it removed. Not much for an old man to look at any more. 'Cept I am glad to see you."

Could she say it?

"Good to see you, too, Rayfield."

102

And in a way it was. She could open and shut yet another prison door; it was okay if this demon wheeled, rather than ran away.

"This here is Emory, Mara."

The realization of who this man was who stood behind the wheelchair shot through her awareness like a lightening bolt. He who had never been allowed to exist, in part because she had willed it so and in part because he had never had a face, suddenly had one. The resemblance wrenched at her heart; no wonder he'd looked so familiar.

"Hello, Mara. Pleased to meet you."

Ironically, it was much easier to say these next words. As much as she'd dreaded this time, this meeting, her words rang true to what her heart felt.

"I'm glad to meet you too, Emory."

It was embarrassing to be the reason for the relieved smile that escaped from its place behind his composed veneer. Mara saw the face of a little boy, braced for and expecting rejection while at the same time hoping to be accepted, before he was quickly replaced by the man who offered her his outstretched hand. She repented for her bitterness and asked God to forgive her as she walked behind the wheelchair to hug her brother to her breast.

Chapter 14

"… So I've been in engineering since I graduated from college. I've thought about going back for some refresher courses, but I have a son who will be graduating in two years, and we're saving money to send him to school."

Mara was sitting on the arm of the sofa, listening to Emory. They had all come back to Buddy and Mara's when they left the cemetery. She was glad that Zena had chosen not to attend the interment; Mara needed time to process this whole thing. Inside her head she was rushing around doing mental housekeeping, dusting things off, putting away things that were delicate and might get damaged. She repositioned some things to create room for others so as to make this place as comfortable as possible for everyone. Mara sat looking into the male version of the face that had once belonged to her mother, maintaining a calm façade that belied the emotional gymnastics taking place internally. She smiled pleasantly and poured coffee while her circulatory system strained to contain the pressure of the blood bounding against its walls. As she took toll of the debilitation that the years had exacted upon Rayfield, something that felt surprisingly close to compassion replaced the hardness in her heart.

"So had Mother Pearl been sick for a long time?"

"You knew Mother Pearl before, Rayfield. She hadn't changed much. She was up and about, still takin' care of herself until about a year and a half ago. That's when she had her first stroke. I wanted her to come live with me and Buddy then, but she was havin' none of that. She finally had to go into the nursin' home after this last stroke."

"Mara would bring her home to spend the night with us from time to time, until here lately. She was in and out of the hospital just before she passed," Buddy added.

They talked about some things, and deliberately avoided others, painting over as much of the emotional graffiti as this one meeting would permit. It would take time to renovate this relationship with Rayfield, though chances were it would never be restored to it's original state, which was only functional at its best. Mercifully, Buddy volunteered to be part of the reconstruction process.

"So Rayfield, did you ever get married?"

"Yeah man, I did. Met her a few months after I got out of prison. I lucked up and got a job on the assembly line at Deltran. She worked in the office, but we had lunch at the same time. I started talkin' to her, we went out for a while …you know how it went."

His eyes darted over to where Mara was struggling not to remember "how it went".

"But we didn't go in bars or anything like that …she was a God-fearing woman."

Mara put the rancid memory of her mother's fear of Rayfield in a garbage bag in her mind, making a note to put it out before it started to smell.

"My mothuh had been raisin' Emory, but we brought him to live with us after we got married. Then we had two more kids of our own… Emory's got a half-sister that I had before I met, "… he hesitated, and then pushed ahead. … "before I met Mamie … and he's got a sister and a brother under him."

Mara got up and started up the steps, mumbling something about going to the bathroom. When she got there, she leaned against the door, closing it as the mental garbage bag burst, unable to contain the pain and bitterness of years of being alone. She raged against the realization that they'd had each other, that they'd all had a life, while she'd fought to collect the broken and displaced pieces of her own. She covered her face with a bath towel to muffle her sobs and catch the tears that wouldn't stop. She cried … for Mamie, and Mother Pearl, for Buddy, and Emory. Her tears were for Versiel, for Hortensia, for Jamar and Jomar too. Mara cried for everybody who had ever needed somebody, for Zena and Naomi, Garfield, Rondell, … and faces without names. Finally, she gave herself permission to cry for herself, for all the Maras she had been, and the ones she'd never yet found the ability to be. She sensed that all of that was about to change.

But the last tears reflected in the mirror before they splashed into the washbowl, the ones that fell as she turned on the cold water faucet were, of course,... for *him*.

****

"No, Buddy told me that his wife died in a automobile accident about six years ago, Zena. He was in the car too, that's why he's in the wheelchair. ... Because I wasn't there when he told him. I had to use the bathroom,... I'm sure I'll get to meet them some time ...No, *they* are not *my* brother and sisters, only Emory. ... He's in engineerin' .... I'm not exactly sure what kind of engineerin', but I know he don't drive a train, Zena! ... He's got a boy and a girl.... They live in Falls Church... Yea-ah, it's a Mer-say-deez Bends and he said his wife drives a foreign car too... That's it, that's the name of it! A Vol-vo... you know those cars don't you girl? ...Un-huhn, he looks just like my mother spit him out!"... well, he does have Rayfield's eyes ....

The healing had begun.

Chapter 15

"Valeta, did Rondell tell you he wouldn't be here today?"

"No ma'am, he didn't say anything to me."

"And Garfield said that he didn't call out while he was here. That's not like Rondell. He would call if he was runnin' late or wasn't comin' in... And he would pick today of *all* days. I need him to pick up those pastry boxes. It'll be too late by the time Buddy gets off."

"Maybe Mr. Garfield can do it, Miss Mara. Why don't you call the church?"

"Because today is the day that Garfield and Pastor Lynch are supposed to go to that meetin' about the Literacy Council. I guess I'll have to go myself. You'll be all right 'til I get back, Valeta?"

"Yes, ma'am, I'll be okay. You go ahead."

Grateful that they didn't have any big orders today, Mara walked outside to the bright yellow mini-van parked in front of the store. She ran her fingers across the bold, italicized, capital letters that spelled out *GRANDMA'S HANDS* on the driver's side door. Under the letters but above the pictures of cakes, pies and cookies, was the telephone number. The design was duplicated on the passenger door and across the back of the van, with a picture of Mara in the lower, right corner of the wide, rear windshield.

It had taken a long time, but she had finally gotten her driver's license. Buddy had insisted that even though Mara knew how to drive, she needed to be legal. She'd had to agree. She had never felt the need to renew her license after all these years. Buddy took her everywhere she needed to go, or she rode with Zena or caught the bus. But Mara had to admit that having her license again gave her a renewed sense of freedom. She was no longer limited; she really could go anywhere she wanted to go.

Not that there was anywhere in particular that she had in

mind to go. She had gotten that need to ramble out of her system years ago. After that little "situation" at Maragon with Irvin before his untimely departure, Mara had decided that he wasn't the only one who needed to be someplace else. She tried to talk her roommate into going with her, but Zena didn't share Mara's sense of adventure. Of course, Mother Pearl was against the whole idea.

"Mara you have not seen your grandmother since you was two years old and she certainly ain't breakin' her neck to see you! She didn't even come to her *own daughter's funeral* so I really don't understand why you got your britches in such a bunch to go see her."

"You don't know why she didn't come to the funeral, Mother Pearl. Uncle Russell said that she *couldn't* make it, not that she didn't want to. My mother is dead and they are the only people that I got and I am goin' to see them!

And she had done just that. Mara gave two weeks' notice, took her severance pay, her retirement benefits and the little savings she had left in the bank and bought a bus ticket to Dothan, Alabama. Her *real* uncle, Russell, had moved back soon after Rayfield went to prison. She hadn't bothered to tell anybody that she was coming. She made herself believe that they would be happy to see her. She realized how wrong she was as soon as she heard her grandmother's voice when she called from the little bus depot.

"You are *where*? ... Russell, did you know that this child of Mamie-Ruth's was coming here? ... Well, I *certainly* don't know why she came unless *you* gave her the idea that she could when you went to her mother's funeral!"

She hadn't even bothered to put her hand over the receiver.

"Well, I don't have any money for taxi cabs. If you got this far then I'm sure you can find a way to get here."

Money for taxicabs wasn't all that Coreen Bothert didn't have. She had no love for Mara and no inclination to pretend that she did.

"I don't know what possessed you to come all this way

108

uninvited. I didn't ask for any grandchildren when I found out that your mother had gotten herself that way, and I sure don't need any at this late date."

Mara should have recognized the emotional detachment that she had experienced from Mamie-Ruth, but she was too young to have a frame of reference. It was nearly tangible, like a genetic code of sorts, detectable under the microscope of human sensation. It had obviously been passed down from this woman to her own mother, and Mara wondered where in her familial lineage the mutation had occurred. Where had this inability to nurture, to encourage, to demonstrate love and compassion, taken root? It was evidenced in her Uncle Russell, almost helped to justify why he had been capable of victimizing her. If she could have understood it then, Mara would have realized that like her mother had been, he too was a victim.

But she couldn't. All that she did know was that she was not loved here, that Coreen had been unable to forgive Mamie-Ruth for defiling the family. What had compounded the insult was that she had done so with a *dark-skinned* man. Mara had 'been lucky' that she took her light complexion after Coreen's side of the family.Her grandmother took pride in her own fair skin and took great pains to keep it that way. She was equally proud of her 'good hair' and often remarked that Mara had taken that "nappy hair" after her father, whoever he had been. Of course, Coreen knew who he was, but the fact that Mamie-Ruth had never talked about her father, caused Mara to know nothing about him. Unfortunately for her, this was just one more vantage point from which Coreen could dispense torture.

Distorted pride kept Mara from getting on the next bus out of Dothan, to escape from this and run back to the warmth of Mother Pearl's sensitivity. Instead, she took a job at the drug store in town, an investment in her own torment. She brought her money home to Coreen, who was more than willing to take it and scoff at how little there was. She slept on blankets on the floor in Coreen's room, reminded daily of what an imposition it was for her to be there. But being there afforded her some convoluted sense of safety. Though neither of them had ever acknowledged what had happened between them before, Mara wasn't sure that if given the opportunity, Russell wouldn't be willing to pick up where he had left off.

The whole situation was insane, and Mara knew that she was crazy to stay and participate in it, but she had nowhere else to go. She was considering her plight the day that Ira Pittman came into the drug store to buy razor blades. She was working the counter.

"Miss, do you have any double-edge blades?"

"Yes, we do. Any special brand?"

"I'm not sure. What brand does your husband use?"

Nineteen-year-old Mara blushed at the thought that she could possibly have a husband. There was no such animal, not even a prospect. She went to work and came home. The bus driver and the pharmacist were about the only men who had said more than "good morning"' to her since she'd been here.

"I don't have a husband."

"Then give me whatever kind you got that won't give me bumps. I want my face to be smooth when it brushes up against that pretty little face of yours."

Smooth. That was Ira Pittman. Smooth even for a country boy. It was almost as if he knew how starved for attention and affection she was, and he wasted no time taking advantage of the situation. Mara seemed to have no recollection of how she had been so recently strung along by Irvin back at home. Not when Zena answered one of her letters to tell her that Arlene had given birth to "the cutest little girl". Not even when Mara experienced her grandmother's shrill accusations; it was déjà vu--except Coreen's railings about Mara and Ira were much worse than Mother Pearl's had ever been.

"If you brought yourself *all the way* to Dothan so that you could show me that you're a little tramp just like your mother was, then "thank you", but I'm not interested in seeing it. You don't even know that man, or anything about him! ... And don't think that you can turn his head with your city girl ways. He wants what every other man wants, and if he can get the milk for free, he sure as hell is hot won't be buying the cow."

But milk wasn't Ira's beverage. He liked a little wine, before *and* after dinner, *and* work, *and* anything else he might do in the course of the day. It was romantic at first, like that movie, "Splendor In The Grass". He would pick her up in his car, and they would ride, long rides on those winding back roads. Sometimes they would sit in the car and talk; other times he'd take the old quilt out of his trunk, and they'd sit under a shade tree. But riding or sitting, on the road or under a weeping willow, there was always a bottle of *something*. For Mara, drinking helped to muffle the volume and dull the sharpness of Coreen's badgering and insults ... *and* to diminish her ability or desire to say no.

So she yielded to the banality of the fermented grapes when they whispered that Mother Pearl and Coreen were lonely old women, and that she didn't want to end up like them. She acquiesced when they reassured her that it was okay if she gave herself to Ira on the blanket or in the back seat. The grapes suppressed her questions, like where his house was, and why Ira never took her there. They only permitted her to see what they wanted her to see, lulled her to sleep almost the same way they lulled Ira to sleep that night on the way to their favorite spot. When he woke up, he was in the hospital; when Mara woke up, it was to acceptance of the realization that he had had a wife all along. *And* that the woman who asked the nurse, "What room is my husband in?" had every right to ask. *And* that no matter that she had been in the car with him, that she *didn't*. Mara awakened to the reality that Coreen was right, she was just like Mamie-Ruth.

So she did what Mamie-Ruth had done; she left Dothan so she could go and be who she was, out of the condemning eye of Coreen. Mara went on a journey to find love... only she didn't know where it lived. She packed her meager belongings and dragged her life wherever her money would take her, but somehow love still eluded her. Mara hid in cities that wouldn't reveal where she was, made Zena promise that she would never tell. She worked in menial jobs that could never speak to who she was, involved herself in too many of the kind of relationships that reinforced who Mara had come to believe she was.

Mara avoided churches in the places where she went--- acted like the God that she'd heard about in Sunday school those many years didn't exist. She ignored His presence, barricading it in a subliminal compartment that muffled His attempt to communicate with her. God's presence shared space with the equally suppressed emotions Mara wouldn't allow herself to feel about Mother Pearl; it was too dangerous to acknowledge the ache of missing her that was in Mara"s heart.

Mara had already learned to fear her feelings; the sun had risen to illuminate too many shadow-concealed betrayals in the short life she'd lived. So she ran---Mara ran and she hid---in twenty-four hour periods that somehow became the months that turned into years. She ran, rejecting and neglecting the will to be more...until finally, tired of running and hiding and hating what had now become her truth, she crawled from beneath the woodworks of her life.

One day Mara awakened to her harsh reality, resisting the impulse to cower beneath its overwhelming intimidation. She tried to figure out what was familiar about the cracked lips, drooling saliva on the dingy pillow case beside her. It was...yeah...that *was* last night when she had met...what was his name? Looking past him, her eyes fell on the images reflected in the mirror on the back of the door. Where had she seen this picture before?

The breeze from the fan on top of the old chifforobe teased the strip of faded wallpaper dangling from the ceiling. Lifting herself, Mara rested on her bent forearm as she reached to scratch the sudden itch on the inner aspect of her thigh. She felt the swelling from the mosquito bite through the stickiness on her leg. Looking down, Mara registered her nakedness just before she saw the crimson circle on the sheet.

Suddenly, camera-shuttered images flashed in her mind, dragging her back over the miles she had traveled. Abruptly, she was transported back in time---dropped right in the middle of the nightmarish memories she had been running away from.

In an instant she realized why the lips looked familiar...recognized the room...saw that *other* blood. She remembered the chifforobe that sat in the corner of Mamie-Ruth's bedroom. Mara's eyes twisted toward the back of the matted head crushing the pillow next to her's, then jerked up to try to make out his face in the door-mirror. She recognized both of the images of Rayfield and Mamie Ruth that stared back at her---but she couldn't understand how they had gotten here.

Then Mara saw the mouth that was reflected in the mirror frame the word...

"Mama?"

Waves of emotion broke through Mara's defenses as revelation flooded her. She threw herself off the side of the bed to her knees, the blood forgotten for a time, her physical nakedness not as important as was her need to expose all of who she was before God. Mara dismissed her still snoring roommate, focusing all of her attention on her *Daddy*.

She prayed, talking to Him through her tears. Mara took comfort in God's omniscience, grateful that even if she couldn't express it, He still knew and understood everything. She poured out her heart, emptying it of the pain, the fear, the confusion... and *all* of the shame. That day, naked and kneeling, Mara embraced the truth of the 23rd Psalm.

"Because the Lord is my shepherd, I have everything I need... He makes me to rest in the meadows grass, and He leads me beside the quiet streams.. He restores my failing health, and He helps me to do what honors Him the most; that's why I'm safe...that's why I'm safe...that's why I'm safe...safe in His arms..."

When it was all over, Mara held on to the bed and pulled herself up from the floor. She was surprised to discover that her roommate was gone. What *was* his name? Picking up her washcloth and towel from the back of the chrome and yellow vinyl chair as she walked toward the bathroom, Mara knew that remembering his name wasn't a priority. Bending to look under the bathroom sink for her sanitary pads, she realized that there were a lot of things that God was going to help her to forget.

The next day, Mara went in the back door of Scaperelli's Italian Cuisine for the last time. When she finished stacking the last of the green Melamac coffee cups and made sure that all of the glass ashtrays were accounted for, she hung her apron on the hook on the back of the kitchen door. She took off her paper cap with the hair net attached, and squared her shoulders before knocking on Angelina's door.

"Who is it?"

"It's me, Mara, Miss Scaperelli."

That was still her name, but she wasn't the same person anymore.

"Come on in, Mara." Angelina looked up from the invoices she was going through. "What can I do for you?"

Mara knew that what needed to be done for her had already begun.

"I just came in to tell you that I won't be coming in tomorrow."

There was something that felt good about having the courage it took to tell someone else that she had made a decision for her life.

"I'm going home."

Mara pulled her navy-blue car-coat off of the hanger attached to the coat rack in the break room. She knotted her scarf under her neck and checked her bosom to make sure her wallet was secure---and smiled, knowing she had picked up that little habit from watching Mother Pearl in her pantry. Mara walked the six blocks to the bus station and then crossed the lobby floor to the wall of lockers. She never went back to the Rest-A-While Hotel; she had packed her bags last night and left early enough that morning to stop by the bus station, place her bags in the locker, and purchase her ticket. Mara reached for her wallet, taking out the locker key and her ticket. She collected her life from the small opening, and leaving the key, walked over to sit on the bench to wait for her bus. Like the prodigal son, she had taken stock of where she was and who her dining partners were; like he had done before her, Mara left the pig sty and went home.

It was good to see the big smile on Zena's face when she picked her up thirteen hours, a bus change and a fifty-five minute layover later. Mara had prepared herself for Mother Pearl's "I-told-you-so"---couldn't fight back the tears when all she got was a tearful nod and Mother Pearl's arms wrapped around her. She couldn't say so, but she didn't need to; they both knew how much Mara had missed them--- there would always be a place for her here.

Mara moved back in with Zena, "but just until I get on my feet". She got a job and applied for her own place in the projects---she moved in and met Milton and Verseil. Mother Pearl gave Mara her old bed.

It was good to be home ...until she discovered something. Mara didn't realize it at first; it would take a little while. But that was how God was; life was a progressive unfolding of truth...even one's own. It wasn't until after Parris was born, after Milton was killed, after Hortensia never came home. It was even after Nathaniel what's-his-name, after she looked for and saw that brand new dimple, long after she left 'him' and walked away from the hospital. It was after that, all of those years later when Mara was unpacking her suitcase yet another time, that the light came on. When she checked the pouch along the side as she had done so many times before, her hands touched something. Instinctively Mara recoiled from this package, the manifestation of the guilt she'd carried everywhere she had run. Then she remembered her new found strength; God's forgiveness enabled her to reach into that narrow pocket. It was then, when she pulled out and unfolded the pages, and tearfully read the adoption forms, that Mara realized something. No matter where she had been, no matter how many times she had folded and hung and checked to make

115

sure that she had not forgotten anything, Mara had somehow never remembered to include one very important thing …her love for herself. Again she was overcome with gratitude at the renewed realization that God had loved her when she hadn't been able to.

With the adoption papers in her hand as confirmation of this new revelation, Mara made a promise to herself to obey God's Levitical instruction. Reaching back to mind-touch those Mother-Pearl-Sundays, she tripped over many of the things that had happened since then. Mara knew she had much to learn in order to be obedient to His command.

*"… And love your neighbor, **as** you love yourself."*

Chapter 16

After she picked up the pastry boxes, Mara rode by her house on the way back to the bakery. She often did this since she'd opened the store because everyone knew that she wasn't at home during the day anymore. She and Buddy had talked about the possibility of moving to a better neighborhood, but for now her bright yellow van was their security system. No one ever knew when she might show up.

But as she turned up her street today, she saw the flashing lights of the patrol car. It was double parked in front of Kaitlin's house, forcing Mara to slow up as she drove pass. Kaitlin was the young White woman who lived in the apartment at the opposite end of the block. Mara knew her from seeing her walking her children to school, and from seeing her go in and out of the apartment building directly in front of Mara and Buddy's house to see Rondell. Kaitlin sometimes came in the shop when he was working.

Mara was wondering why the police were there when she saw one of the officers come out of the house holding on to the arm of someone whose hands were handcuffed behind his back. Mara was surprised to see that the handcuffed person was Rondell, and she unconsciously braked the van when she saw him. Just then another police car pulled behind her flashing its lights, forcing Mara to drive on. She pulled her van into an open parking space and started walking back to find out what had happened. But the policemen, three of them, were motioning for the growing crowd to stay back. As she looked up the street, Mara saw more policemen and the yellow tape that denoted a crime scene outlining the apartment building across from her house. Sighting Luce in the crowd, Mara walked over to where she was trying to balance herself on the crumbling brick wall bordering the front yard.

"What in heaven's name is goin' on, Luce?"

"I not sure eg-*sact*ly what happent, but I hear somebody

say'n that Rondell and that guy was een the apartment fightin', and the next thing they knew Rondell was runnin' over here to Kaitlin's house."

"Why do they have that police tape around there like that? Is anybody hurt?"

"Miss Mara I'm not bein' smart or nut'ing', but I really don't know what all happent. I had to go to the exchange to get my food stamps, and I get off the bus and walk around here just before you was drivin' up."

Realizing that she would have to wait like everyone else to find out what happened, Mara surveyed the crowd. The ongoing transition in the neighborhood that took place all around her, without her awareness or assent, never failed to amaze her. There were people who she recognized from the neighborhood or the bakery or the church, but there were many that she had never seen before. Taking note of a group of about six or seven blue jean outfitted young males, she recoiled as she realized that three of them were holding dog leashes or ropes attached to the necks of pit bulls.

This was the most recent nuisance plaguing the neighborhood. Buddy had called the police on several occasions when circles of people, teenagers and adults, congregated in back yards or alleys to witness vicious canine fighting matches. Often the mutilated dogs were left, abandoned and bleeding, when the approaching police siren scattered the crowds. More times than she could count, Mara had stepped off her porch and froze in terror at the sight of one of these animals, loose and roaming the street. As she examined these young men gathered on the corner, Mara made the probably correct assumption that not one of their dogs had the required license. She verbalized her thoughts to her Hispanic neighbor.

"I'll be glad when they do something about these dogs."

"I know dat's right, Miss Mara. Somebody going to get hurt by one of them, *es-spe-ci-ally* somebody's keed going to school or sum'ting, you know? It better not be one of mine is all I can say or *some*body is going to be in *beeg* trouble."

For right then it appeared that it was Rondell who was in big trouble. Seated in the back of the patrol car, it's lights still flashing, Mara saw him alternate between nervously swiveling his neck to peer into the crowd, to hanging his head on his chest as he waited for the car to leave. At one point his eyes caught hers, and sensing his panic, she nodded her head and attempted to comfort him with her look.

When finally the car edged through the crowd and down the street, Mara followed it with her eyes. As it disappeared in the direction of the precinct, she thought she saw *that* face just before he turned his head and walked around the corner. As she judged the distance back to the van, she knew that *he* would be gone long before she could get there.

****

"Buddy, you don't believe any more than I do that he'll run away."

"But Baby, that's a chance that we can't take. Because *if* he does ... then we stand to lose the shop."

"Well, we can't leave him in there. You know what they'll do to him in that jail."

Mara and Buddy ping-ponged the pros and cons of offering the bakery as collateral to secure the money for Rondell's bail. Though ultimately she would defer to his decision, Mara hoped that Buddy's compassion would stretch this far.

"It would be different if his charges were worse, Buddy. The lawyer said that he probably would get probation because it was self-defense."

Buddy smiled as he shook his head.

"Rondell is tougher than that other one thought he was. Who would'a imagined that he would be the one to end up in the hospital? I guess Rondell "rocked his world" for real, huhn, Baby?"

"I guess he did. He told me that he learned how to fight when he was a little boy. Good thing he did ... came in handy. But that still won't get him out of jail. That takes money, Buddy, and Rondell don't have none."

"Well, I guess you need to get your coffee can out then, don't you?"

****

"Miss Mara, I thank you and Mr. Buddy for doing this for me. I can't tell you how much I appreciate what you all did."

"Just make sure that you show up for your appointments with the public defender and for your hearin' or I'm goin' to have to answer to Buddy Singleton."

"I wouldn't do that, Miss Mara. I know people probably judge me because of the way I live my life, but if you really knew me, you would know that I'm not a bad person."

Listening to him, Mara recalled the message Pastor Lynch had preached on Sunday.

"... Most people compare themselves with each other, and they think, I'm not so bad. What they don't realize is that not being as bad as someone else isn't what's important when you compare yourself with a holy God. There are a lot of good people going to Hell..."

She wondered what Rondell thought about God, wondered how God fit in his life. She had seen another side of him once he'd started coming to the shop to see Valeta, a side that didn't jive with the behaviors she knew he practiced. Sure, he was openly gay and made no pretense to the contrary. But when Mara needed someone to fill in for Valeta or Garfield when they needed some time off, she had witnessed a sensitivity that she recognized as a desire for something else. She knew that to take advantage of his current vulnerability relative to this legal situation would be to exploit him in worse ways than any of his past involvements had. There would be time for them to talk about God later ... right now he needed a friend. That she volunteered for the job perplexed even Mara. But Zena's reaction was infinitely worse.

"I don't know which one of you is the bigger fool, you or Buddy, Mara Singleton! What has shook loose in your head that you would get yourself involved in some nonsense like this?"

"It's not nonsense, Zena, it's serious. And don't no fools live in my house. You need to keep that in mind when you say my man's name in the same sentence with the word *fool.*"

"That's just a figure of speech, Mara. You know I didn't mean anything by it."

"I'm not sure what you meant ... I just know what you said, Zee. We been friends a long time, but friendship don't give you the right to call Buddy no fool. We all did foolish things,... I'll be the first to say so. But when you *know* better, you *do* better. Knowin' is the hard part for most folks. The way I see it, Rondell is just like everybody else ... he just knows what he knows. And neither me nor you understands what that is or where he learned it from. He's far from stupid though, Zena. I'll tell you that."

"No, he's got good book learnin', it's his common sense that ain't much to shout about. ...I guess you know what you're doin', Mara. And maybe it's not for me to understand. I'm just worried about what might happen."

"God took care of everything that's happened in my life so far, and most of the time I didn't see how. So I'm goin' to have to trust His track record on this one too."

"You ought to change the name of that bakery to Grandma *Moses'* Hands. You don't just lead people through the wilderness, you giv 'em bread to eat too!"

Mara looked across Zena's dining room table to where her friend was studying the cards lined up on the vinyl tablecloth. They were playing 500 Gin Rummy and Zena was deciding how many cards she wanted to pick up.

"Zee, let me ask you somethin'."

"Um-hm, go 'head."

"I'm not 'zactly sure how t'say this, but how come you always change it when you say somethin' to me? I mean, like when you and me don't feel the same way about somethin'.

Zena felt an immediate sense of discomfort, but never lifted her eyes as she reached for the king of hearts.

"Wha'd'you mean Mara?"

"I mean like, just now. I meant what I said about you not callin' Buddy a fool, but if you really feel like it's not a good idea about Rondell, why did you change your mind?"

It was a time that Zena had both dreaded and hoped for.

"Who said I changed my mind?"

"Maybe you didn't change your mind, but you did change the *sub*-ject. You always do that, an' what I'm askin' is why?"

Taking the time to short spread her three kings, Zena switched cards and placed the four of clubs on the "dis" pile. She folded her cards together, laying them on top of the daisy pattern, and took a deep breath before answering.

"Well, Mara, I guess there's a few reasons why. ...It's, well ...I'm not ..."

"Zee, like I said, we been friends for a long time. There ought not to be nothin' you can't say to me."

Zena abandoned caution and made the decision to dive into the deep.

"Mara, bein' able to say somethin' to you is one thing. Handlin' what you might say back is the hard part for me. ...I know that you just call it sayin' what's on your mind, but sometimes...sometimes, it comes out kinda rough."

"But Zee, you know me. I would never delib'rately say somethin' to hurt your feelin's."

"Just b'cause you don't mean to doesn't keep it from hurtin'. And it's not only me. I listen to how you say things to Buddy, and I wonder how he lives with it."

"Now you're goin' too far again. What happens b'tween me and Buddy is our bizness."

"That's what I mean, Mara. You say that you and me are friends, but the only way we can stay friends is if I say what you want me to an' that's all! But Buddy is my friend too...And ain't no sense in you lookin' like that---friends is *all* me and Buddy are an' you know it! Don't get me wrong, I'd love to have a good man like Buddy, but I know he is not my man, he's yours! Still and all, just because I'm your friend, I can't preten' like I don't see how he looks sometimes. ... I don't think you realize when you embarrass him. ...Mara, Buddy loves you! And he's a strong man, you're his only weakness! When he looks at you...sometimes I swear he could eat you *up* he's so glad that you're his wife. Like he would be lost if he woke up and it wasn't no Mara. So he just tries to make sure that he does whatever he can to make you happy, to make sure you're always around."

Mara was stunned into silence by her friend's words. Seeing her marriage from her friend's perspective gave Mara pause. Zena's bowed head as she swallowed her saliva and her pride further shamed her. Licking her lips, Zena went on.

"... An' ... an' ... I guess ... I feel the same way. ... Mara, I don't have many friends, you know that. I mean I work with a lot of people an' I probably know most of the people that you know. But I don't make friends easy, especially after... you know. Even before that it was hard for me to trust people. ... I don't even know what made me take to you so fast way back then. It just seemed like you was strong, like you wouldn't take no tea for the fever. ... An' I guess that made me want to be around you, ... made me want to be your friend. ... So I tried to act like you did, like I was strong. ...

Zena paused a minute, as her thoughts came together.

"Mara, do you remember that day in the lunch room, when Irvin started talkin' to you?...Well, I do. I remember because I had been likin' him since the first time I saw him when I came in for my interview. When he started talkin' to you, I made a fool out of myself... tryin' to act like I knew how to talk to men. He didn't want no bother out o'me."

Smiling as she remembered, Mara said, "Fact of the matter is, Irvin didn't really want no bother out of *no*-body, Zee. Not you or me and es-*peshully* not poor Arlene!"

123

"I guess that's right. It's funny now, but it wasn't funny then. All I could do was act like I was happy for you. Then when you found out about him and Arlene, I thought you would be all upset. But it seemed like it didn't even bother you. Right after that, when you said you were movin' out and goin' down south, I really wanted to go with you, but I was afraid. ... I never told you this, but I cried for two weeks after you left because I missed you and was mad at myself for not havin' nerve enough to go. I had to watch when the only real friend I had left."

"But the times when I wrote to you, it seemed like everything was goin' good for you. I was the one doin' bad."

"I had to live the life I had, Mara. I couldn't just give up and die. So I worked hard and I worked all the time. I met some people along the way, but even then most people were too busy tryin' to live their lives to get involved with somebody else's...at least not mine."

"I got t'agree with you on that one, Zee. I saw some things and did some things that I wouldn'a never thought I'd see or do, tryin' to find somethin' and not knowin' what I was lookin' for. I'm hearin' you say what it seemed like to you, but b'lieve me, life wasn't real good to neither one of us back then. But you already know that, we talked about it before."

"Yea-uh, we did. And even though I felt bad that things didn't work out the way you thought they would, I was glad when you came back. I figured we would pick up our friendship where we left off. ... But it didn't go that way. It was different; you was different. I mean, you explained some of it to me and I understood it for the most part. But you came back ... *different* is the only way I can say it. ... It was like, ... like you needed a friend, but you acted like you could take it or leave it. You wouldn't let y'self get involved, almost like you didn't have no feelings. So I decided that since you was a friend when I needed one, then I would return the favor. ... And I'd be a friend whoever and however you came. ... But you didn't make it easy, Mara. A lot of times I had to keep remindin' myself that you were only tryin' to protect yourself."

Tears filled Mara's eyes as she tried to make her friend understand *now* what she herself had been unable to piece together *then*.

"I was, Zee. I had been through a lot, an' I didn't have nobody. My mother was dead and I didn't have nobody else to love, except Mother Pearl. Everybody that was supposed to love me didn't, ... or they had loved me the wrong way. They stepped over the line. I couldn't afford to lose no more of me, I had to protec' myself. So I put up fences and walls. I didn't really know how to do it no other way, so I stayed inside myself, in a way of speakin'."

"The problem was, nobody could get inside to where you were. When you did stick your head out, it was usually to bite somebody, and most of the time it was me. So I just stayed around, lettin' you take little bites out of me, until I couldn't take it no more. Then I'd stay away for a while. ... But I always came back, because I promised myself and God that I'd be a real friend. ... Then I guess I stayed away too long, b'cause when I got back, you had Milton and Verseil. Then it was Nathaniel, and I didn't even know him. He was in your life and gone before I even heard about him."

The memory of that time still bled somewhere inside Mara. She hadn't intentionally excluded her friend. It was just that it had all happened so quickly. Like a tornado, that situation had spun into her life and back out again, leaving devastation in its wake. Mara recalled Zena's attempts to console her when she had recounted the Nathaniel story, of how panic-stricken she'd been when she'd discovered she was pregnant. But she had pushed Zena away---closed her and Versiel and the rest of the world out of Mara-land. She had chosen to live there alone ...inside herself...alone except for *him*. *He* had lived inside her too, for a time...And then she'd given *him* away.

Mara recalled the intermittent numbness and pain, the bitterness and confusion of that time. She cradled the emptiness of that incident in her bosom, rocked it even now.

She had given in to her pain then, and she almost did now, but she couldn't. Now it was Zena's turn.

Mara stared at her friend, watched as the tears she hadn't known existed, coursed down Zena's face. It hurt to know that she was at least part of the reason why they were there. As she listened to Zena, Mara realized that she was only part of the problem, that her friend had wounds from other issues that needed to be healed. But that would have to come later.

"So I stayed away. If I needed to know how you were doin', as much as I didn't want to, I'd get in touch with Versiel. I used to call your job t'make sure you went to work. By the time you started to come back from the dead and I could finally start comin' around again, I guess Versiel needed you. … And then she died. I didn't know what to do, even though I knew how much it had to hurt you when she passed."

The courage that had fueled this purging was ebbing away now, leaving Zena empty of what it took to look at her friend. From beneath the hoods of her swollen eyelids, she looked past Mara to stare at the framed certificates of her own vocational achievements hanging on the dining room wall. Zena could hardly raise her voice above a whisper, so fearful was she of the potential impact of her next words.

"I was … I … I felt bad, but I was almost … glad … when she died."

Had it been at some other point in her life, Mara might have been shocked or angry at Zena's confession. But a sensitivity mechanism within her understood and was able to translate the language of the emotions that formed it. She could relate to that degree of neediness, had walked a mile in her friend's shoes. Rather than condemning her, Mara's knowing nod provided a bed of compassionate consolation where Zena could unburden herself and rest.

Time stood still like a parent patiently witnessing the halting first steps of a toddler; proud of the effort, admiring of the progress, yet aware of the necessity of not expecting too much. Determinedly past and present inched closer to each other.

126

Zena continued,"… I … I had you … We were friends again. It was almost like before."

"You needed me" were the words that they both knew remained unspoken. Mara recognized need as the paste that had often bonded them to each other; Zena needed to be needed, and she had needed Zena. But Mara's needs were temporary; when they had been fulfilled, like paste, they dried up and couldn't be relied upon to hold things in place. When Mara's needs changed, so had their friendship … *again and again.*

"Not too long after that must be when I met Buddy, huhn Zee?"

Zena nodded.

"I was sad, I was happy, and I was jealous all at the same time. … Then, that *thing* happened.. It was too much. I remember sittin' in the park that day, not too long after I got out of the hospital, watchin' you and Buddy. I was as beat up on the inside as I was on the outside. I just kept thinkin' that it seemed like I didn't have no place where I belonged and nobody that I belonged to. And I had just lost my friend again."

"Zena, you didn't lose me. As a matter of fact, meetin' Buddy was what helped me to start carin' about.. carin' about *life* again. I had forgot how to care about me, and God sent Buddy to me so I could learn to love my-self! I didn't know how, an' I guess I was doin' like you said. I was busy tryin' to live my own life. … I'm sorry, Zee. I didn't mean t'be, but I guess I was selfish. It was just 'cause I needed so much, I didn't think I had much to give. … An' I really am sorry if the things I say and the way I say'em hurt you. I had so many people to just walk on me, when I finally started standin' up and fightin' back, I forgot who's on my side."

It was okay. Even if they couldn't say it right now, they both knew it was okay. The weeds had been pulled and the soil turned in preparation for the new seeds of their friendship.

Handing her friend a wet paper towel and then a dry one, Zena sat down and picked her cards up from the table.

"Here, wipe your eyes so you can see it when I Gin Rummy on your butt. That's the best two out of three, so you owe me a potato pie. I'd appreciate it if you could have it here by tomorrow evenin'. Garfield is comin' by to look at my vacuum cleaner."

Chapter 17

"So this is Kiata, and the real cool guy over here is Keshon. This is your Aunt Mara and her husband Nelson."

Hearing Buddy referred to by his real name sounded strange to Mara. He didn't like his name and preferred the nickname, but hearing it spoken, especially in this setting, reaffirmed her pride in what the name had come to mean to her. Buddy and Nelson Mandela shared the same name and as far as Mara was concerned, were men who offered the world shining examples of courage and strength of character. It was this strength that under-girded her now and encouraged her to face this particular challenge.

She and Buddy had left yesterday to make the seven-hour drive to Falls Church, Virginia, where her brother Emory and his family lived. They had arrived last night, but elected to stay at a hotel. Though she was willing to cross this chasm, Mara decided that wisdom dictated that it be done with moderation.

As they had driven down its streets, the imposing sight of the city's magnificent structures and scenic beauty overwhelmed her. Mara had been many places in her past, but she usually saw them from another perspective. That her brother lived like this took some getting used to. With irony did she reflect on the realization that these were the kinds of homes that Mother Pearl had cleaned, God rest her soul.

Battling the million or so thoughts and emotions in competition for her attention, she granted first place to the awe and appreciation she felt as she looked at her niece and nephew, her *family*. Deflating formality, she hugged first Kiata, then Keshon and was grateful as they in turn, hugged her back. Immediately they were at home in her heart.

"And this is my wife, Karlynne."

Mara was thankful that Karlynne was carrying a casserole dish that she had to put down, because it afforded her the seconds she needed to compose herself. By the time Karlynne lifted her head to smile at her sister-in-law, Mara also had a smile on her face that belied her surprise at Karlynne's long, blonde hair and blue eyes. She should have known, *would* have known if she'd had more time to consider Kiata's sandy braids or Keshon's hazel eyes. But right now was all the time that she had to settle it in her consciousness, so as Mara reached out to hug her, right now was the time she used to welcome Karlynne into her heart too.

"I don't know what's in that casserole dish, but it sure smells good. Do you need me to help you with anything?"

****

Maybe it was being in a strange place, sleeping in a strange bed that had done it. Whatever it was, Mara liked it. They had sat out on the balcony, watching the fireflies and listening to the night sounds after leaving Emory's house. It had started to rain, a soft, refreshing, summer shower, so Buddy had made a small fire in the fireplace. She turned back the crisp, clean sheets and turned on the news while she waited for him to come into the bedroom. But Mara never did hear about the robbery at the Sovran bank or know what the temperature was going to be, because somewhere between the lead story and the weather report, something else happened.

At home, she and Buddy maintained a healthy sexual relationship that probably rivaled that of younger couples. The ardor accompanying the volcanic passion that had been their lovemaking in the beginning of their marriage, had evolved into a physical act of warmth and security. But that night was different, somehow. Buddy made love to her with an appreciation and a fervor so deep that it felt as if they were indeed the one flesh that God had intended. In his knowing and his giving of himself to her, Mara was able to drink from the reservoir of love that Buddy poured out; she felt safe, ... and she was satisfied. More importantly, she took comfort in knowing that he too was fulfilled.

When she awoke and looked at the clock, it was three fifty eight in the morning. She pulled the sheet over Buddy as she quietly maneuvered herself out of bed to go into the bathroom. Reaching in to adjust the water in the shower, Mara saw herself reflected in the mirror. The person who stared back at her had lost many of the physical accessories that had been the confirmation of her physical beauty in more youthful times. The waistline had disappeared, taken hostage by the same pounds that had converged upon her curves. Her breasts no longer faced forward to challenge the life ahead, but pointed instead toward the earth, nearly defeated, but futilely attempting to defy its inevitable, magnetic claim on her. The still full, thick head of graying hair had long since abandoned stylish coifs in exchange for a more practical and manageable "do". As she surveyed the damage, Mara cupped her breasts in her hands and sucked in her stomach, revealing the small scar hidden beneath its paunch.

"It's okay, God. You're just getting' this old body ready to come home.Buddy hasn't handed in his resignation yet, and even if he does, I've still got You."

But as she stood in the shower, steamy tears shared paths with the water on her face as her heart spoke what her mouth hadn't; a longing for the "who" that was the reason for the scar.

Just before she climbed back into bed to fall asleep in Buddy's arms, Mara knelt on the rug in front of the fireplace to talk to her Father.

"God, I'm amazed at ev'rything You do, even though I guess I shouldn't be because You are God. I... I have to... to keep remindin' myself that the love You have for me is a perfec' love and that no matter what I think I deserve, Your mercy and Your compassion makes You keep on lovin' me and keep on givin' me Your best.... Thank You, God, for what I *do* have ... for givin' me back the things I used to think were lost. Thank you for my family, thank You for how You are changin' me so that I can give love, and thank You for blessin' me with people to love me... In Jesus name, amen."

Chapter 18

"As long as they make you sit here and wait, seems to me like they would put some cushions on these hard benches."

"They keep the soft chairs in their offices so that they'll be comfortable while they take all day to mess up your paperwork."

Mara and Rondell were sitting in the hallway outside the hearing room. She watched as disproportionate numbers of young, 'hoodie' sweat-shirted Black males slumped on the wooden benches, or leaned with defiant scowls against the peeling walls. Periodically a white-shirted assistant would holler a name from the lists on the yellow legal pads he carried, then defender and defendant would retire to an available corner to plan their trial strategy. No wonder the jails are filled with Black men, Mara thought.

While they sat in the courtroom waiting for his case to be called, Mara and Rondell were forced to observe the cases that were being conducted. One of them, a domestic relations case for assignment of child support, had Mara's full attention. The couple, a thirtyish White man dressed in dirt-stained jeans, a khaki work shirt and steel toed boots, and a smartly dressed, blonde-streaked and tanned young woman, sat at opposite tables in front of the judge. As each presented their case, the female judge listened while she scanned the papers that were submitted as evidence to support their respective arguments.

The young construction worker, legally representing himself, tried to convince the judge that what he earned was nowhere near what his girlfriend was requesting for child support, and handed in a stack of bills he was paying to prove it. Further, he contended, she had the house, *his* house, inherited from an uncle, and a new BMW. Mara felt the plunge and turn of the knife when the judge, citing the total of the paid bills as proof that the man's income exceeded what he said, awarded the young lady over five hundred dollars a week in child support. Mara shook her head as she thought about Naomi and others like her, struggling to take care of their families on welfare or minimum wage. Mara knew that the weekly amount the young woman had been awarded, equaled Naomi's bi-weekly paycheck as a nursing assistant.

When it had been his turn, the bailiff had Rondell place his hands on the Bible while the court secretary handed the judge his paperwork. Mr. Kinsey, Rondell's public defender, had convinced the judge that Rondell acted in self-defense in the alleged assault against the person whom Mara now knew as Angelo. The charges had been dismissed, but now they were waiting for the paperwork to be completed so Mara could make arrangements to claim her bail refund. Remembering Buddy's remark about the fight, she alternated between concern and amusement as she observed Rondell's reaction when Angelo exited the courtroom, rolled his eyes in their direction, then swished down the hallway and through the revolving doors in a huff.

Curling his top lip and rolling his own eyes, Rondell registered his own disdain.

"Hmmph ...He can save that drama for his mama, because I-am-*not* impressed! He just *ought* to be glad that his arm was the only thing I broke that needed to have a cast put on it."

"The way I see it, instead of glorifyin' what you did, *you* ought to be the one that's glad. God gave you favor in that courtroom today, young man," Mara admonished him.

"Yes, ma'am."

Sensing that her reproof had really humbled him, Mara decided to use this opportunity.

"Rondell, you and me, we have never talked about this... this... whole situation. Remember that day that you said that you felt like people prob'ly judged you because of your lifestyle? Well I want you to know that I didn't really judge you, but I can't say the thought never crossed my mind as to the reason why you do live this life. How come you even got involved in this kind of... relationship?"

He looked at her and then looked down at his feet.

"I'm askin', not pushin' so if you feel like it's none of my business or it's somethin' that you don't want to talk about, then that's how it'll have to be."

"No ma'am ... it's nothing like that. I know that you're asking because you're concerned about me. I ... I guess ... it's like ... I don't know ... I really don't know how to explain it, Miss Mara."

"I mean, I heard people say that they felt like they were born like that ... or.."

Cutting her off, Rondell said,

"Miss Mara, I know some people believe that, but I don't. I know God didn't make me like I am. This is something that I chose to do on my own."

"But why, Rondell?"

Taking a deep breath and another moment to collect his thoughts, he tried again for the millionth time to answer his own questions as he attempted to answer hers.

"Miss Mara, when I was a little boy, my mother used to be a prostitute. I used to watch her when she would be getting herself ready to go out and trick. At first I was too young to understand where she was going because she would just tell me that she was going to work. The only thing I knew was that she would leave and be gone for a long time. She wouldn't come home until in the morning, or sometimes she would be gone for days. We lived in an apartment on the second floor, and I could look out the window and see her when she would go out and get in those big, pretty cars and drive away. I would miss her so much, and I wanted to go with her or be wherever she was."

Staring off into then, he went on.

"But when she'd be getting ready, I would sit on her bed or in her room on the floor when she was putting on her make-up or combing her hair ... it was always long, and thick, like yours. She always wore pretty clothes and high-heeled shoes ... and she liked perfume, she had all kinds of good-smelling perfume. I always thought that I had the prettiest mommy in the *whole* world. And ... I guess ... I guess I wanted to be like her, she was the person I admired the most."

Mara saw his eyes mist and was conscious of the fact that they were in a public hallway. Sensitive to what she understood to be happening, she knew that here was not the place. Reaching between them for where she'd put her purse, she pushed him to a standing position and then extended her hand to him.

"Help the ol' lady up and let's go see if that paperwork is finished yet."

****

It had been a long time since she had been here. She and Rondell were sitting at one of the picnic tables in Ryan Park. There were other tables scattered throughout the park and under the pavilion, but Mara had picked this one because it was her favorite. Nearby was the row of cherry blossom trees that created the shaded pathway she had walked down almost twenty years ago. She smiled at the memory of Buddy waiting at the end of the row, wiping the moisture from his face with his handkerchief. She'd teased him later about perspiring because he was nervous about getting married, but he reassured her.

"I was sweatin' because it was hot. I wasn't *never* nervous about marryin' you."

Mara had asked only a few people to come--Mr. and Mrs. Wyatt, Mr. LeGrand, some of the people from her row, a few of Buddy's friends. Mother Pearl had been sitting up front in one of the folding chairs next to Zena, both of them fanning and hitting at gnats. Mara remembered that Zena almost hadn't come, that she had really been happy to see her sitting next to Mother Pearl. It was good that the sun had been so bright that day, so her friend's wide-brimmed hat and sunglasses didn't look out of place. Zena's bruises were almost gone, but she still had a yellowish ring around her right eye. If anyone had looked closely enough they could see the tiny holes where the stitches on her cheek had been removed. The ones in her head, on her back and her arms were covered by her hat and the shawl that she had draped around her. Those wounds were getting better; it was the scars in her heart that were taking longer to heal.

When Mara had gone to see her in the hospital, Zena told her that she never saw who it was that stabbed her in her head. She didn't even realize she had been stabbed, thought it was a punch that knocked her down, until she heard the people's voices around her. Zena hadn't even known she was unconscious until she managed to open her puffy left eye "to try to see who the voices belonged to". She couldn't get the right one opened; that's where one of the cuts was. It was better that she hadn't been able to see, better that she had slipped away again, because if not she would have known that she was naked and Zena was too modest for that. It would have been worse for her to know that the people who witnessed her nakedness were White, some of them executives from Maragon whom she saw every day.

Zena had worked late that night, like she had on many nights in the fifteen years she had worked there. Now Mara was aware of Zena's envy of her sense of adventure and her decision to leave... that she wished she had left with her. But even those years ago her friend had been level-headed, and the years of hard work had not been fruitless. By the time that Mara came back home, Zena had worked her way up and out of the file clerk position and had been working in the claims division for a little over two years. Her diligence in that department led to her being elevated to the position of assistant to the supervisor. The night of the incident she was in line for promotion to department supervisor and had worked late to finish processing the claim she was working on.

When she had finally walked to the parking lot around the corner from the building, Zena was already trying to figure out what she was going to wear to work the next day. Just as she checked her watch to see if it was too late to pick up her clothes from the cleaners, she felt the pain in her head.

Zena wasn't surprised when the police told her about the note that was stuck on her forehead with chewing gum. She knew that there were people who didn't like her, who thought that she shouldn't get the promotion, not because she hadn't worked hard and deserved it, but because she was Black … and they didn't want to work under her. Zena knew that just because there were affirmative action programs in workplaces like hers nationwide, it didn't mean that prejudice and racism didn't still exist in this one. She knew that just because the note was written and punctuated properly, it didn't negate the ignorance that had not been edited out of the mind of its educated author.

"Black baboons like you don't make good supervisors. They belong in the jungle with no clothes on, swinging from trees. Stay in your place, NIGGER!"

The note, the beating, her missing clothes…none of that surprised Zena. What she didn't understand was why they hadn't destroyed her car or stolen her money. Whoever it was who had done it, had stolen everything else that meant anything to her.

Chapter 19

"I still don't see why that made him want to *act* like a girl, Mara. Why didn't he just grow up and marry somebody like his mama?"

"Buddy, some people respond to certain things one way, some people another. Maybe if his daddy had been around, or at least treated him like somebody when he was, Rondell would'a looked at things different... I don't know. I sure don't have all the answers for everybody's problems ... you're the one who's always tellin' me that."

"Well, as far as I can see, it ain't stopped you from tryin' to solve 'em yet. I guess God knew what he was doin' puttin' you and me together. We didn't need no kids of our own because we was goin' to be mama and daddy to everybody else's."

For the most part, Buddy was right. Mara knew that he embraced her conviction that many people needed parents, even though they themselves were adults. They had achieved a chronological age that far surpassed their intellectual, emotional or mental maturity. Many looked in the cupboards of the world around them for food to nourish their social skills, without the insight to discern that most people's shelves were as empty as their own. "Parenting your inner child" was a philosophy that Mara had heard discussed on one of the talk shows. She had her own interpretation and shared it with Rondell that day in the park.

"The way I see it is like this, Rondell. If you didn't have a mother or a father around, or they didn't teach you how to do this "life thing" the right way, then when you get old enough, God kinda' gives you another chance. He lets you be your own mother and father. So now you got to do the things for yourself that they didn't do or weren't around to do. You hafta take a look around and see what the best choices are so that you help yourself and add something good to the world. You gotta look at other people's mistakes and see how they got there, and do the opposite of what they did."

Sitting across the bench from Mara, Rondell considered what she said. They had stopped by the Burger Box when they'd left the courthouse. He wasn't sure where she was going when Mara turned the van onto the freeway until they'd ended up here at Ryan Park. It was nice and quiet down here at the waterfront, with the river kissing the rocks around its edge.

"You mean like, just because my mother got pregnant with me didn't make her know how to be a mother?"

"*Tha-a-t's* right, honey. She wasn't livin' the right kinda life to be good at bein' anybody's mother."

"That's why she would sleep with all those men and then give my father all of her money. I never understood that; he didn't marry her and he wouldn't do anything for me … I mean, if she made the money, why didn't she keep it all for herself and me?

"As best as I can tell from where I sit, she didn't know who she was, didn't have no sense of herself. She needed somebody else to tell her when to come and when to go… at least she probably thought she did."

"I hated it when I realized that she was the one who paid for all those different cars he drove and the diamond rings on his fingers… I used to lay in my bed and cry when I would ask her for something, and he would tell her that *he* had something else to do with **her** money, even if I needed it for school … That's why I got caught stealing in the sixth grade … so I could have some money to go to the zoo with the other kids at school!"

Rondell hadn't been lucky, or blessed enough to have a Mother Pearl like Mara did. As they'd finished eating their burgers and fries, he'd gone on to tell Mara about how he had been placed in foster care, and had lived first with this family and then that one when his mother went to jail. He told her about feeling like he didn't belong anywhere and about being mistreated by people whom the state government paid to take care of him. When he'd had enough of getting knocked around by people who spent his allotment on new furniture for their houses, and then bragged to their friends, "They give you six hundred dollars a month for each one," he had run away. He ran to the very streets that had victimized him once through his mother, and would double his trouble when he enlisted in its ranks for himself.

It pained Mara to hear Rondell tell her about the life he'd lived and the things he'd done to survive. He had found himself the object of other people's fantasies, those that were purely sexual as well as those that were motivated by power and violence. Frequently he'd wake up in some strange place, the pain of his shame worse than the pain of the physical injuries he suffered. The cars, the faces, the hands that paid for the seamy hotel rooms ripped holes in his soul, leaving it damaged and bleeding. Mara could identify and empathize with him; she'd been there and done that. She wanted him to know her God because she knew that Rondell had prisoners too.

That Rondell had been intelligent and loved school was the life line that saved him. Even as he dived again and again into life's cesspools, his love for learning was the buoy that kept him from drowning in them, eventually forcing him to return to the surface. When he did emerge, he managed to obtain his GED. In the last two years he was encouraged to attend junior college through a program for homeless young people like him. This most recent incident with Angelo had been one of Rondell's near drownings, and he knew that he had to do something different this time.

Witness to his pain as he shared his chronicles, Mara conjured up a picture of young Rondell, waiting for his mother. She imagined that she saw a familiar dimple in Rondell's cheek, but she quickly dismissed it, recognized it for what it was. She was wiser now, to the guilt that attempted to pirate her, forcing upon her a bill of lading for the emotional cargo which had already been purchased and stamped "paid in full". This time she wouldn't give in.

"...Forgetting those things which are behind me, I press toward the mark of the higher calling which is in Christ Jesus ..."

"God does somethin' else too, Rondell. He gives us a chance to have Jesus as our Big Brother, to take up for us when the worl' tries to beat us up. And He sent the Holy Spirit around to walk us through the rough spots to help us learn how to live better. I'm not tellin' you what to do, that's not my place. But you might want to give that some thought."

"Yes ma'am, I will."

****

"So even though he's on public assistance, he can work a few hours at Grandma's Hands, ... as long as he doesn't make over a certain amount. That way he can help me out, and he won't miss the little chump-change Angelo was givin' him. He's gonna have his associates degree in designin' computers, or some such, in a little less than three months. Then he said he wants to go on and get a four-year degree. Don't you think that's good, Buddy?"

"Rondell is majorin' in computer design and yes, it most cert'nly is good, Baby, *es-specially* if you don't expect me to pay his tuition or his rent or anything."

The make-believe consternation on Mara's face in response to Buddy's comment quickly transformed itself into a warm smile. Planting her hands on her full hips, she said,

"You don't have to give me none o' your smart mouth, **Mister** Nelson Singleton. Since when did you get to know so much about computers? ...And for your information, Rondell has grants to pay for college, he works part time for me, and he's on Section Eight, so he don't need you. He can pay his own rent."

But she knew he would pay it if she asked him to. Buddy knew it too. He couldn't think of too many things that he wouldn't do for Mara. She wasn't just his life partner, she was his best friend ... even if she didn't always act like it.

Buddy knew that most people couldn't understand what held them together, wondered why he was still around. Mara had a way about her that, to an onlooker, belied the true intentions of her heart. Some would call her hard or abrasive, something he had been unable to see in the beginning.

That first day, at Mona's wedding, she had been quiet, withdrawn. He'd thought she was shy, was drawn to her because of it and his own need for serenity. As he'd gotten to know her better and she became more comfortable with him, he experienced other, less endearing facets of who she was. He'd been confused, as much by his own response as he was to this "other Mara" he was seeing. It was confusion that he didn't want, certainly didn't need. There were times when he considered running away, divorcing himself from the whole thing. But he hadn't run; he'd stayed, and asked her to marry him, though he wasn't sure why. Maybe it was because he really wasn't in the best emotional health himself. Perhaps he had discovered that her hard exterior was just one of the coping mechanisms Mara employed to safeguard herself. Though she had verbally and psychologically "scratched" him more times than he could remember, something made him willing to look beyond the obvious. Maybe it was because he was needy--- because he understood the pain of separation. Or maybe it was because he knew that he had quit on life too often.

Whatever the reason had been, Buddy was glad he hadn't run away. The reward for his perseverance had been small, but grew powerful; it was because of who Mara was, who she fought to be in God, that he'd been in position to receive it.

He had almost decided to skip service that Sunday. He was running late and had one more delivery on his list. When he realized the pie was for an elderly deacon at the church, Buddy looked at his watch and knew he had just enough time to catch him before service was over. He'd gotten in the door just in time to hear Pastor Lynch's closing comment.

"Remember this, saints of God, ... hurting people *hurt* people."

"Amen, Pastor! That was *good* Word!"

He smiled at his wife's declaration, saw the back of her head in the third row where she was seated. Mara hated sitting in the back of the church.

"Too many dis-*tractions* f'me. I can't afford to miss *nothin'* God is sayin'!"

Neither could Buddy, and he was glad he hadn't missed this. The pastor's words had finally given Buddy the ability to begin to make sense out of the contradictions that were this woman he had married. They encouraged him to *"run on, and see what the end was gonna' be!"*

Chapter 20

"You can't handle the dough too much, makes it tough … and you have to be careful to have it *just* moist enough … then you sprinkle flour on your pastry sheet … this is somethin' new, this pastry sheet. When I learned how to make pie crust, we use'ta use Cut-Rite waxed paper, … after you sprinkle your flour, you put your dough in the middle so you can roll it out. Now what I do is, I put flour on my rollin' pin, and I sprinkle a little on top of my dough, like this, so it won't stick … then I roll it from top to bottom … and then from side to side, like this. I keep doin' that until it's about a quarter inch thick, and then I …."

"Well I didn't know I had to be a math teacher to make pie crust! How in the world do I know if it's a half inch or a quarter inch, Miss Mara?"

"It's just like anything else you do … the more you practice, the better you get. After a while you just know, Kaitlin, … 'specially after you do like I did and make a few pie crusts that look like layer cake!"

The females in Mara's kitchen joined with her as she laughed at herself. That they had the ability to laugh was a good thing, because life didn't give them an awful lot to laugh about. Mara knew that most of these young women around her table lived under the weight of the many opinions that existed about the lack of difference between the Black, female experience and that of their White counterparts. How many times had she heard, "When I look at Black people, I don't see color." Or "I don't see what all the big hullabaloo is about; I think if you really work hard, you can achieve the same goals as us." But Mara had her own perspective.

She and Buddy were lying in the bed one night, watching Politically Incorrect on the televison. Mara had to get a dictionary to look up the word "entitlement" that she'd heard the TV talk show host use as the panelists explored "the historical roles of the Black woman". At one point, the

144

discussion centered around the reason why Oprah Winfrey's character Sethe, from the movie "Beloved", had killed her own children. One panelist's observation was that "Sethe, a slave with limited language, tried to explain that she had killed them in a heroic, albeit warped, protest of the slave master's institutionally supported belief that he had some right to own, rule and destroy people's lives". The discussion escalated to heated debate as they talked about whether or not Angela Bassett's character in the movie "Waiting To Exhale", had the right to be angry after being abandoned by her Black husband. The fact that his wife had been the one who supported and sacrificed for him, after which he elected to share his subsequent wealth and good times with a White woman, Mara felt, substantiated her position about Black women and White women. Few could understand the dynamics of sacrificing for and then being rejected by your own people after being brutalized and systematically exploited by another. It was one of life's cruel realities.

"White people just don't get it; they don't understand, Buddy. I can operate in their world and then come back and live in mine with no problem; they made me learn how to do that. But White people can't do the same thing; they can only live and operate in their world and I'll tell you why. Because for so long, that was the only world that ever meant anything to them. What happened in my world was never important to them. It has always been up to Black people to try and find a way to get along with White folks. It's us that had to fit. But it's changin'...And the only reason why it means anything to'em now is because their White daughters are sleepin' with our Black sons...an' they ain't hidin' it."

The good thing was that even though she had her feelings about this, Mara had learned that she had no room in her life for hatred. From her perspective, the world she lived in continued to silently support the issues, systems, and symptoms that were socially carcinogenic and threatened its very life force---but these were considerations outside her sphere of influence. Impacted by them, Mara refused to be negatively driven by them. She talked to God about it---

shared her observations with Him, told Him how she felt about what she saw. She could do that, she trusted Him. Her God was colorless and he wasn't bound by gender except as He had divinely elected to manifest Himself in the male flesh of Jesus. She trusted His Word that encouraged her to ask for wisdom, that assured her that she could come boldly, seeking, --- grace and mercy. As often as she detected the presence of bitterness in her interactions, Mara purposed not to become what she despised. She traded in her bitter for better...and it was her better that she chose to impart to these women.

Pastor Lynch had challenged his members to duplicate themselves in others. This explained why Valeta, Jovanda, Luce, Rondell, LeTeseya, and Kaitlin were all gathered in Mara's kitchen. She was teaching them how to bake her now famous sweet potato pies, the legacy and the recipe that Mother Pearl had left with her. She realized the wealth of such a legacy and that perhaps, as a result, she, too, had been given a realm of influence in these lives. If her influence was to have its most positive effect, she knew that it must be smoothed on with an applicator of love within an atmosphere of understanding. Though the kitchen at the church was much larger, the warmth of her own kitchen offered all of the above, and provided a place for learning.

"Each one, reach one", was the philosophy that Mara had adopted and was what it had taken to get them here...even Kaitlin. Assuring an environment that encouraged appreciation of their diversity while celebrating their commonality, was a gift that only God could have awakened in her.

"Jovanda, make sure that the oven is on three-fifty, and LeTeseya hand me that lemon flavorin'."

"So *thet's* yo' secret ingredi-ent, Mom Mara! Ah've been wonderin' what it was!"

"First I had to be a math teacher, now I have to be a mad scientist and discover the missing ingredient to the special formula! What do I have to be next?"

146

"When you're in my kitchen Kaitlin, the only thing you have to be is true to yourself. You know that."

Mara had learned that being herself was something that Kaitlin had a hard time doing. This was something Mara could identify with. In spite of the fact that their neighborhood was an ethnic gumbo, there was evidence of individual values and cultural traditions that gave it a distinctive flavor. Somehow though, who Kaitlin was, the fact that she was "a White girl" had been lost in her assimilation of the values and traditions of those who lived around her. Like Garfield, she appeared to have no family of her own and adopted the sisters and brothers, aunts and uncles of her neighbors. Though Mara had seen her talking to a few of the other White people on the block, her preference appeared to be Black people; Mara still hadn't settled this little idiosyncrasy inside herself. Kaitlin's children, two obviously bi-racial little girls, were always clean and well groomed when she'd walk them to school, but like many of their playmates, had no visible father.

Mara had often watched Kaitlin in the past, cornrows secured with rubber bands making sure that her curly, brown hair didn't unravel, as she'd shared a blunt with Rondell. But more recently, the fact that he was attempting to turn over a new leaf also seemed to have a positive effect on Kaitlin. She usually stopped in when Rondell was working, and like many of the others, was a "check-day regular" at the bakery. But it was the day that her seven year-old, Jabria, ran up on Mara's porch, that a greater closeness was fostered between the two of them.

Mara had come running when she heard someone screaming and banging on her door. She'd opened it just in time as one of the clothes-line-collared pit bulls rounded her hedges in pursuit of Jabria and Luce's daughter, Carmelita. Mara pulled the terrified little girls in and locked the storm door even as the dog stood snarling, with his front legs on the glass. As the baseball bat wielding Luce ran toward the steps cursing, the pit bull turned his attention and charged toward her. Startled, Luce lost her balance and fell backward

147

down the steps just as shots rang out. Mara looked out to see Caleb, gun in hand, running across the street, aiming in the direction of the dog. As one of the five shots and then another found its target, the pit bull flipped over, bleeding onto the patch of grass between Mara's house and her next-door neighbor's. Mara saw Mr. Paluszka open his door, step one foot onto his porch, and look over to where the dying pit bull was lying next to the steps where Luce was sprawled. He then stepped back in, closed and locked his door, and disappeared into his house, unwilling to be involved. Though she shook her head at his actions, Mara understood.

Mr. Paluszka was one of the last original members of this neighborhood. He was retired and lived here alone, despite his children's repeated attempts to get him to sell his house and move into a retirement village. Having lost his wife to Alzheimer's disease almost four years ago, he kept to himself, speaking to no one... except Buddy. Somehow her husband, with an ability that only he had, managed to engage him in some semblance of a friendship. Mara had often looked out in the backyard and seen them discussing a recent ball game or that year's tomatoes. She had long since given up trying to talk to him, when after several "good mornings", she had never received more than what sounded like a grunt. But gauging Mr. Paluszka's life from his perspective, Mara realized a grunt was probably the best he had to give.

Having migrated here with his family from the Ukraine, Mr. Paluszka had worked full-time for thirty-seven years at the steel mill and part-time driving a cab for eighteen of those years. He and his wife raised their three children, sent them through college, and saved to buy this house in this neighborhood, looking, Mara was sure, toward his future and retirement. When that time had finally come, his wife no longer recognized him, and the neighborhood had deteriorated to the point that he had been forced to become a prisoner in his own home. When his family came to visit, his grandchildren played inside one section of his fenced-in backyard. The other section was a paved carport that he'd had built, with motion sensors to keep his car safe from vandals. It was no wonder that he didn't want to get involved in the lives of people who littered his yard with cellophane bags and left Colt 45 bottles on his front porch.

As Mara unlocked the door to join the crowd forming on the sidewalk, she saw Caleb helping Luce to her feet. She almost lost her balance again as Kaitlin hysterically pushed past her looking for Jabria.

"She's okay, sweetheart. She's in my house with Carmelita. Go on in, she's in there."

As Kaitlin rushed into her house, Mara continued down the steps to where Luce was examining a bleeding area on her leg.

"Look at thees, Miss Mara. I think Caleb shot me when he was shooting at the dog!"

Sure enough, Mara saw an area that looked like it probably had been grazed by a bullet.

"I think maybe he did, Luce. Do you want to me to take you to the hospital?"

Looking at Caleb with noticeable admiration, she said, "Oh no, Miss Mara. If I go to the hos-pee-tal, then they will be asking me too many questions. And then maybe, they will be takeeng my Pop-pee Caleb to jail."

Chuckling at how Luce had lapsed into a deep Spanish dialect, Mara said,'

"Come on in this house, girl. I need to check on Kaitlin and those babies, and I think I can clean your leg up with some peroxide. Caleb, you better stay out here to tell the police what happened."

But Mara knew better. She knew that Caleb probably didn't have a permit to own that gun, and when the police finally did get here, probably no one would have any idea how the pit bull that was found in the alley behind the houses got shot. As long as the police didn't knock on her door, this time, Mara probably wouldn't have any idea either.

Chapter 21

"Thank you, Miss *Maa-a-ra*."

Sitting in the living room with Kaitlin's other daughter Kamri, Jabria and Carmelita sang their appreciation.

"I'm just glad I was still here because I was on my way over to Zena's."

"I'm glad you were here too, Mrs. Singleton. Jabria would never have been able to make it home. That dog would have torn her apart."

"They should keep those dogs locked up! Remember when you and me was talking about that, Miss Mara?"

"We sure did, Luce, but they don't have to worry about *that* pit bull any more And Miss Kaitlin, I don't know where you got that Mrs. Singleton bizness from. Everybody calls me Miss Mara, so you might as well too."

"Thank you, Miss Mara, but I can't help it, that's just the way I was raised."

Just then they heard Mara's front door open as Buddy came in, his face creased with concern, followed by Garfield.

"They told me about what happened out there. Is everybody all right?"

"Everybody's okay, Buddy. Luce just had a little place on her leg, but it's not bad."

"And I need to go and see about my Pop-pee," Luce said, getting up to leave.

"Don't go just because we came in Luce. You women can finish your little hen party. I can take Garfield out in the backyard to whup him in this game of checkers, can't I, Garfield?"

Garfield just smiled as Luce replied, "Oh, no, Meester Buddy. I really have to see about Caleb and finish cook-king my dinner. Carmelita, come Mee-ra, we need to go home now."

"I want to play with Jabria, Mommy. Can she come to my house?"

Seeing Kaitlin's reation out of the corner of her eye, Mara interceded.

"Why don't you go see about Caleb, Luce, and leave Carmelita over here. They can all have some cookies and milk and play until Kaitlin gets ready to go."

"They can play out in the backyard while I'm whuppin' on Garfield. I'll keep an eye on 'em," Buddy offered, reaching out to take two of the girls' little hands in his big ones as Garfield picked up the smallest one.

After they'd left, Kaitlin turned to Mara.

"Thanks, Miss Single ... I mean, Miss Mara. I would rather that Jabria stay with me after everything that happened."

"You don't have to explain it to me. I saw it in your face, that's why I told Luce to leave them here."

"Are you sure that they're okay with Mr. Si ... Mr. Buddy, and Mr. Garfield?"

Mara heard what Kaitlin was being polite enough not to say.

"Buddy loves kids, we just never had any. And whatever anybody told you about Garfield, let Miss Mara tell you *this*. Garfield is one of the most gentle people I have ever met, and believe me, I have met all kinds of people. But I trust him with *anything*."

"I'm sorry if I sounded funny, but you can't trust hardly anybody these days, Miss Mara, especially when it comes to my daughters... you know what I mean? And I remember when he ... when Mr. Garfield used to be homeless and lived across the street under the porch."

"It's funny that you would say that Kaitlin, because I was thinkin' about that very thing last Sunday in church. Our pastor, Pastor Lynch, chose Garfield and my Buddy to be deacons, because he said that they were the kind of men that Jesus would'a picked.

Now don't get me wrong, they got their faults, everybody does. But those are two men who love people and would do whatever they could to help them. ... I was kinda thinkin' that you and Garfield are alike in some ways."

Kaitlin scrunched up her face in disbelief at Mara's observation.

"Alike *how*, Miss Mara?"

"Well, I know that Garfield has a family 'cause everybody came from somewhere, and I acksh'ully met one of his brothers. But you would'a never thought he had anybody when you saw him sleepin' under the porch."

"*And*?"

"*And* I know that you must have a family somewhere too, even if they never come around."

She watched as Kaitlin's eyes filled with tears as her head fell involuntarily on her chest in reaction to Mara's comment. Reaching for the box of Kleenex, she moved over to sit next to Kaitlin on the sofa, putting her arms around her to comfort her. She waited, allowing Kaitlin to cry into her generous bosom until she finally lifted her head to blow her nose, her eyes red-rimmed and swollen. Kaitlin threw her hands up, letting them fall again into her lap, as she fought to contain all that she felt.

"Miss Mara, I have tried *so hard* to do this by myself! My family won't even call me to see if I'm all right … **you** care more about what happens to me than they do …and they don't do anything for my babies, …they **never** did **anything** for Jabria or Kamri! They act like they don't even have two granddaughters … *just because their father is **Black***! And that's not right! My girls can't help who their father is, it's not their fault! It's not **anybody's** fault who they are or how they were born! … And I can't help it that the person I fell in love with wasn't White, …and rich, … and perfect … and boring … like my sister's husband!"

Unable to keep the tears dammed up, she fought between them to get everything she had been holding inside of her out.

"And it's **not -my- fault** that he left me … I'm not stupid …I don't care what they say … I thought he really did love me … he said he did, … I loved him, Miss Mara!"

As Mara again cradled White Kaitlin in her Black arms, God caused her to realize that His love, demonstrated in her compassion, had no color. She looked up as Buddy came in, a look of concern again on his face. As he took in the whole picture, he turned and went back toward the yard. He knew that God and his wife were doing the things that they did best.

Chapter 22

"Well, I thought I was just goin' to have to call and make an appointment, Miss I-am-an-important-business-woman! Mara Singleton you need to slow yourself down so I can catch up with you!"

"Zena, I'm gonna have a talk with God and see if He can't add a couple more hours to the day. I have been busier in these last months than Republicans tryin' to count votes in Florida!"

"Girl, that's a mess ain't it? They can send a man to the moon, they know how many freckles on a bullfrog's butt from a hundred miles away, but they can't figure out how to make a system to count votes in a presidential election! Maybe after they spend a few more millions goin' to outer space, somebody on Mars can tell'em how to do it when they get there!"

"You better stop talkin' like that or they'll have somebody tappin' your telephone."

"I hope they do, and I hope he's Black, a widower, rich, and lookin' for a good woman!"

The two of them laughed together like they hadn't been able to for some time.

The friendship they shared had endured many things, finding a new strength, and Mara knew that it was in spite of their differences. She believed that the respect that they now had for each other had achieved a depth that was hard to unearth. Much depended on Mara's recently developed philosophy that friendship was like marriage, "... And you gotta do the same thing to stay friends as you did when you first started bein' friends." As far as Mara was concerned, she and Zena had finally found their way through the maze that few friends were willing negotiate, and their relationship was a testimonial to that. Sitting in Mara's kitchen that evening, it was her hope that they would soon be embarking on yet another phase of their alliance.

"So how in the world do you think you can open up another Grandma's Hands? Where are you gonna' be able to find the time, Mara?"

"Well, Zena, it's like this. The only people I know that like my potato pie better than I do is Buddy and you. He's already helpin' me, in fact you can say he is my delivery service. And it's high time for him to stop workin' so hard ... Buddy's not gettin' any younger. And neither are you, Zee."

Sensing her friend's reaction even before she saw it, Mara forged on.

"Hear me out, hear me out. ... You been at Maragon since we first met, umpteen years ago, and I'm the first to admit that you did better than anybody thought you would. 'Cept me, of course ... I always knew you'd do good. But you *have* been there a long time, Zena. You already got your time in,.. you can take your retirement and come on and help me run Grandma's Hands Too. I've been teachin' Rondell, Kaitlin, Luce and a few of the girls from the church how to make pies. But I need somebody who's as bossy as me to run things, and you're the only one I know who can out-boss me."

The two friends laughed as Zena rolled her eyes in mock anger at Mara's comment. A few minutes passed as Mara pretended to be busy at the stove so as to give Zena a little time to mull over her proposal.

"Well, it's somethin' to think about, Mara. You say you and Buddy have talked about this and he thinks it's a good idea?

"Think ish a goo' idea 'bou' wha'?"

Both women turned their attention to where the back door had opened. Buddy lurched through it, nearly causing both him and Garfield to fall on the kitchen floor. Garfield was beside him, trying to support the weight of an obviously intoxicated Buddy.

"I hear' you two hens talkin' 'bout me. Wha'sha matter? Buddy ain' no man no more when he ain' go' no job, huh?"

"Aw Buddy, no ... not now, Buddy, you was doin' so

good!" Mara cried, slumping down in the kitchen chair.

"Aw Buddy, nah' now," he slurred, mimicking Mara.

Zena walked over to where Buddy was reeling against the kitchen stove.

"Watch out, Buddy! That stove is hot! Come on, Garfield. I'll help you get him up the steps and into the guestroom. Then you can get his clothes off, and I'll throw'em in the washer. ... Mara, I'll be right back down, but don't forget to check on your spareribs..."

It had been years since Buddy had taken a drink. There was a time, between relapses, when Mara had lived in fearful anticipation of the next one. Her fear was not because Buddy had ever been physically violent toward her ... even drunk, they both knew that she would never have stood for that. Rather, it was the reconstruction process that they always had to go through later. He'd get drunk, come home, sleep it off, and then try to make it up to her, try to convince her that it would never happen again. And she believed him, not because she was gullible or even that he was a good liar. She believed him because she knew that he wanted it so desperately to be true.

So they would begin rebuilding upon the foundation of their love and dedication to each other's well being. He had to work his way back up the ladder to reach a functional level of self-respect... again. And she had the responsibility of not being a hindrance to that climb. This was war, and they were in the trenches together. He had her back, and she had his. He was always there to help her avoid the minefields that threatened to implode and destroy her. And when "the enemy" came against him, it was Mara who prayed and ushered in God's standard. And so they lived, as happily ever after as they could manage... until the next time. It had come a few years ago.

It was one morning at about three a.m., after she had struggled to get Buddy in off the back porch; Mara was on her knees. She was cleaning up the lunch he'd eaten sometime earlier in the day and talking to her "Father".

"God, I don't know how much more of this I can take. I

know you gave me this man, and he's a good man God. But he's got somethin' goin' on his heart, God, that I can't fix; that's *Your* job. So God, I'm askin' You to fix what's broke in him. If he had a brother or a sister or somebody I could ask, I wouldn't be askin' You. But I'm all he's got, and besides You, he's all I got.. So I need You to work this thing out in him, please, God. Because I can't do what You want me to do if You don't. I can't take him with me, and I don't want to leave him God, b'cause I believe You mean for us to do Your work together. So God, can You please help my man? In Jesus' name, amen."

Mara hadn't seen the shadow of Buddy standing in the doorway behind where she was kneeling. She didn't know that God wasn't the only one that heard her petition. What she did know was that God does answer prayer because, to her knowledge, Buddy had not taken another drink from that day to this one.

Listening to her two friends upstairs as they worked in concert to try to straighten out this crooked place in her life, Mara nodded her head in silent appreciation of their presence, before and right now. Bowing her head in her hands, she contemplated what this situation could mean for her ... for them. If this was the resumption of a life that she believed they had left dead and buried in another grave-marked era, it had resurrected with ghostly timing. Could she do this again? Did she even want to? She had just asked Zena to abandon her safe, secure existence to join her in this now potentially disastrous one. Could she expect Zena's loyalty? Should she?

As Mara faced the prospect of starting the reconstruction process yet again, she automatically questioned her ability to handle this. After all, she wasn't young anymore. But just as immediately, she knew that she was strong enough to do it. She was a fighter. This was still war, it was just another phase of the battle. And he was still her man. Buddy was a proud man, ... a dreamer, but proud ... a simple man, but proud ... a hardworking man, but proud. His pride was not arrogance. Mara believed that it had come from faith in himself and his commitment to doing his best.

But now Buddy's best couldn't be the measurement; because he was God's man before he was hers. Now God wanted to do *His* best, and Buddy's faith had to be in God's commitment to do His best through him. And it was God who would give them the victory.

She was taking her ribs out of the oven when her two friends came back into the kitchen. She looked up at them with new eyes.

"Me and Garfield got him situated Mara, he'll be all right in the mornin'. Do you want me to stay here with you for a while?"

"Yeah, Zee. Maybe the three of us can play a few hands of pinochle. That's if Garfield won't mind playin' with us hens."

****

The early dawn crept in under Buddy's eyelids, forcing him toward consciousness. His grimacing face telegraphed the message sent by the forces that joined against him as the nausea in his throat rose to meet the throbbing in his head. Tightening his lids, he swallowed in an attempt to control the biological responses to the cheap wine that was assaulting him internally. Fighting to ignore the taste of the alcohol-laced bile being evicted by his stomach, he tried to make his hand cooperate by covering his mouth. Realizing that something was holding his arm down, he struggled against the sheets that Garfield had tucked around him. He loosed himself and rolled over the side of the bed just before everything that refused to stay down found its way into the plastic trash can next to the bed. The calm before the next eruption gave his lips only time enough to form "Jesus!" before he threw his head over the side again.

Physically unable to move, Buddy lay there, an unwilling actor in this scene that he had directed and produced. His senses assailed by the sights and smells, he was both physically and emotionally sickened. He had done it again. As the why and how began to form into a reason, he knew that there was no reason, good or *bad* enough to justify *this.*

Chapter 23

"Naomi, that is *wonderful*! God is faithful to His promises! It took a little while, but you know what the song says, … 'He may not come when you want Him, but He's right on time!"

"And now that Jomar is in school all day, I don't have to pay for daycare any more either, Mara. Plus they'll still give me my food stamps until I finish school."

"Now that's God all the way, Naomi. So I guess I have to buy a weddin' present and two graduation presents!"

Mara's happiness for Naomi was genuine. If anybody she knew deserved a break, her friend did. That Naomi's daughter Valeta was getting married was not for Mara to question, that was God's business. At least they were doing things the right way; Valeta and Arlay were in Pastor Lynch's pre-marital counseling class. They would be finished just about the same time that Valeta would be finishing her GED class, and Naomi would be starting nursing school. This time next year, they could all kiss welfare goodbye.

"Mara, you don't have to buy anything for us. I can't ever thank you enough for what you did for me when my Jamar got killed. Then how you helped Valeta when she was having the twins. And if it wasn't for you and Zena helping me … I would never have known anything about that Victim Survivor's Fund. Girl, if anything, I might buy you a present when I graduate!"

"Well, I'll wait until you graduate and start bringin' home those big nurse's paychecks. I think a pair of diamond earrings would look nice in my ears," Mara kidded.

"If anybody's gonna buy my wife diamonds, it's gonna be me," Buddy butted in from the supply room. "But you can make some of these deliveries for us if you want to do somethin'."

"Leave Naomi alone. She's got more than enough to do, Buddy. And you know you don't have to do this run; you can send those last orders by Rondell. He'll be in by three forty-five."

Turning to Naomi she said, "Believe me, Honey. Closin' the plant may not have been good for everybody, but it was the best thing that could'a happened for Buddy. He took it hard at first, you know how he is about bein' the provider. But God is good. They gave him the option to relocate to their other plant in Rehoboth, or he could take that early retirement package. That's all he needed to hear. He signed his name so fast he was home before the ink dried! So now he's mister-in-charge-of-delivery-and-operations, and lovin' every minute of it." Mara didn't bother to mention Buddy's relapse.

"That's good, Mara, that's good. But I wouldn't expect anything less. You and Buddy deserve everything good that's happening for you because you've helped a lot of people."

"Go on now, Naomi. I could only do what God blessed me to do; so it was Him, not me."

Naomi knew that Mara meant what she said; this was no false, trumped up humility. She would take no credit for herself. God had done it all. Oh, Mara knew that a lot of people would take the credit for pulling themselves up by their bootstraps, but she knew it was God that gave them the boots. The Bible said that it was He who gave the power to create wealth; it all began and ended with Him.

God's demonstrated abundance in their lives extended outside of Grandma's Hands to include Mara's relationship with Emory and his family. She looked forward to their weekly telephone calls, on Sunday evenings when rates were low, of course. Kiata tried to get Mara to use her "aunt influence" to convince Emory and Karlynne to let her talk to "this really cute guy at school, Auntie Mara". She had been surprised to find a letter from Keshon from time to time. He was away at college and wrote to thank her for the box of goodies she'd sent to his dorm or the money she slipped in a card for him, "so you can buy yourself a burger."

What was of greatest amazement to Mara was the relationship that had developed between Karlynne and herself. Perhaps it was the fact that they now shared the mutual experience of loving Emory and that Karlynne had never once acted threatened or intruded upon. Or maybe it was the times when Karlynne had made the drive to spend time with Mara, to get to know her. It felt good to share her home with her family. It was even better to share her Bible with her sister-in-law as they sat on the pew, shoulder to shoulder, worshipping God together. Mara dared not ask God for more.

It was during one of Karlynne's visits that a thought occurred to Mara.

"Karlynne, what did your family say when they found out about you and my brother?"

"Well, they didn't have to 'find out'. He came to my house and met my parents. Do you mean because Emory is Black?"

Mara smiled at the thought of what Buddy's response to Karlynne's question would have been if he'd been there. "No, because he was from outer space... of course because he is Black!" She fought against saying it out loud, nodding her head instead.

"Well, my parents weren't what you'd call 'thrilled' about it. They weren't prejudiced against Black people, but they were concerned about the problems that it had the potential to create for me and for Emory. And there was the matter of what our children would have to deal with, being bi-racial."

"That's what I was thinkin' about. It's like they have to learn to live in two different worlds."

"I guess that's one way of looking at it. But Emory and I decided that they only had to learn to live in one world, and that was the one we created for them. If we showed them how to love themselves and respect the differences in everybody, then they had a head start. We knew that it wouldn't always be easy or fair for them; both of us have had to deal with prejudice and racism. But Em and I just decided that we would give Keshon and Kiata the tools that they would need to be able to deal. They're doing okay, so far."

Mara thought for a moment, then said, "I got somebody I want you to meet, Karlynne. If anybody can, I think maybe you're the one who can help her."

Karlynne caused Mara to rethink her philosophy about White women. Maybe they *could* live in her world too.

****

"That's fine for you, Miss Karlynne, but my mother won't listen to anything I have to say. I don't even talk to her. She thinks I'm stupid."

"What other people think about you is only important if you let it be. It's what you think about yourself that's more important, Kaitlin."

"I don't really know what I think anymore. I guess that's the reason Miss Mara wanted me to talk to you. I mean, I know that I need to have a positive self-image, but it's hard when your own mother won't have anything to do with you .... You know, people always act like having children makes you a mother, but I know the difference in the love and commitment I have for my girls and how my mother treated us. I mean, she made sure we had nice clothes and a good education, but she never wanted us to think for ourselves, to be people with our own values. She just wanted everybody to look at what a wonderful job she did raising her beautiful, upper-middle-class daughters."

"Is that the reason why you made sure you did all the things she didn't want you to do? Was it because you wanted to hurt your mother that you made sure you were nothing like your sisters?"

"No, not really. I mean, I made some mistakes, but I honestly loved Durel as a person, not for his money or what he could do for me. I knew that my mother didn't want me to

163

date anybody that wasn't White, but I thought he loved me and would be there for me and the baby. And that my mother would see that material things weren't important, that he was a decent person, even if he was Black."

"So you feel like he failed you and made you look bad. But if he wasn't there for you after your first baby, why did you get pregnant again, Kaitlin?"

"Because it was too late then, I didn't have my family any more and I thought that I could make him want to be with me and the girls. Miss Karlynne, you're married to a Black man, so you know how hard it is. Even when they want to do the right thing, it's hard for them to get a good job. And when he was with me, Durel's friends stayed on his back, telling him that White girls are just for *layin' and playin'* and that he needed to be with a Black woman!"

Fortunately, Karlynne had the wisdom to realize that Kaitlin had issues that couldn't be solved in one conversation, but at least now there was an open door for communication. They could explore the differences in their situations later, she would make sure of that. Neither could she overlook the common thread that linked Kaitlin to her own daughter. But it was Mara who knew that there were some things that had to be handled now.

"Kaitlin, Miss Mara wants to say this to you, sweetheart. Everything that you said about your mother could be true. But sometimes mothers are so busy tryin' to figure out what *is* the best thing to do that they end up doin' the wrong thing. I know you love Jabria and Kamri, but I know somethin' else too. I know that you smoke weed and those Blunts, too. A mother who wants the best for her children don't put herself, or *them* in that kind'a situation. After all is said and done, you know I'm right."

Neither Kaitlin nor Karlynne knew where Mara had to go inside herself to offer this bit of wisdom, but they both sensed her sincerity. That it took reopening an old wound was worth the bleeding of her heart. Mara knew that heaven was still open and that God was still in the business of healing.

Chapter 24

Surpri-i-ise !!!!"....

Mara was so startled by the shouts and laughter that she dropped the packages of Tidy-Dy-Dees she was carrying. She involuntarily put her hands over her eyes as she tried to adjust her focus against the camera lights flashing in her face. There were arms hugging her and lips on her cheeks and hands pulling her into the room. So eager were they in their efforts that Mara felt herself stumble and nearly fall. But the arms that caught her and steadied her on her feet were attached to the lips that brushed her ear as they whispered,

...*"Happy Birthday, Baby"*...

"Surprise! ...Happy Birthday! ...*Na, na-na-na-a-a, na!*... We got you ...Hah-hah, we fooled you this time, Miss Mara!"

Mara struggled to catch her breath and regain what she could of her composure as she lowered herself into the seat that appeared behind her. It had been decorated with gilded gold foil, multicolored ribbons and a rainbow of balloons attached to the back and the arm rests. There were over two hundred helium filled balloons with attached streamers hanging suspended from the high dropped ceiling of the former gymnasium. Several more brightly colored balloons formed the number "55" as a backdrop to the festively bedecked birthday table, which was laden with bags and boxes of varying shapes and sizes. Around the perimeter of the room, to the left and right of the gift table, tables were heaped with every kind of food; from bowls piled high with fresh fruit and salads to platters of cheese and cold cuts. Lighted cans of sterno warmed aluminum pans filled with string beans, collard greens, sweet potato fluff and macaroni and cheese, while others held sliced ham and roast beef, meatballs, and fried chicken. Directly behind where Mara was seated were two more long tables, one with pans of peach cobbler, walnut and raisin sticky buns, platters of donuts and cookies and homemade pies. The other table held all kinds of cakes including butter pound, seven-up, Dutch apple, German chocolate and strawberry short- cake. Sandwiched between the two was a small round table upon which was a huge, pie- shaped cake with the words *'Happy Birthday, Mara!'* spelled out above a pair of brown, wrinkled hands opened beneath them.

People were seated in every one of the chairs circling the twenty-five or thirty round tables that had been placed about the gymnasium floor. Each table sported gold foil centerpieces with balloon bouquets placed on top of colored table coverings that matched the balloons hovering above them. There were even balloons decorating the paper plates and cups that joined the red, yellow, orange, green and blue plastic cutlery that formed each place setting.

The shear magnitude of the planning and work that had obviously gone into the   preparation for this celebration overwhelmed Mara. Her emotions played games with her as she looked out at the ocean of smiling faces that beheld her grateful confusion. Her heart leapt and cried at the demonstration of appreciation and generosity displayed before her. Nothing could ever have prepared her for this; there was nothing she could think of that she had done that would make her worthy. It was God who made her worthy in the eyes and hearts of these people.

"I came that you might have life and that more abundantly, ... Try Me and see, I will pour you out a blessing you won't have room enough to receive."

Mara reflected on God's Word, and her thanks echoed those of others who had also experienced His goodness. *And for this too, ... I give You praise.*

****

It seemed like everyone she knew was here, all of her friends, her neighbors and her family. They lined up around the room to come and offer her their well wishes; little ones

whose hands she had held when they took their first steps,
and their parents whom she had taught to walk a different
pathway.

"Me and my Pop-pee came to tell you Happy Birthday,
Miss Mara."

"Heppy Birthday, Mom Mara. I jest wont you t'know
how much Ah 'preciate awl you have done fo' me and mah
fam'ly since we moved heeyer. You an' Mister Buddy made
me and Parris feel raht at home."

"Mara, thank you for seeing something in me that I
didn't see in myself any more. You became my friend and
gave me a friend when I needed one, and you helped me
regain my self-respect. Thank you and Happy Birthday."

"Hold on now, Garfield, you been as much a friend to
Buddy and me as we have been to you, ... And it wasn't me,
it was God who gave you back respect for yourself. But He
only did it when you gave your life to Him."

As she stood up to hug him, Mara caught sight of eyes
that she recognized. Before she could associate them with a
particular face, she felt someone pulling on her dress. She
looked down to see Kamri and Jabria standing on either side
of her birthday throne.

"Happy Birthday Miss Maa-ra!" they chimed together,
one extending a small gift bag and the other an envelope.

"Thank *you*, Miss Mara's sweet babies. Give Miss Mara
some shuggah!" she said, sitting back down so they could
reach her face.

Mara's breath caught as she looked at them and heard
herself, for it was then that the realization hit that there was
someone very special missing from this celebration. Looking
at Jabria and Kamri, she realized that they were her "little
White babies", and she had just heard Mother Pearl's voice
coming out of her mouth. She fought back the tears; this was
supposed to be a joyous time. But o-o-oh how she missed
her!

Finding a smile, she released them and looked up to
greet the next person in line. Her smile widened; this was so
like God. Just as a moment ago she had cause for grief,

standing before her now were reasons for happiness. She stood to embrace Kiata, Keshon and Karlynne one by one. Bringing up the rear was Emory ... her brother. She remembered what she had read in her Bible earlier that day, that *"God places the lonely in families ... and satisfies your desires with good things"*...

Holding her brother close she thought, 'Yes He does ... yes He does'....

As Emory stepped aside, Mara realized that the gap in the line behind him wasn't actually a gap. Seated in his wheelchair, Rayfield awaited his turn to talk to her. Mara quickly checked her heart for the forgiveness she hoped was really there. She sat down as Emory pushed the wheelchair closer to her.

"Happy Birthday, Mara Ruthine."

Reaching to take her hand in both of his, Rayfield looked Mara straight in her eyes.

"I hope that this isn't the wrong time for me to do this. If it is I'm sorry, but I need to do it. It's something I should have done a long time ago. I wanted to say something that day in the bedroom, and then later, when you were in court. I wanted to write to you from the penitentiary...I actually did write to Mother Pearl and she wrote me back and said it was probably better for you if I left it alone ... When I finally got out, I would look at Emory and think about you, ... all the time. ...

Deferring to what he recognized as a moment in time, Buddy quietly motioned for those still waiting to greet Mara to give her this time. Few other than Zena could have known who Rayfield was, but any observant eye could see that this was significant.

"Mara, what I want to say is that I am so sorry, I've always been sorry for what happened to Mamie Ruth. I was living a hellish life back then, ... I'm not making any excuses, that's just the truth. If I could have changed anything, I would have. I'm an old man now, Mara Ruthine, and I've had to live with what I did all these years. ... I know that you did too, but it seems like you've found some peace.

… I just needed to tell you I'm sorry so that I could try to find some before I die."

It really wasn't a hard thing for her to do; telling Rayfield that she forgave him wasn't hard at all. She knew what it was to have lived a hellish life, for she had some hellish moments in her own past. Placing her free hand on top of his, she liberated Rayfield to live the rest of his life unfragmented. It was okay. When she checked her heart, she knew he had already been forgiven. It was like discovering a brand new silver dollar under the pillow where your old, baby tooth had been; she got something of value for something that was now useless to her.

****

The food and the gifts and the beautiful decorations weren't the end of the preparations for Mara's party. She beamed as the church praise dancers ministered to one of her favorite songs. The interpretation of "For Every Mountain" by the newly formed mime ensemble was followed by a solo from Kasai, the teen father of one of her nursery babies. There was a dramatic presentation by "HIS prerogative", the church drama ministry, and then some of the teens performed an original gospel rap. Mara heard a drumbeat and saw the gymnasium door open to reveal Rondell, leading the drill team he was captain of. She was so proud to see him marching and strutting … **not** *swishing.*

Naomi, Jomar, Valeta and her twins, Ryan and Ryana, stood to thank Mara and to present her with a beautiful bouquet of yellow roses, so that she could "smell her flowers while she was alive'. When they were all done hugging and crying, Naomi gave the microphone to Kaitlin, who was having a hard time trying to figure out what she wanted to say.

"Miss Mara, could you … Mr. Buddy could you escort Miss Mara up front please?"

Buddy bowed his head, offered her his arm and walked Mara up the aisle and onto the stage where Kaitlin was waiting, her eyes alternating between looking at Mara and down at the floor.

"Miss Mara, I ... I just want to say Happy Birthday and ... and ... and I want to say thank you, for everything. ... You have come to, um, to mean a lot to me, ... almost like a mother, ... no, that's not right. You have been *just like* a mother to me,... and a grandmother to my girls... But, ... I want to tell you that you don't have to do that anymore, ... oh, wait a minute, I mean, I still want you to be my mom, but, ..."

Squaring her shoulders and breathing deeply, she went on.

"Because of what Miss Karlynne taught me about myself, and because you cared enough and weren't afraid to tell me some things I really needed to hear, ... well, now I have my real mother back. ... Mom, could you come up here please?"

Mara turned to see Buddy escorting a somewhat portly, dark-haired, older version of Kaitlin up the steps leading to the stage. Realizing the journey that it must have taken her mother to get here, Mara walked across the stage to meet her half way. The only words that were necessary was the "Thank You" that Mrs. Elfman mouthed as she reached out to squeeze Mara's shoulders and then hug her close.

All over the gymnasium people began standing to their feet and clapping, chanting "Speech, speech, speech!"

Mara took the microphone, waving them to silence. She then cleared her throat and said, "I'm hungry y'all. Let's eat!"

Sitting next to Zena at the guest table eating the plate that Ginger had prepared for her, Mara looked out at all of her guests.

"I don't know how you all managed to keep me from findin' out about this, Zee."

"It was harder to do than gettin' Clinton out of the White House, girl. I thought sure somebody was gonna' let it slip out."

"Well, nobody did. You all sure got me this time... Who would'a thought that all these people would come out like this for me?"

"I told you that they should call you Grandma Moses because you are always there to help people when they're in the wilderness. ... Well, look at this, would you?"

Mara's eyes widened, and her mouth dropped open in amazement as she turned to where Mr. Paluszka was standing with his hat in his hands.

"I am not go-ink to stay, Missez Singleton, but I did vant to stop by and vish you a Happy Birs-day."

Recovering from her surprise, she said, "That's just so much nonsense Mr Paluszka. We finally got you out of the house, now you're gonna sit right down here at the guest table with me and Buddy and have somethin' to eat. Come on, please stay."

With only the slightest hesitation, he pulled up a chair and sat down. Later on when she looked over, he was waving a chicken leg as he, Buddy and Garfield animatedly discussed whether or not Mike Tyson should be allowed to return to the ring.

Chapter 25

"Well, I guess everybody here knows that Mara and I have been friends for just about thirty-five years, and that's no mean trick, let me tell you. Because I'm not the easiest person in the world to get along with ... but believe me, there was a time that you could'a shot a bullet outta' her too, because she was a pistol!"

Waiting until the laughter died down, Zena continued.

"But when it comes to having a friend, God couldn't have special ordered the parts from heaven's best friend factory and built me one any better than this woman we came to honor tonight. ... She has seen me through some times that I wasn't sure I wanted to come through. ..."

There was some residual pain associated with those times that remained with Zena even now, making it necessary for her to compose herself before she could continue. Reflexively, Mara reached out her hand to ease or share the burden of it with her friend, whichever was necessary. But over the years, the strength Zena had gained in the face of her trials enabled her to persevere. She filled her lungs and did so now. She motioned to Caleb, who came carrying a tall rubber tree plant, placing it next to Zena and Mara on the stage. Turning to her friend, she said,

"I'm not going to make this all long and drawn out. Mara, I want to give you this rubber plant because it represents a lot of things to me. It reminds me of you because the leaves are thick and strong, but they're still delicate, and you have to handle them with care. Because it's a tropical plant, it's used to the heat and won't sag and droop when things get hot. Even though it grows tall, sometimes a rubber plant has to get rid of its old leaves so that new leaves can grow. It's ... like ... like God made the rubber plant able to know how much weight it can stand. ... But most of all, the roots of the rubber tree grow real deep, just like you, Mara."

Her throat full of emotion, Zena was almost whispering now.

"You have a deep commitment to people, your friends, your neighbors, your family, ... and we appreciate it. I want to say thank you for being our friend and thank you for being my friend. I love you very much. ,,, *And you make the best potato pie this side of God's heaven!*"

The applause that followed Zena's oration was muted. Most of those gathered were accustomed to Zena's outspokenness, but few had ever heard her speak with such reverence and admiration. Hands all over the room were clutching handkerchiefs or searching purses for tissues to wipe away tears. She and Mara held and hugged each other for a span of time that was indicative of their friendship, but may have been awkward for persons of a more shallow devotion. Buddy was probably the only person who could have known her better, or loved her differently.

As they released their embrace, Pastor Lynch was crossing the stage to where they stood.

"Well, Sister Singleton, I don't know if there is anything left for me to say. Everyone seems to have said all of the things that I might have said, except maybe this. I have watched you from the very beginning, even when I know you were watching me. And I have observed that what Sister Baldwin said is true. Not only do you have a deep commitment to people, but you also have a great desire for God's truth to operate in your life. You have been an asset to this ministry and have made my job here as pastor less burdensome. You've allowed God to mold you and to use you as He sees fit. I can't speak to who you were before, but I can say you have been a blessing to me."

As the sound of hands coming together began echoing in the room, Pastor Lynch signaled for it to stop.

"Hold your applause for just a few more minutes, everybody. ... Your family and friends took up a collection to buy something for you, Sister Singleton. Because everyone else was busy trying to keep you from finding out about tonight, I was drafted to pick up your gift. While I was there, I ran into someone from your past that I am sure you'll know when they come out. When they realized what we were doing for you, this person insisted that they wanted to participate, but desired that it should be a surprise. I believe it is only fitting that they be given the honor of presenting you with this demonstration of our appreciation."

Mara wondered, along with everyone else, who her mystery guest could be. She scanned the auditorium, trying to determine if there was someone who was missing. It occurred to her that it might be her uncle, her *real* uncle, Russell. She hadn't heard from him since right after she and Buddy had gotten married. He'd managed to track her down through Mother Pearl to tell her that her grandmother, Coreen was dead. That she experienced no emotion at the news was proof to Mara that in her heart and mind, in the soul of who she was, her mother's mother had long since been dead. Though Buddy had encouraged her to attend the funeral, she had felt no urge to make the trip. Since that time, neither had she ever felt any guilt because she hadn't.

She glanced over at Zena, but her friend looked more puzzled than Mara. She looked down at the guest table where Buddy was sitting, but with questioning eyes, he just shook his head no. As Pastor Lynch opened the door that led from the stage to his office, Mara felt herself being mentally kidnapped and flung against her will into a place of shadows and potential devastation. Overcome and dismayed, she fought to breathe; she was "there" again. In synchronization, all of her senses geared for escape, searching for a way out. She fought down the urge to run off the stage, out the door, and away from the unknown, so panic-stricken was she at the looming possibility of being publicly exposed and humiliated. It couldn't be "him" could it? Not after all this time.

"No God, no! Not now!"

Almost instantly she recalled those *other* times when she had told God no. She'd thought that she wasn't ready then, either. But God had insisted. He'd been with her, He'd held her hand, walked with her, but He'd insisted that she confront "the bogeyman". And so it was now. Covering her mouth in dreaded anticipation, she waited. For what, she didn't know.

When they saw who it was that appeared in the doorway of the pastor's office, Mara and Zena looked at each other and burst out laughing. Doubled over, each trying to support the other, they missed most of Raylinda's grand entrance.

Overdressed in a tight-fitting, red-sequined, floor length gown and three-inch long cubic zirconia and fake ruby earrings, Raylinda adjusted her fur stole across her dangerously plunging neckline before stepping out on to the stage. Her false hair, complete with intermittently spaced red tracts, was curled and partially piled on top of her head with a wide, jeweled comb positioned in the upswept ponytail. The front was parted and hanging across her left eye while the shoulder-length hair that remained, trailed down her back. Huge costume jewelry adorned her arms and neck, three fingers and the thumb of each hand. Peering at her through water-filled eyes, Mara became fearful that she would trip and fall when Raylinda's red, peu-de-soie platform pumps got entangled in the train of her gown. Luckily, Pastor Lynch recovered from his visible astonishment at the transition of the woman he'd met in the store, to the one that was now falling across his pulpit, in just enough time to catch her. The people looking on began to clap and cheer his efforts.

In a world of her own creation, Raylinda was oblivious to anything except how stunning an impact her presence created. She completed her saunter, and stood next to Mara, waiting for the commotion to die down. Clearing her throat, she began.

"Mara, I haven't known you for as long as some of these other people, but we have known each other for a long time. When your pastor told me what was taking place, I wanted to be part of your special night. The last time I saw you and Zena, I told you about my new husband. I am very lucky that he is financially in the position to be able to give me anything I want. When I found out that your friends wanted to buy you a gift, I decided that I would be the one to pay for it. It would be my gift to you and, *since you probably need it*, they could still give you the money they collected. So I would like to present you with this pair of one-half- karat diamond earrings."

With a grandiosity that only she could manage, she reached out with her freshly polished and bejeweled nails to hand Mara her gift. Sober now, Mara took the jewelry box that Raylinda offered her and opened it to admire the earrings. Choosing to ignore her snide comment, she felt sorry that Raylinda was still Raylinda. Snapping shut the lid, she reached over and hugged this person from her past, thanking her for the earrings. In her heart she both lamented and thanked God that Raylinda hadn't been someone else.

Later, as crews of volunteers worked to take down, clean up and put away, Mara stood in the vestibule, saying goodbye to her guests. Recognizing his scent, she smiled as Buddy came up behind her and slid his arms around her waist. Placing her hands on his, she looked over her shoulder at him.

"So what happened to *your* speech, Mr. Singleton? I thought sure *you* would'a had somethin' to say."

"They aren't as lucky as me, Baby; I get to take you home. I figured I'd let'em have their time. I can tell you what I want to say while we're in bed and you're layin' in my arms. ... But I did tell you that *I* wanted to be the only person to shower you with diamonds! I think I might be jealous about those earrings you got in your ears."

"Well, don't be jealous my brother, it is *not* too late. These earrings that Raylinda gave me is only a drizzle. You can come on with the shower *whenever* you get ready!"

They were still laughing when Raylinda sashayed up to them.

"I am *so* impressed at how nice this turned out, ...*even though it wasn't a catered affair.* Everything was so nice, even those *original* little centerpieces. ... And Mara Ruthine ... everybody said such nice things about you; you're just quite the local celebrity, aren't you? ... Where is that Zena? I was *so* moved by what she said. It's good that you're still here for her; she needs a good friend. ...Tell me, don't you love these earrings? I have some similar to them, except mine are a whole karat. ... Buddy you are just one, strong man to still be with Mara after all these years! What's your secret, I want to tell my Alvon."

"I meant to ask you, Raylinda, how is your mother? And where is that new husband of yours? I thought he was with you; I was hopin' t'meet him. I think I'm disappointed."

"I bet you are, Mara Ruthine. Meeting Alvon would have made this night even *more* special. ... Well, Mama is doing fine, I stopped in to see her today after I had my nails done. Unfortunately, Alvon couldn't make the trip with me; he had some contracts he needed to close on. He's a real estate developer you know. As soon as we get settled into our new home, you and Buddy have got to come down and spend some time with us."

Raylinda had been looking out at the street all during the time she was chattering. Taking notice of her behavior, Buddy asked,

"Raylinda, did you drive or is somebody pickin' you up?"

"Oh, no Buddy, I couldn't drive with these shoes or this dress on. Actually, Alvon has had an office here for quite some time. He's interested in developing some land near the Walmart where I ran into you the last time, Mara. Of course, he has someone else managing things on this end, one of his assistants. He dropped me off earlier but I told him that I was certain I'd be ready to leave by ten. He's usually very punctual, he should have been here by now."

"Well if you need us to drop you off someplace, just say so. Mara drove her van and my truck is parked in the back."

Repulsed at even the prospect of having to ride in Buddy's truck, they both heard the relief in her voice as she said,

"Oh, there he is now, in the Lexus, the champagne-colored one. Could you tell him that I'll be there as soon as I go to your pastor's office to get my fur and my purse? I thought it would be safer if he locked them in there. I know this is a church, but we're not in heaven yet you know."

"*The champagne-colored one*, like there's nine or ten Lexuses out there," Buddy parroted Raylinda, after she waltzed through the door.

"That's him, Buddy! That's the man!"

"What man, Mara? Where is he?"

"The one that I told you about, the one I been seein' everywhere! I guess he didn't wanna park in front of the fire hydrant ...he pulled the car around the corner. Here he comes!"

Concerned at Mara's rising voice and growing alarm, Buddy turned to look out at the man approaching the building. Suddenly Buddy's skin turned ashen as the blood drained out of his face. As they faced each other, it appeared as though both men were looking into a mirror. The only difference was that one of them was younger and was dressed in a starched white shirt and navy blue, pinstriped suit, while the older image was wearing a green collar-less shirt and a pair of khakis.

Mara couldn't believe it. There was irony in the fact that it was Buddy who had always told her she could trace sperm better than anybody else he knew. Scenes flashed in her head ... the bakery, Walmart, tonight in the auditorium. *That's* why she knew those eyes. They were younger, clearer, less weary eyes that hadn't seen as much, but there was no doubt that they were her husband's.

The door opened as Raylinda whooshed into the vestibule.

"Neal, what happened? I thought you would've been back before now."

Chapter 26

"No Buddy, I don't understand. I'm tryin to, I really am. But I don't understand. We never keep any secrets from each other. We never did."

It was true. Buddy knew everything about her past; Mara had told him everything. He had given her a platform for trust and, hesitantly at first, she had been allowed to reconstruct her dilapidated life. She had been blessed that her life was salvageable; some people never got the chance to turn things around. They just kept operating in ignorance, repeating the same mistakes, engaging in the same negative patterns of behavior that produced the ruts that they couldn't get out of. Over the years, God had blessed her with the tools and provided the materials for Mara to restore and decorate walls in her life that had been crumbling and bare.

But now she had discovered a crack that had the potential to destroy the foundation of her and Buddy's life together. That he had known it was there all along and chose to ignore its existence further weakened the structure.

It had been awkward that night in the church vestibule. So absorbed was she with her own issues, Raylinda hadn't realized it at first.

"Neal, this is tonight's honoree, my old and dear friend, Mara Ruthine and her husband, Buddy Singleton. ... I just realized something. I have never known your first name. ... I've just always called you Buddy. I suppose I would have known what your name is if I had gotten an invitation to your little wedding ceremony, ... but we won't talk about that now, will we? Tell me Mara, is your name Mrs. Buddy Singleton?"

"No, her name is Mrs. Nelson Singleton. ... His first name is Nelson."

This announcement came out of the mouth of Buddy's white-shirted reflection.

"Nelson? Buddy, I would have never figured you to be a 'Nelson'. ... Neal, how in the world did you know that his name was Nelson? I've been knowing these two for ... well, how long I've known them is not important, ...how is it that *you* know Buddy's right name?"

Mara's attention had been focused on her husband from the moment he saw the young man walking up the church steps. Buddy's reaction spoke louder than any words could have. As recognition flooded his eyes, so did the realization overflow his consciousness that his past had now become his present. Watching him, Mara witnessed the departure of something that left her questioning who the person was that remained.

"Because he's my father."

This declaration invited even the silence of Raylinda as she looked first at Neal, then Buddy, into the face of her friend and back again to Neal. As interpretation of the meaning of Neal's words fought through Raylinda's preoccupation with herself to concern for their impact on Mara, she turned again to look at her friend. What she saw in Mara's countenance defied any effort to comfort that was less than sincere. Subdued by the roar of the silence, Raylinda waited.

"Are you ready to go, Mrs. Richardson?"

Flustered, she responded.

"Well, I guess ... I mean, if you ... Buddy ...uh, Mara ... I'll talk to you some other time, okay? ... Oh, and Happy, ... uh, Happy Birthday."

Neal walked to the door, held it open for Raylinda to pass, helped her down the steps, into the car, and left.

It was 11:30 p.m., August 5, 2001, a day that would forever be chronicled in Singleton history. Though it wasn't Pearl Harbor or Desert Storm, the potential for the destruction that would be left in its wake could only be imagined.

It was good that Buddy had his truck out back. Mara made it a habit never to give rides to strangers.

****

In their living room, Buddy sat in his reclining chair, across the room from Mara. The plaque on the wall that read "God Bless Our Home," looked as out of place as the birthday presents piled up on the sofa. The grandfather clock in the corner had a foreign tick now, and the drapes that she'd hemmed just last week looked like they belonged to someone else. From where she was sitting on the arm of the sofa, everything that had identified this as home now felt strange to her,... everything including Buddy.

He tried to look at her, but for some reason his head weighed two hundred pounds. It was heavier now than it had been all of those times after he'd sobered up, when he'd had to lift it to look at her and say,' I'm sorry'. The burden of this situation bowed his back and buckled his confidence. Mara hated to see him like this, ... it pained her to see him hurt. But right now she had to tend to the wound in her spirit.

"Buddy, you have to say somethin', you can't just sit there."

But he did. He sat, and sat, and sat, head hung, eyes down, as if he could find the answer to Mara's questions in the designs on the fake Persian rug. He sat until the dawn of something crept up within him like the morning of an overcast day. When finally his neck took over and did what his heart could not, he lifted his head, looked at the woman who had been his reason for breathing, and spoke.

"I'm sorry, Baby. ... I'm sorry. ... I know you need more than that, but that's where I need to start. I know I've said I'm sorry before, an' I know I prob'ly said it too many times. But I always meant it then an' I mean it now. ... I'm sorry. ..."

Buddy looked away from her to the picture that was sitting on the end table next to the couch. It was a picture of the two of them standing in front of Grandma's Hands.

"Mara, that day when I met you, I really wasn't plannin' on meetin' nobody. I was just comin' to the weddin' because I knew Mr. Wyatt from work and he asked me to. Even after we talked, I really didn't think nothin' would come of it. It wasn't because I didn't like you, but you seemed like you really didn't want no bother. ... Then after we ate the water ice, you kind'a loosened up more. ..."

Shaking his head at the recollection of his confusion, Buddy continued.

"To tell you the truth, I really didn't know what I was s'posed to do. But I liked you, so I just figured I'd play my cards and see what happened. ... So then we, ...Well, you know pretty much everything that happened after that."

Mara thought she did too. Neal was the obvious proof that she didn't.

"Baby, in the beginnin' when we would talk, you wouldn't hardly tell me nothin' about yourself. You told me about Mother Pearl and about what happened to your mother, but you never talked about you. At first I didn't know what to make out of it, but then I just told myself that it was ... *okay*. I figured you would tell me what you wanted me to know when you got ready. So I just waited, because by that time I knew I had real strong feelin's for you."

She remembered. It was then that she'd come alive again. Buddy had awakened things in her that she had reckoned dead, feelings that caused a quickening in her even now. She remembered trying really hard to inoculate herself against the infectiousness of his smile, but to no avail. He'd won her. He became the repository for her respect and her love. Eventually unlocking the crypt that entombed it, she had appointed him guardian of her trust. Though there had been challenges that threatened his position, she had never really regretted her decision ... until now.

"When I could tell that you felt the same way about me I.. I still didn't want to put no pressure on you, ... and anyway, whatever you did before I met you wasn't that important to me. I was only worried about the woman that I was lookin' at right then. The only thing that meant anything to me was makin' that sad face a smilin' face. ... I love it when you smile, Mara. All I ever wanted to do was make you happy so I could always see you smile."

She knew that what he said was true, and his words produced a warmth in her that had always managed to soften the inflexibility of their hardest problems. But even though she knew he wasn't trying to manipulate her now, she resolutely resisted giving in to the effect of those words.

"Then tell me why you never told me about this Buddy."

Searching inside himself for words, Buddy wasn't at all sure that the ones he found were the right ones.

"Baby, do you remember the first time we made love?"

She would have to be crazy or dead not to. It was around Christmas time and they had been sitting in her living room. She loved Christmas, even though she didn't have any children to buy toys for. She always baked for the holiday, and her house smelled like cakes and cookies and sweet potato pie.

There was another smell that was always in her house at Christmas time. Mara always had a live tree; she loved it when she first walked into the room and was met with the fragrance of freshly cut pine. And she loved the lights, the ones that shone through the tan-faced angel that perched on the very top, and the little twinkling ones that she always stuck deep between the branches on her tree.

There was something else that Mara always did too. Under the branches of the tree, with the revolving color light pointed right at it, on top of a blanket of soft cotton, was where she placed her Nativity scene. As she and Buddy sat watching television, the Christmas lights twinkled their kaleidoscope of colors, and the light alternated red, then yellow, then green, then blue, on the little carved ivory figures of Mary and Joseph. The little white light bulb in the top of the miniature barn shined directly over top of the manger where the figure of the baby Jesus lay.

Mother Pearl had given her the Nativity scene that first Christmas after Mara had returned from her "journey to find herself". She had one just like it that Mara had seen under Mother Pearl's own tree, next to her gifts, every Christmas that she could remember.

"Don't you ever forget to remember this, Mara Ruthine Bothert. It's okay to buy gifts to put under the tree as long as you realize that God gave us the best gift of all. He sent His son to die on the cross for the same folks who don't even think about Him on His birthday. ... *Jesus is the reason for the season!*"

She and Buddy had been watching a rerun of that old movie "Imitation of Life", the one that made her cry every

time she watched it. She'd felt a little silly crying as Hattie
Mayfield's daughter clung to the horse-drawn carriage,
crying for her dead mother inside. But Buddy hadn't known
that Mara had seen the movie at least six times before. When
she came back from getting some toilet paper to blow her
nose, she was surprised to see him crying openly. That's
when he told her about his mother dying when he was only
four and that he had been raised by his grandmother. He
hadn't seen her in a while, and seeing Hattie Mayfield
reminded him of her.

In the compassion of the moment, she had told him
about Coreen. Reflecting on all of the negative things that
had happened in the aftermath of that brief encounter with
her mean-spirited grandmother had caused Mara's dam to
break. He'd held her, and held her. He'd held her until her
eyes were empty and her heart was full of appreciation for
the tenderness and sensitivity of this man. And then Buddy
kissed her.

At first she resisted. That first kiss was the descendant
of a long line of first kisses in Mara's history. Kisses that,
like the one that Judas gave Jesus, had been expressions of
betrayal. She had *just* told him about Coreen, and connected
to her grandmother were the memories of her uncle, her real
uncle. She couldn't tell Buddy about Russell, not yet. She
needed to know that he would understand, that he wouldn't
take advantage of her.

When he sensed her resistance, Buddy had let her go,
her head still resting on his extended arm. They sat like that
for a long time, until the news came on and went off. Until
she felt him move a little and knew that he was probably
getting ready to leave. And Mara knew that just like before
with Nate, she really didn't want him to. Only this time she
knew that she wasn't going to say "no', that she didn't want
to say "no", not *this* time. Somehow Mara knew that this
time wouldn't turn out like before. So this time she didn't try
to push him away---this time *she* reached for *him*.

She hesitated for just a second as the light turned,
stopping to shine red on the Nativity scene. Could the red
light shining on the purity that the scene represented be a

signal to her to stop, that there was danger ahead? Mara immediately felt the conviction in her heart, conviction that she wanted strength enough to obey. But she was still weak; she still longed to belong. Jesus had not yet become enough. So it was there, in her heart that Mara prayed that Jesus would forgive her ...and that God would understand and save her as she pulled Buddy to her.

He hadn't known the extent of what she was risking that night. Buddy hadn't known that he was auditioning for the part of leading man in her life. He didn't realize that if, after this placing of herself on the Christmas altar, he became one of her betrayers, it was Mara who would be sacrificed. Buddy had no comprehension of who God was, or what He expected of him. If he had known, perhaps he would have been strong enough to resist for the both of them.

"Yes, Buddy. I remember."

"Mara, after that night I knew that it was different between you and me because you started to tell me about *you*. It was like ... like ... You know that closet upstairs in the back room? Remember when you got mad 'cause of all the junk that was in there, and you cleaned it out? And then when Karlynne and Kiata came for the weekend and you found out I had been stickin' my stuff in there? Well, it was kind'a like that. When you started cleanin' out the stuff that was piled up in your life, I knew you wanted it to stay clean. I had some stuff that I needed to put someplace, but you had just started to get your life in order, the stuff that you wanted to keep, and the stuff you wanted to get rid of, the garbage. I just didn't want to junk up your life with my stuff."

Mara felt terrible. As she rewound the video of "Buddy's life with Mara", reality glared painfully in her face. At nearly every intersection where they had encountered crisis, the crisis had been her own. Buddy had signed on each time only as a volunteer lifeguard; his job was to save her from drowning. As the scenes flashed vaudevillian in her psyche, Mara had a front row seat in a Charlie Chaplinesque replay of their life together. From this most recent situation backward, she observed Buddy's positive influence at the outcome of nearly all of her negative circumstances.

Interspersed within her calamities were the cameos of Buddy's drinking episodes. It shamed Mara to see that she had only been able to view Buddy's problem in light of how it had affected her. Like a transgression policeman, Mara was stationed at the beginning and at the end of each offense, giving direction and motivation for his every action, controlling the flow of forgiveness when his crime caused an emotional bottleneck for her. He had never had what she had. Mara had seldom provided him with a platform free of time constraints and judgment from which to repair the breach. So instrumental was he in her reconstruction that Buddy had only been allowed to patch the holes in his own walls. Even now her concern hadn't been for him.

This time it was Mara's turn to examine the floor. She descended the basement steps of her reasoning, remembering something she had packed away that might be useful to her now.

Back in a corner, covered by dust and shrouded by mental cobwebs, she pulled out that conversation she'd had with Zena a while ago. After her own defensive come-back to her friend that she'd gone too far regarding Mara's marriage, she'd self-righteously tucked this part of their confrontation away. At the time she'd prioritized addressing Zena's feelings, with a well-intentioned promise to sort through this information later. But like last year's summer clothes, she'd put it off, opting instead to supplement her mental wardrobe with the things that fit fashionably in this season of her life. Now, faced with the inevitable, she either had to chuck the whole thing or examine the contents for "keepers".

Reluctantly she unfolded the things Zena had said about her and Buddy. It burdened her to accept that her friend had been right. Though of course she could try to justify her behavior, a passage she had recently encountered in her personal study time led her away from that choice. She had firmly embraced the Living Bible's translation of Proverbs 16:2 as one of her life application scriptures.

"You can always prove that you are right, but is God convinced?"

She knew He wasn't.

As she sat there searching her internal shelves for the right thing to say to Buddy, Mara acknowledged that the first thing that was necessary was another of the things he'd given her. Looking up at him, she honored her husband.

"I'm sorry, Buddy. I was wrong."

The shock that was reflected in Buddy's eyes at this affirmation relaxed into that smile that had so frequently been her sanctuary. All at once she had a greater appreciation for the words that Jesus had spoken to Simon Peter. Knowing that Peter would repeatedly deny his relationship with the Messiah, His words exemplified God's eternal commitment to the heart that acknowledged Him.

"Blessed are you, Simon, son of Jonah, for this was not revealed to you by man, but by my Father in heaven. And I tell you that you are Peter, and on this rock I will build my church, and the gates of hell will not prevail against it."

Acceptance of God's revealed truth had always produced an unshakeable foundation to build upon, and this time was no different. Just as God had transformed "the little stone" into "the massive rock" that He'd constructed His church upon, He would use Mara's submission as fortification for restructuring this marriage. Now that the ground-work had been laid, she would look to Him for the rest of the things they could use to help rebuild her man. Only this time she would scrutinize the materials she discovered for Godly quality and endurance, … she needed for Buddy to be around for a long time.

Chapter 27

"Hand me those glasses please, Zee. The ones with the gold trim around the top."

Carrying them by their stems, Zena handed Mara the goblets.

"These are goblets, *not* glasses, Mara."

"Goblets, glasses, mayonnaise jars,… they're all the same t'me."

"Oh no they're not. Who do you think you're playin' with? I know this is your good china. You're puttin' your best stuff out for them to eat off of today."

"Do you think everything looks okay?"

"It certainly does, … everything looks *beautiful*. … And anyway, as good as you cook, if they had to eat off of paper plates, they probably wouldn't even notice."

"*Shut up, girl!* … But that macaroni and cheese sure smells good if I do say so myself, and I can't wait to cut one of those pretty, golden, sweet potato pies."

"Because don't '*nobody*' love your potato pie better than *you*!"

The two friends laughed as they continued preparing for Mara's guests.

"Where's Buddy?"

"He went to the market to pick up a couple of bottles of sparklin' cider."

"How's he doin' Mara? Do you think he's ready for this?"

"As ready as he can be, Zee. He's been waitin' a long time for t'night."

It had been a long time, almost twenty-three years. Mara had understood it all when Buddy finally told her what had happened.

As it turned out, Mara wasn't Buddy's only wife. He had married Loreatha, his high school sweetheart when he was nineteen. He didn't have to marry her, he did it because he loved her. And that way, after he completed basic training, when he got his assignment to be stationed in Germany, she could come where he was. They could get a place on the base and after a year or so, maybe start a family. At least that's what the recruiter had told him. Only it hadn't turned out that way. When his assignment came it was for someplace called Viet Nam. And a year or so later, Loreatha was still home in Tallahassee and he was still there.

But one thing the recruiter said was true. Buddy and Loreatha had started a family. When he finally got the letter from her telling him that she was pregnant, she was already four months along. When the baby came, Loreatha named him after his daddy. She sent Buddy pictures of his son that he carried in the little Bible he kept laced up in the top of his boot. Still, Buddy hardly recognized his son when he saw him after they finally shipped him back stateside. His son was almost two years old before Buddy got to pick him up and swing him around. Everybody said that he had Loreatha's big, pretty eyes and Buddy's smile.

Buddy bought a house for them with his GI loan. He got a job driving one of the big rigs that picked up new cars and delivered them to the dealerships. It paid pretty good money, but sometimes Buddy didn't get home for two or three days. He and Loreatha decided to wait before they had any more kids. She had enough to do taking care of the house and Nelson Jr. When Buddy lucked up and got a couple of short runs, he'd get home in enough time to take Loreatha out for a movie or a few drinks. They could always leave Nelson Jr. with Buddy's grandmother, Hattie; she didn't mind it when her little "Junebug" had to spend the night.

The winter before Nelson Jr.'s fifth birthday, Loreatha stopped taking her birth control pills. Though she had some problems with this pregnancy, eleven months later she gave Buddy another son. They named him Neal. If it was true that Nelson Jr. "had Buddy's smile", Neal went one step further. To use Grandma Hattie's words, "he looked like Buddy just hawked an' spit him out!" For some reason, Loreatha hated to hear her or anybody else talk about how much Neal was like his daddy.

That September, Nelson Jr. started first grade. Buddy had seniority over some of the newer car haulers by then and was able to pick the best of the delivery runs. So that day he was able to park his rig and stop by the school in time to fix Nelson Jr.'s baseball cap before Loreatha walked him in to meet his new teacher.

One of the other mothers was one of Loreatha's friends from high school, Dorsey Linthrop. The two of them started walking to school together. Dorsey had a daughter who was in Nelson Jr.'s class. Loreatha's habit was to drop little Neal off at Grandma Hattie's on the days that the weather was too bad to take him.

When Neal was three years old, Loreatha started leaving him at Miss Hattie's in the morning, but she didn't pick him up until time for Nelson Jr. to come home from school. At first Grandma Hattie didn't say anything to Buddy; she didn't want to 'stir up confusion'. She had pretty much figured out where Loreatha and Dorsey were spending their time, but when she smelled 'that rot gut' on Loreatha's breath, she knew Buddy had to be told.

"I'm sorry Buddy, but I'm bored at home all day. I need to do something besides taking care of babies and washing clothes!"

"What do you feel like you want to do, 'Reatha?'"

"I was thinking about maybe going back to school."

They were able to compromise when she signed up for a course in real estate. She could attend class from ten in the morning until two in the afternoon, and still be home in time for Nelson Jr. to come home from school. Of course, Neal would stay home with Grandma Hattie.

Initially, this arrangement worked out okay for everybody. Though Buddy still had to make long runs occasionally, he usually got to spend time at home with his wife and sons. Loreatha really liked the real estate business and did well in her class. When she completed that one, she convinced Buddy that she should take the advanced course.

"There's a new pre-school program called Head Start; Neal could go there in the morning when Nelson Jr. goes to school. I can pick him up and drop him off at Miss Hattie's on my lunch break and still be home by the afternoon."

Buddy was a little bothered that she didn't get to spend as much time with Neal as she had with Nelson Jr., but he finally gave her the money to enroll.

By the year that Neal started third grade, Loreatha was one of the best real estate agents in the area. The fact that this was more important to her than being a good mother was a discussion that usually turned into an ugly argument between her and Buddy. When it did, Loreatha would walk out to avoid the confrontation, leaving Neal in the house with his father. Sometimes she would come home after midnight, other times she would come in just before it was time for Buddy to start up his truck.

When he began questioning her about where she'd been, Loreatha told Buddy that she stayed over at Dorsey's apartment. Then she dropped the pretense of caring and stopped giving him any information at all, leaving him to think whatever he would. Buddy started stopping by the package store on his way home, and he and Neal would sit and watch TV until drunk, he'd fall off to sleep. Fifteen year old Nelson Jr. wasn't home a lot; he was hanging out a lot with his "homies". He would come in, wake his brother, and tell Buddy to "git your drunken self up and go to bed!" Sometimes Buddy made it into the bedroom, most of the time he didn't. He hated sleeping in their empty bed.

The more he drank, the harder it was for him to wake up.

"Keep on getting drunk and oversleeping, they are going to fire you as sure as my name is Loreatha! You're already on probation! But you'd just better know that if you get fired, I'm leaving!"

"You c'leave any ol' time you geh' ready, but you ain' takin' my sons no playsh!"

"I can't take *your* sons anywhere because you only got 'one', and as far as I'm concerned *he* can stay right here with his drunken father and his Grandma Hattie!"

191

Devastated is the only word to describe the impact that Loreatha's announcement had on Buddy. She had made a fool out of him without him ever questioning it for all these years. All he had ever tried to do was to be decent, to be a good husband and a responsible father.

"Who was Nelson Jr.'s father, Buddy?"

"My Gran'ma Hattie told me she heard that Loreatha started seein' somebody no sooner than they shipped me to Nam. When she found out that she was pregnant, Gran'ma didn't know whether it was by me or not, but she wasn't gonna write me over there in the middle of the war to tell me that. I found out later that the guy had worked for some insurance company. As a matter of fact I thought that it was kinda strange in a way because it's the same one Zena worked for. I never did know because it seems that when he found out that Loreatha was pregnant, he got transferred someplace else."

Recognizing the pattern and adding up the inevitable two and two, Mara could only shake her head. Grateful she had been spared that particular misfortune, she smiled and made a mental note to explain it all to Buddy, later.

"It's a small, small world,"

Not understanding what she meant, but engrossed in his story, Buddy continued.

"So when Loreatha started writin' me and tellin' me about a baby that was comin' I didn't know no better. I thought the baby was mine. Gran'ma Hattie told me later that she never did think the baby looked like me."

"Sayin' that baby had yo' smile. That was Loreatha's lie, straight from the pit of Hell! After you came home, I just thought that it would be better to let sleepin' dogs lie."

That had been Gran'ma Hattie's explanation for why she'd never told him. But even after Loreatha dropped her bomb, Buddy had been willing to work things out. Nelson Jr. had been his son all these years, there was no way he would treat him any different now. And there was still Neal that they had to think of.

But Loreatha was having none of it. She confused Buddy's strength with stupidity and acted like it. She wasn't interested in staying married to him and told him so.

"I don't need to work out anything with you. What I need is to get out of this mess and start living my own life. You can keep your son and this little house. I can take care of me and Nelson!"

So it didn't take Buddy by surprise when she packed up what she wanted and moved out. What did surprise him was who she had become before she left. The transformation in the woman he had been married to for over sixteen years baffled him, but not as much as the change in his oldest son.

When he rode by, he saw Nelson Jr. hanging on the corners with his "homies", drinking wine out of a brown paper bag. Like father, like son... it was a sad reality that Buddy was powerless to change. He would learn later that surrendering to his powerlessness was the way out, but that knowledge was lost to him then.

Buddy's life swirled down the drain in a tidal wave of alcohol. The probation turned into a disciplinary suspension, requiring him to complete an alcohol treatment program to keep his job. Unable to free himself from the cycle of his addiction, Buddy spent his days closed in the house with his constant companion and confidant, successive bottles of Demantray Gin.

"Buddy, you have got to get yourself some help, son. I'm not getting any younger and with his mama gone, Neal needs somebody to look after him."

It was good that God blessed his grandmother with good health and a long life, because it was going to take years before Buddy would manage to pull his life out of the bottle. Even after his boss drove over, picked Buddy up and deposited him on the doorstep of the treatment center, the fact that he walked in and turned and walked back out, would ultimately cost Buddy his job. The day finally came when he took the last of his severance pay, put three hundred dollars in an envelope that he slipped through Grandma Hattie's mail slot, bought two bottles of Demantray and a bus ticket and attempted to ride away from his misery. Buddy knew he should say something to Neal, but he couldn't face him.

It astounded Mara to understand how her husband had managed to bag up the garbage of his past so that its putrid, tell-tale odor seeped out only intermittently. To know that she might have been responsible for any of the pressure that caused the leakage, produced in her something that only Buddy's forgiveness could soothe. Of greater amazement was that their paths never crossed until they both had journeyed from destruction to salvation.

Buddy's Demantray ran out about three hundred miles from home, but his bus ticket took him as far as Albertaville. The bus station attendant gave him directions to the YWCA where he was able to get a bed. A flyer in the bus station led him to a job as a laborer on a construction site.

Life was looking brighter until Buddy woke up broke and hung over behind a trash dumpster the day after his first payday.

"When I realized where I was and what I did, I was so 'shamed. It was like I had brought everything I was runnin' away from wit' me! I started tryin' to find my way back to the Y so I could get m'things 'cause I thought I had lost my bed."

When Buddy walked into the lobby around lunchtime, luck was with him because the person who usually monitored transient beds had called out sick the night before. Instead of doing bed checks, his replacement found a corner and went to sleep as soon as the doors were locked. No one even realized that Buddy hadn't slept there. They probably thought that he had gotten up and left earlier in the day.

"That night when I was layin' on my cot, I prayed and asked God and whoever worked for Him to help me get my life in check. The next morning I found a church not too far from the Y. I went in, sat down and listened to what the preacher had to say. The YMCA had AA meetings every Sunday evenin' and that night was my first one."

Monday morning found him standing in line with some other men at the construction site, waiting to see if their names would be called for work.

"I sure will be glad when the strike is over. A man can't pay his mortgage like this."

"What strike? I'm not from 'round here."

"Oh, I didn't know. I work on the assembly line down at the automobile plant, but we're out on strike right now. The only problem is my house note and the gas and electric still need to get paid. I'd rather be working on my job, but Mr. Need Mo' told me to stand right here."

That was how Buddy and Chester Wyatt had come to be friends. Chester would swing by the YMCA every morning to pick Buddy up. They rode together for the rest of the time that they worked on the construction job.

"When the strike was over, Chester went back to work. But that first week he went back, he stopped past my room and gave me a job application. Some of the guys didn't come back after the strike. He told me to put his name down as a reference and he would talk to the shop steward for me."

Buddy had been working at the plant for about eight months when he and Mara met at Mona's wedding. The rest was the history that Mara knew, with the exception of the money that showed up in Grandma Hattie's mail slot each week.

Chapter 28

"He always meant t'go back an' get him. In the beginnin' he needed to get back on his feet, but he was havin' a hard time with that drinkin.' It got so bad that he asked Mr. Wyatt to hold on to his paycheck for him. Come to think of it Zee, that's prob'ly why he only had enough money in his pocket to buy me a water ice."

But Buddy had done better. He had gotten a room in a boarding house. By the time that he stood at the end of the rows of cherry blossom trees in Ryan Park waiting for Mara that following summer, he had managed to save over twenty-five hundred dollars. After the ceremony they drove to Ocean City for the weekend in the used Oldsmobile Ninety-eight he had just bought. That was the second time she saw him drunk. The first time was on New Year's Eve.

That was the Christmas when they'd first made love. Everything was so perfect. When they woke up in Mara's bed and looked out the window the next morning, it had just started to snow. It was Sunday, so neither she nor Buddy had to go to work. But they didn't lay around in bed all day. What had happened between them the night before was special; Mara wasn't going to allow it to become common.

Buddy got up first to go to the bathroom. By the time she had located a rubber band for her hair and brushed her teeth, he had started the coffee. He had the radio on and was humming "Goin' up yonder".

"You gon' cook breakfast too?"

"I can if I need to."

She wondered who else he had cooked breakfast for, but she wasn't about to ask. Mara wasn't ready to talk about how many times she had cooked breakfast the morning after. She was thirty-five, and Buddy had just celebrated his thirty-sixth birthday in October, so it just stood to reason that he had sat down to more than a few plates of bacon and eggs.

Buddy drove her to the market to pick up a few things that she really didn't need. He just wanted to be available to her, and she welcomed the attention. They grinned like teenagers as they went slipping and sliding back to the car, and she sat close to him while he was driving. They stopped past Zena's house and the two girlfriends sat in the kitchen and giggled like high school girls while Buddy shoveled Zena's sidewalk.

When they got back, Mara was sad for a moment as she looked over at the house where Versiel and Parris had lived. She wondered how Parris was doing. Then, as Buddy bent over to make a snowball to throw at some of the children on her row who were outside playing, she wondered if somewhere somebody had "him" out playing in the snow. She quickly ran back to the moment; this wasn't the time to think about that.

She and Buddy spent the rest of that day and, except for the time they each went to work, the rest of that week together. Friday was New Year's Eve, and they had all planned on going to the cabaret Chester and Buddy's union held every year.

While Buddy checked their coats, Mara found a place to put the chicken she'd fried on the table with the food everybody else had brought. She was talking to Zena and her date, but she noticed that when he came back, Buddy had a bottle of Demantray that he put on the table next to the paper bucket of ice.

Though they danced and had fun, Mara saw Buddy refill his glass several times. By the time that they were ready to make a toast to the New Year, Buddy was already toasted. Mara was appalled at how loud he was talking and how he was hanging all over her. He fell down when he tried to walk to the coatroom, and when he got up he'd urinated on himself. It turned out that Chester had to get someone to take his wife while he took Buddy home, and Mara ended up riding with Zena.

Buddy was so embarrassed that it was almost two weeks later before he called her. He apologized and made his first in a long line of promises never to do it again. And he had kept that promise … until that weekend in Ocean City after their wedding.

Mara was beginning to think she had made a terrible mistake when she saw him pull a bottle of Demantray from under the seat of the car as they were riding. He managed to get them to the motel without crashing into anybody, but he didn't know where he was when he woke up the next morning. That was the day that Mara gave Buddy the first in her long line of ultimatums that, over the years, proved as empty as Buddy's promises. Somehow she had stuck it out; he was a good man. But she thanked God for that night when He had finally answered her prayer.

****

Mara measured first one cup and then one-half cup of sugar into the iced tea she was mixing. She checked to make sure that the top was secure on the canister, placing it back on the shelf before continuing to fill Zena in on the story.

"He ack'shully did go back one time. I thought he was out on the boat fishin' with Chester, but he told me that he drove back to see Neal and his Gran'ma Hattie."

"So what happened that he didn't see him?"

"He told me that when he got to his grandmother's house, she was so happy to see him that she cried and carried on."

Mara stared off as she remembered the look on Buddy's face.

"She had been lookin' at some pictures from Neal's ninth grade prom and thinkin' about how much he looked like me. I was so proud when I saw how much my son was growin' up. Gran'ma Hattie said that Neal was doin' all right, but he'd had a hard time handlin' it when I left. She showed me a newspaper clippin' about Nelson Jr. getting' arrested."

"Buddy said he felt so bad about what had happened to his sons that he just left again. See Zena, he didn't wanna hurt'em any more than he already had hurt'em, so it seemed to him like it was better if Neal didn't even know he was there."

"I just got in the car and drove away, Mara. Part the way home I pulled over and cried. I didn't know what I should do. I had never told you about Neal, so I couldn't come back from a fishin' trip with a son."

"I know that's right girl! That would'a been a fish that was too big for even you to fry!"

Not really amused by Zena's attempt at humor, Mara wanted to think that she could have handled it if Buddy had been able to tell her about his son. Maybe if he had, she would have been able to support him when he'd gotten drunk instead of going to Neal's graduation. Maybe she could have gone with him when he drove to the prison to see Nelson Jr., and he wouldn't have had to face Loreatha's disdain by himself. If he had told her, she could have stood by him at Gran'ma Hattie's home-goin' like he had stood by her at Mother Pearl's later. Instead she had shook her head when he finally staggered home at 4 a.m., and wondered "when was he goin' to stop this dad-blamed drinkin'!"

Mara considered all the times she thought she had the answer; all the times she hadn't paid attention because she thought she knew. From the time she left Mother Pearl's, to when she ran away from Coreen's. From her situation with Nate, to when she ignored Zena and lost Jomar. From her faulty judgement of Rondell, to her misunderstanding of Kaitlin. She remembered her terror at her birthday party, when she thought it must be *"him"* who was on the other side of the door. It was like looking at her life on a giant movie screen; she was able to see just how many times she hadn't had the right answer.

But this time she was listening, with her heart. She hadn't stood by Buddy then, but as sure as Jesus "tarried", she'd be with him when he had to face his son this time! She had cleaned out a closet just for Buddy... so finally he would have somewhere to put *his* stuff.

Chapter 29

When the knock came on the door, Buddy's eyes immediately found Mara's. If it had been any other time, she would have gone to answer it, but this time she knew that Buddy had to go. She was standing right behind him when he opened the door and was again struck by the remarkable resemblance between this father and his son. Moving back to give them both space to step into the room, she watched the two of them negotiate the awkwardness of this meeting. They shook hands until Mara alleviated the clumsiness of the moment by reaching out to hug "their" son to her breast. She had already embraced him in her heart.

The distance between father and son was far greater than the few feet that separated them as Buddy sat in the recliner and Neal on the sofa. Mara tried to fulfill her role as hostess, but the mouth that was so like her husband's politely declined anything she offered him.

The three of them sat there making small talk until Zena came in. She had gone home to change her clothes, but nothing short of an earthquake could have stopped her from coming back.

"Pleased to make your acquaintance, Neal. You know, old folks say you're born for good luck when you look as much like your father as you do."

"Well, it takes more than good luck to make it in this world. A man has to have a plan, and the courage and determination to stick to it and see it through."

It was impossible for Neal's verbal jab not to have caught his father square on the jaw. But like she had promised, Mara was in her husband's corner.

"And havin' a little God in your life can't hurt either, Neal. Sometimes things turn out different than what you plan and you need Him to help you out; but that's somethin' you might hafta get a little older to understand…Zena, how 'bout you and me go on back in the kitchen and check on the cornbread…an' give Buddy an' Neal a little time to talk?"

Mara knew that it would take longer than the time it took for the cornbread to brown, but they needed a place to start.

When the doorbell rang a while later, Zena offered to answer it. Mara knew it was probably because her friend thought she might get to hear what was being said between the father and his son, but she just shook her head as Zena shuffled toward the vestibule. She smiled when she heard that it was Chester and his wife, Deloris. She wiped her hands on her apron as she walked out of the kitchen to greet them.

"*Mara!* Hurry up and come in here! Oh dear *God!*"

Alarmed at Zena's voice, Mara rushed, not knowing what to expect. She almost fell as the throw rug in the hallway slid beneath her slippered feet. Grabbing the woodwork around the doorway to prevent her fall, she righted herself before stepping into the room.

"What in th'world is it, Zee? Why are you hollerin' like that?!"

Zena, Chester, and Deloris were standing in the middle of the living room floor. Quickly glancing around the room, Mara noted Neal and Buddy's absence.

"What's the matter, Zena? Where's Neal? Is it Buddy?"

Chester moved to the left and pointed to the television. At the same time that she was following his finger, Mara heard the muted voice of the news commentator.

"Ladies and gentlemen, what you are seeing on your TV screens is live coverage of the collapse of the second tower at New York's World Trade Center. It has been tentatively reported that these two airplane attacks are the work of terrorists…There is total chaos as people are running in an attempt to escape the burning debris…"

The world around Mara was truly falling apart.

****

"So where in the world did you go, Buddy? When I came outta the kitchen the livin' room was empty! I mean, excep' for Zena had just let Chester and his wife in; Chester never did get to meet Neal. He stayed until nine thirty waitin' for you."

"I'll tell Chester what happened when I see him at work. But we needed to go someplace so I could talk to my son."

Mara was glad to hear the old Buddy talking.

"We rode around for a while. I showed him Grandma's Hand's, and where I used to work, then I took him to the trash dumpster."

"Now you sound *real* crazy Buddy. What would make you take him to the trash dumpster?"

He had done it for a few reasons. Buddy needed for Neal to understand where he had been twenty years ago, that back then nothing existed inside his father to affirm his own worth. Like so many people did, Buddy defined himself by what he believed he saw reflected in the eyes of those he was in relationship with. All that he valued he had been unable to sustain; he was a man without a sense of purpose.

"It was bad enough that your momma didn't want me when she left, … she didn't want nothin' that reminded her of me. She even left you. When I think about it, it's a wonder that she didn't change Nelson Jr.'s name."

"She didn't…he changed it. When he went to jail, they told him that Nelson was his slave name. He calls himself Edriese X now. That wouldn't be so bad if he would do something positive with his life. He's got three kids, and his girlfriend is on welfare."

"That's what I mean. If you don't know who you are, then people can make you believe anything. If I didn't know who I was, then what was I gonna be able to tell you? I never even saw my daddy, he was just a name, like you read in the newspaper ev'ry day. But at least he wasn't around to mess up my life like I was messin' up yours. … I know you remember what I was like before I left."

"I remember you and my mother arguing, and the two of us being in the house all the time. I felt kind of responsible for you. So I can almost understand that part. ... But how could you not come to Grandma Hattie's funeral? You knew that she loved you if nobody else did."

"I did come. I went to the funeral home to see her laid out. I even put my suit on, and told myself I was gonna walk in the church... But I couldn't...I couldn't bring myself to walk in the door... I was standin' outside. I saw the guards when they brought Nelson Jr. to the church in handcuffs. ... I felt like ... like I had failed both of my sons. ...I didn't want him to see me when he came back out, so I just left. ... I bought me a bottle, got in my car and...and ran away again."

The trash dumpster represented something else. It was also the place where Buddy had found a reason to get up, where he had asked God to help him. He pointed to a spot on the now cracked and gravelly cement.

"I woke up on the ground right over there one Saturday mornin' about twenty years ago. When I saw where I was and what I was doin', I knew that if somethin' didn't happen to change how *Buddy* felt about Buddy, it didn't make no difference where he went. He would always be wakin' up beside trash dumpsters. That night I asked God for some help. I needed it."

Being parked by the dumpster had another purpose too. Now that Buddy was emptying out his closet, he knew that there were some things he wanted to keep, and some things he would need to get rid of. When he finished, he hoped that Neal would make a decision to throw away some of his old garbage too.

****

"Come on Buddy! If you don't hurry up we won't be ready when the limousine gets here!"

Well, they'll just have to wait for me, won't they?"

"I know he loves his daddy, but I hope you don't think Neal is gonna stop everything just so he can wait for you to get there."

"I'm comin', I'm comin', Baby."

"Aw, Buddy! Where in the world is my mind? I almost forgot the present. Bring it when you come please. It's on the table in the dinin' room."

The mailman was coming up the street just as Buddy was locking the door behind them. Mara took the mail and stuck it in her purse before the chauffeur helped her into the long, white car. Looking around at all of the accoutrements inside the limo, and inhaling the newness of its upholstery, Mara was impressed.

"You could almost live in here as long as you got enough money to buy the gas to run this thing. I think I might be in the wrong business, wha'd'you think, Buddy?"

"I think one wife in the real estate business is enough for me, that's what I think."

"Oh, yeah, I guess so. I forgot about Loreatha. ... You think she'll be there?"

"Maybe so, maybe not, you never can tell. She might want to come just to see how things turned out after all these years. I don't s'pose she'd be comin' 'cause she cared anything about Neal."

"Well, if she does show up it's fine with me, so long as she keeps her distance. When she sees how good you look today, she just *might* be in'nerested again."

"That's one thing she never got to worry about, ... and neither do you."

"I was just makin' sure I didn't haf'ta go back in the house and put my tennis shoes on."

"Mara Ruthine Singleton, *'you'* are a mess!"

Buddy looked over at her and smiled that smile that she loved. She was right; he did look good. His skin was so pretty and clear. He looked younger somehow. Maybe it was because he was so proud of his son. Maybe it was because he'd cleaned out his closet.

Her husband and Neal had come a long way in their journey to heal. They had a way to go yet, but Mara trusted the God that had brought them this far to insure that they would get there. Today, Buddy was going to stand beside his son, *their* son, as best man in his wedding..

"God *is* good, **all** the time."

"Did you say somethin', Baby?"

Not realizing that she was thinking out loud again, Mara reached over and ran her hand over the back of his neck.

"Just thinkin', … just 'thinkin'."

She was thinking that Buddy was her best man too.

As they continued the ride to the church, Mara reached over to fix the bow on the present she'd wrapped for Neal and his bride-to-be, Capri. The card that she had stuck under the ribbon had her sweet potato pie recipe tucked inside. Capri should have the recipe, she was family now too. Looking at the envelope, Mara remembered the mail that she'd put in her purse. She took it out and flipped through it until something caught her eye.

The return address on the envelope read "Carter Johnson Medical Center". Mara's heart started racing, her cheeks flushed, and she suddenly felt moisture on her nose and top lip. Had it been any other time she would have thought that she was having a hot flash. But it was what was typed on the envelope that precipitated this internal change in temperature. Carter Johnson was the name of the hospital where she'd gone over twenty years ago. The one she'd walked into and then away from, broken and empty.

She looked over at Buddy, looking so handsome in his tuxedo. As the breeze blew in through the open window on his side, Mara caught a whiff of the cologne he was wearing. It wasn't one of the new ones. It was Aramis, her favorite. She opened her purse and put the envelopes back inside. Today wasn't the day, and this wasn't the time to think about *"that"*.

She turned to look out the window on her side. As she did, the limousine stopped for a traffic light, and Mara realized that they were in front of Grandma's Hands. She leaned her head forward, enabling her to see through the window to where one of the showcases held cakes and cookies, and the other one, pastries. Her sweet potato pies weren't there and wouldn't be until the next morning when Rondell and Kaitlin took them out of the ovens. Mara wouldn't be there to oversee things; Buddy had made arrangements for the two of them to go on their own little honeymoon after the reception.

Rolling away as the limo pulled off and turned the corner, Mara could see the back of the row of buildings where the shop was. She was glad that Garfield did such a good job of keeping the area clean where her trash dumpster sat inside the fenced-in lot.

Turning to stare straight ahead, she looked at the back of the chauffeur's head. Mara remembered those days in her now ancient past when she'd seen the back of a bus driver's head, the many times she had been a passenger as she gave someone else the responsibility of determining her destination. She had been roaming in search of something then; she hadn't even known what it was. She had been running away from bad choices---the ones she'd made herself and the ones other people had made for her. She was making her own choices now, with God's guidance. He had the steering wheel now.

Inside, in her deep, dark place, Mara heard the sound of a key turning to open another prison door. But this time she wasn't afraid. She was aware that God was with her now just as He had been in the past. She welcomed Him as always, but this time there was no apprehension about what lay ahead. She knew that He wouldn't have to make her face what was behind the door.

****

Mara, Zena, and the Wyatts had stood paralyzed in front of the television in her living room that day. Even though the pictures that stared back at them had forever changed the world around her, September 11 couldn't shake this new foundation that Mara stood on. As businesses went under and the temporal guarantees failed the many who had placed their faith in them, Mara experienced something else.

Mara understood that she was blessed. She grieved for those who had lost so much, for those who had yet to wake up to the reality of whom and how much they'd never have again. She cried at the testimonials to the lives of the heroes who had braved the danger. She watched as they painstakingly searched the rubble, as people tried to clean up the fallout, as others tried to crawl from beneath the aftermath of someone else's horrible choices. Mara watched as the differences that she had viewed as obstacles, the Black and White that previously had separated her from *them*, became the gray that united them.

Mara fully recognized that she was blessed. What she had suffered could in no way compare to the loss and devastation that had intruded on the lives of thousands around the world. What Mara *did* realize was, like the people who survived, she, too, had cleaning up to do. What she *was* able to compare was that the same God who was there to comfort those who were blessed to be saved from the fallout, was there to help her. She was grateful that her life and the rubble around it was just as important to Him as those other lives.

God loved her and had shown her how to love herself. She knew that Zena loved her. She had a family and friends who loved her. She had never doubted Buddy's love; his love for her had been a constant. But in God, even his love for her had changed; it had simply grown, matured, because he had loved her from the beginning.

Secure in the love that surrounded her and that which emanated from inside her, Mara understood that she had another closet to clean out. She knew that there were some things she would need to get rid of---some attitudes, some prejudices, because she had to make room for what was coming. Like she was loved, Mara was called upon to love in return. She trusted God that He knew the right time... that He would tell her. She knew that when she told Buddy, he would be there to help her, like he always was.

She didn't know everything, but Mara knew that.